ECHO BAY Christmas

Gina Robinson

THREE JAYS
PRESS

Three Jays Press LLC
SEATTLE, WASHINGTON

Gina Robinson
www.ginarobinson.com

Book Layout ©2013 BookDesignTemplates.com
Cover Design by Jeff Robinson

Echo Bay Christmas/ Gina Robinson. — 1st ed.
ISBN 978-0615854526

For Grandpa and Grandma
Rocky Point Lodge was one of the happiest places of
my childhood.

Also by
GINA ROBINSON

THE BILLIONAIRE MATCHMAKER
SERIES
Part 1, LAZER FOCUSED
Part 2, HARTE STRINGS
Part 3, PAIR US

THE BILLIONAIRE DUKE SERIES
Part 1, THE BILLIONAIRE DUKE
Part 2, THE DUCHESS CONTEST
Part 3, THE TEMPORARY DUCHESS
Part 4, THE AMERICAN HEIR

SWITCHED AT MARRIAGE ROMANCE
SERIAL
Part 1, A WEDDING TO REMEMBER
Part 2, THE VIRGIN BILLIONAIRE
Part 3, TO HAVE AND TO HOLD
Part 4, FROM THIS DAY FORWARD
Part 5, FOR RICHER, FOR RICHEST
Part 6, IN SICKNESS AND IN WEALTH
Part 7, TO LOVE AND TO CHERISH

NEW ADULT ROMANCE
RUSHED
CRUSHED
HUSHED
RECKLESS LONGING
RECKLESS SECRETS

CHAPTER ONE

Welcome to Echo Bay, Idaho, Population 24

Tara Clark frowned, perplexed, as she drove past the carved sign with its gilded gold, partially snow-obscured lettering. Dark green, rectangular, with a painted 3D graphic of a bear fishing in a lake, and anchored by river-rock pillars, three fourths of the village could picnic in the shade of the monument. Usually the overly grandiose thing amused her to no end.

Echo Bay has another year-round resident?

She shook her head and bit her lip, trying to digest the news.

A sign-worthy move-in? And Grandpa, let alone Gram, who spreads news as easily as Twitter, hasn't shared the skinny with me? What's up?

It was not like her grandparents could have forgotten about it. As owner of Echo Bay Resort and village mayor, her grandpa Harry Jansen was keeper of the sign. Harry never waited for the federal census to make a change.

He always said a community should keep better track of its members than to count them once every ten years. That was the problem with big cities like Seattle, where Tara insisted on living, and the neighboring town around the lake from the resort, with its six thousand or so nameless souls. No sense of kinship.

Harry changed the sign whenever the situation required or he darn well felt like it. That he'd recently been in the mood and not told her surprised Tara, especially since she'd been talking with her grandparents at least weekly since October.

Tara turned off Echo Bay Road, easing off the gas and downshifting to avoid braking on the slick roads. She pulled into a spot in the resort's plowed parking lot just as the first snowflake in the latest squall floated onto her windshield and melted on impact.

She couldn't believe her grandparents had finally agreed to a firm meeting with the hotel management company. Tara and her parents had been worried about Harry and Margie working too hard for years, encouraging them to retire. Then this fall Tara and her mom hit upon the idea of hiring a hotel management company to run the daily operations, freeing Harry up to fish and Margie to putter around the kitchen. They hoped Harry would be amenable to a partial retirement, at least.

Harry and Margie fought Mom every time she brought the subject of retirement up. So Tara and her mother decided it was best if Tara approached them with the idea and handled the details with them. Harry was determined to leave Echo Bay to Tara as her inheritance from him and her grandmother. Because she had a stake in Echo Bay's future, Tara and her parents hoped Harry would listen to her and take her ideas into consideration.

In October, Tara broached the subject and Harry reluctantly agreed to meet with Northwest Resort Management Services and hear them out. Then proceeded to postpone every meeting Tara set up. Until now, just before Christmas. If Tara would come to Echo Bay for the holidays, Harry promised he'd hear what Northwest Resort Management had to say.

It was loveable blackmail, and touching in its way. Her grandparents had been begging her to come for Christmas for years. It wasn't that she was hardhearted toward them. Tara visited Echo Bay several times a year, but she hadn't come for Christmas, or any time during the winter months, in nearly ten years. Not since her brother Chad's fatal snowboarding accident on Christmas Eve at the Basin, the local ski resort. The same Christmas Eve that precipitated her broken engagement with her brother's best friend, Ryan Sanders. The memories were just too painful.

And then there was Ryan. He was a local boy, a town favorite. He'd moved away after the accident, but his parents still lived in town. Tara never came to visit her grandparents when she knew he'd be visiting. She blamed herself, and him, for Chad's accident. To say things had ended badly between her and Ryan was putting it mildly. He'd broken her heart, and she still wasn't sure it was completely mended.

Ryan usually came home for Christmas. Her grandparents had been vague about whether he'd be home this year. The best she could hope for was that she wouldn't accidentally run into him. She had no intention of going to town if she could avoid it. She hoped he'd give her the courtesy of the same space and privacy she'd shown him over the years and stay away from Echo Bay during her visit.

Tara looked out the car window. Her breath caught. Her heart raced. Everything looked so familiar, so much like it had that fateful Christmas she'd been trying so hard to forget.

Tara turned off the engine and stared at the lodge. *This place is going to outlive us all.*

It was only three-thirty in the afternoon, but already dusk was falling quickly. Along the lodge roofline, multi-colored lights sparkled through the gray-white gloom of a growing snowstorm. An oversize evergreen wreath, complete with a red bow, hung on one of the double front doors, as it had every Christmas Tara could remember. Doors that jingle, jingle, jingle-belled whenever someone entered. Eager for Christmas, Gram always hung jingle bells and mistletoe above the doors the day after Thanksgiving.

Behind the resort lodge, the dam-controlled lake failed to reach its summer-level shores, leaving docks high and dry. A wind blew across the surface, rippling its depthless, light-absorbing gray waters that never, ever froze, even in the coldest winter. Beyond the lake, obscured by snow clouds, the mountain rose like Mount Crumpet.

In clear weather you could see the ski runs. Tara swallowed a lump in her throat, glad for the first time during this long, slow trip for the cloud cover. She pulled her coat collar up around her chin and grabbed her purse.

The heir to Echo Bay returns.

White-clad evergreens, white pines mostly, swaddled the lodge. The scene looked like something you'd see in an ad for a Christmas ski vacation.

She pushed open the door of her compact SUV and stepped into the wind and snow.

The jingle of bells over the doors carried on the stiff breeze to Tara's ears before she'd slid three steps across the icy lot. Gram stepped out onto the covered front porch. Just as Tara knew she would, Gram had been watching for her.

"Harry! Harry, she's here. Tara's here!" Gram, wearing nothing warmer than her signature cardigan sweater, called over her shoulder into the lodge.

"Gram!" Tara ran, slipping and sliding, into her tiny grandmother's hug. "How are you! So sorry I took so long getting here. The weather's atrocious—"

"Oh, stop making excuses." Gram, who stood a good six inches shorter than Tara, put her arm around her. "Get on in here out of the weather." Gram chuckled and her face lit up with her pleased smile.

But Gram felt thin and slight in Tara's grasp. *Frail.*

As Gram turned and shooed Tara inside, Tara noticed with a start how stiffly and slowly she walked. Gram wasn't healing as quickly as she should have from her hip replacement last summer.

"Everyone, she's here. My granddaughter's finally here!"

Tara's grandparents lived in an apartment at the back of the lodge. Gram treated the lodge's lobby, front desk, and great room as her personal home. As hostess, it was only polite to introduce a member of the family to the other guests. *All the other guests.*

If the people lounging around the lobby knew what was good for them, they'd flee before Gram caught them and recited Tara's every accomplishment at them until their eyes glazed over. As a kid, Tara used to be embarrassed by Gram's obvious pride in her and the way she showed Tara off. Now Tara thought it was sweet, a sign of Gram's love for her. But the guests might have a different opinion.

Fortunately, before Gram got far, Kathleen, Tara's favorite cook, next to Gram, scuttled out of the kitchen with a dishtowel slung over her shoulder. The opposite of Gram, square and wide with short, wavy gray hair, her face lit up when she spotted Tara.

Tara gave Kathleen a hug. Then Stormy, Kathleen's daughter who'd waitressed at the lodge for over twenty years, joined in. Finally Harry appeared and demanded a hug all his own. Suddenly everyone was talking at once.

"Give the girl some space," Harry joked. "Let her get some air. She'll be with us for a while. There'll be plenty of time for yakking."

"There better be." Kathleen, warm and pink from the kitchen, dabbed her forehead with the dishtowel. "We've got catching up to do and plenty of news to share."

"Like what?" Tara teased, knowing she'd be hearing hours of local gossip soon and hoping to find out about this new resident number twenty-four without being too obvious. "Nothing ever happens in Echo Bay." She winked at them.

"Big-city snob. Better watch yourself or I'll spit in your soup." Kathleen let out a hearty laugh.

"Hush now." Harry frowned at Kathleen. "Don't let the guests hear you. They don't know you're joking."

"Oh, sure they do!" Kathleen shook her head.

Tara glanced around the decorated lobby, happily surprised. The tree wasn't up yet, but the place looked good, well kept. Since her last visit in July, they'd replaced the rusty screen in the large stone fireplace. A window looked like it had recently been changed out. After her last visit, Tara had been worried that her grandfather was slipping and things were beginning to fall apart. "Wow! The place looks great."

Harry beamed.

Gram waved her praise aside. "Oh, we still have more decorating to do. We saved the tree for you."

"Excellent!" Tara feigned enthusiasm for her grandmother's sake. She and Chad had always helped Gram decorate the tree together. Without Chad as her accomplice in teasing and joking and horseplay, she doubted there would be much joy in the act of trimming the tree.

It was lonely being the only sibling left, with no older brother to share secrets with and go to for advice. Tara felt the hole of Chad's absence and the responsibility of being the only living grandchild all the time. But it was worse during the holiday season.

Stormy must have sensed Tara's sadness. She grabbed her arm and changed subjects. "We got a new bread man. He'll be here tomorrow."

"Another one?" Tara raised an eyebrow. She lowered her voice and leaned in conspiratorially toward Stormy. "What did you do to the last one?"

Stormy laughed and whispered in her ear, "Wouldn't you like to know?"

"This one's cute," Kathleen said. "About your age. Though I prefer the candy man, myself."

Harry rolled his eyes. "The candy man's too slick for Tara." He shook his head. "Give me your keys, kid. I'll go get your bags and leave you to these hens."

"I'll get them, Grandpa."

He waved her offer aside. "I'm not too old to carry a few bags. Do it every day." He grabbed his coat from a peg near the front desk. Then he grabbed a small envelope from the desk drawer, took out one key and handed another to Tara. "Gram put you in your favorite room, good old ten."

Tara's mouth went dry as she stared at the key. It took her a second to be able to speak. She'd specifically asked Gram not to go to any trouble, and not to put her in a view room, one that looked out across the lake at the mountain.

"Grandpa, there's no need to throw away good money by giving me a room with a lake view. You'll lose hundreds of dollars a night. Save it for a paying guest. I'll sleep on the hideaway in your apartment." She held the key out to him.

"Nonsense!" He took her hand and closed it around the key, giving her hand a squeeze. "That room's always yours during the holidays. We aren't breaking with tradition now."

Harry walked off before she could argue with him further. "Go easy on her, girls," he called over his shoulder. "Our Tara's just barely got here. Don't go fixing her up with some local yokel before she's even unpacked." He winked at her.

Tara turned to Gram and arched a brow. "Who does he mean?"

"Oh, forget that old fool. He doesn't know a thing, not a thing." Gram shook her head, looking exasperated as she watched him walk off.

Harry and Margie had been married for over fifty years. It was safe to say Harry knew his wife pretty well. And so did Tara. She stared at her grandmother, waiting for the truth to come out.

"Did I tell you we have a salad dressing man now?" Gram sounded too casual about him to be trusted completely. "He'll be here later with a case of Copper Creek's finest. For our cookbook experiments."

"What cookbook?" Tara asked, trying hard not to sound as surprised as she was. People were always asking Margie for her recipes. Usually she found a way to avoid giving away the secrets to her specialties, especially her pies. "Finally putting a collection of your secret pie recipes together to sell in the gift shop?"

"Sell my babies?" Gram shook her head and laughed. "No, no, no. Since when would I do that?" Then she beamed. "Kathleen and I are helping Copper Creek Salad Dressing put a book together for their customers. One with regional flavor. And we're going to get credit as collaborators and the lodge will get a mention, too. It's good publicity for us."

Kathleen cut in, "We invent and test recipes using their products. They're going to print them up into a cookbook to hand out to customers—theirs and ours." She nudged Tara and winked. "It was the dressing man's idea."

A terrible thought crossed Tara's mind. "Oh, really? Is this dressing man pimply-faced Charlie Hopkins? Because if you have any crazy idea you're going to fix me up with him, you're all seriously insane."

Charlie was her age and the heir to the Copper Creek Dressing fortune. His parents had a big house on Horseshoe Bay. She'd had a single disastrous date with him when she was sixteen, orchestrated by her grandparents.

Stormy cocked a brow. "He had his face sanded. He's got great skin now."

"And a wife and three kids," Gram added, shaking her head and laughing. "Fix you two up, what an idea!"

CHAPTER TWO

Ten years in the food business. An MBA. New vice-president of production and product development for Copper Creek Dressing. The youngest VP, next to Charlie, the owner's son, and Charlie obviously had nepotism coloring his meteoric rise. Ryan Sanders was a bona fide salad dressing executive. Yet three months back in town and already he'd been given the ignoble title of the "dressing man" by the ladies at Echo Bay Resort.

Ryan shook his head. Sometimes you didn't get any credit for being a good guy. You certainly didn't get any respect.

Not that he didn't know what Margie Jansen, Harry's wife and co-owner of the resort, was up to. Todd "The Beer Man" Barney, the delivery guy for The Basin

Brewery, had already warned him. He hadn't needed warning. He'd known Margie his whole life. A new bachelor in town, especially a prodigal son, was fair-game fresh meat in her book.

He'd seen Margie's machinations firsthand and wasn't particularly concerned. As far as he knew, she'd never managed to make a match that stuck longer than a year. As for him, he was doing just fine with the women he met on the slopes.

It would take more than Margie's scheming to keep Ryan away from Echo Bay Resort. He and that old place went back too far. When he was a kid, his mom cleaned rooms at the lodge while he ran wild through the resort and hounded Harry to take him fishing. When Ryan got a little older, he went from angling for trout to trying to hook girls. Harry spent the better part of Ryan's high school and college years trying to make sure Ryan's rod didn't end up anywhere near Tara. And failing miserably. There'd been no keeping Ryan from Tara, or her from him.

To be fair, Ryan's friendship with Tara's older brother Chad had complicated Harry's task, making it nearly impossible. Ryan was always with Chad. And wherever Chad went, Tara followed. Before it was alluring, it was simply annoying having Chad's little sister always tagging along. Then, suddenly, Tara blossomed and Ryan's hormones kicked in.

By the time the attraction between Tara and Ryan became obvious, no mere grandfather could break them up. Especially not with Chad watching Ryan's backside.

Yeah, well, water under the bridge.

Chad and Ryan had had such big plans for Echo Bay Resort. When Harry retired and Chad inherited and took over, he and Chad were going to carry on Harry's legacy and improve on it. Ryan sighed. The thought of what could have been made him melancholy, just like thinking about Chad brought back the old grief and guilt. *Miss you, buddy.* If only he could tell Chad how seriously sorry he was.

Ryan still planned to own the resort one day. Harry was refusing to sell, but he was getting old. It may have been pure optimism on Ryan's part, but he thought he was winning Harry over. Just the other day Harry mentioned how he could see Ryan owning the place. Ryan had to convince him before he got senile, or, heaven forbid, died. Tara would sell the minute she inherited. To anyone *but* him.

Ryan forced his thoughts back to the present. He had to be the only vice-president who made deliveries. Anything for the cookbook and his cause. He loaded the case of dressing for the resort into the cargo area of his SUV and slammed the door closed just as his buddy Dean, Copper Creek's production manager, came out of the building.

"Snowing again! Fifth day in a row." Dean laughed, scooped a handful of snow into a ball, and pelted a tree at the far end of the parking lot. "Woot!" He did a victory punch in the air. "Going to be a great ski season this year if this keeps up. Finest powder around."

"Heading up tonight?" Ryan grabbed his broom from the backseat and began sweeping snow off his vehicle.

"Yeah. Gotta get a little night boarding in. You?" Dean started his car and turned the defroster on full, then popped back out with an industrial-strength scraper in his hand.

Ryan shook his head. "Making a delivery."

Dean laughed at him. "Ah, dressing man. *Right*." Dean clapped him on the shoulder. "How long are you going to play up to Margie and kiss Harry's butt?"

"Kiss butt, what are you talking about?" Ryan shook his head and grinned. "I like the old man and enjoy hanging around the place."

Dean gave him a long, skeptical look. "Have fun, then. But don't get your hopes up. Harry's never going to sell to you. He'll leave the place to Tara."

Ryan shrugged and shook the rapidly falling snow off his head. "Maybe." He didn't like admitting Dean could very well end up being right. And he never talked about Tara.

Dean tossed his ice scraper into the car. He slid into his driver's seat and kicked the snow off his boots on the running board. "Doing the Santa Ski on Christmas Eve?"

Ryan nodded. "Couldn't miss it if I wanted to. The entire ski patrol's required to be on duty. With bells on. Literally. Jingle, jingle, jingle."

Dean laughed. "Hope you already bought your Santa suit. Walmart's out."

"Got mine online in October."

"Great! Maybe wearing the suit will finally score you a few babes. Girls love sitting in Santa's lap."

Ryan scooped up a handful of snow, enough to pelt Dean. But Dean was too quick. He slammed his car door shut before Ryan got a shot off. Dean honked, laughing and mouthing *ho, ho, ho* as he drove off.

"What's this? What's a Santa Ski?" Tara picked up a cardboard tri-fold sign from the center of the booth table and held it out to Gram, who sat across from her.

At Gram's urging, Tara had just ordered the mega-calorie Copper Creek Bleu Cheese Burger from the newly revised resort menu. Gram needed her opinion on it before it got starred-most-favored-recipe status in the crazy cookbook she was writing. Tara still couldn't believe Charlie or his dad Bob actually paid Gram enough interest to ask her to do the book for them, even at the mysterious dressing delivery man's bidding. But who else would think of it?

Except in the off-season, Gram rarely cooked in the small kitchen in the private quarters at the back of the lodge. Friends and family alike ate in the restaurant. Close family, like Tara, usually helped themselves in the kitchen or behind the counter. But the first day back, Gram insisted Tara be treated like a guest and let herself be waited on.

Tara suspected Gram's insistence also had something to do with the dressing man's imminent arrival. Though Gram refused to name him, Tara had the distinct impression Gram was dying for her to meet—and eventually date—him. Gram didn't want her grabbing something and hiding out in her room.

Tara was just curious enough about the dressing man and his influence on Gram to hang around and get a look at him.

Outside it was dark. Much to Tara's relief, the only view out the window was the white of falling snow. She wasn't ready to see the mountain yet. It reminded her too much of Chad and all she'd lost. Even the happy memories she had from good times there made her melancholy.

"Oh, that Santa Ski's the brainchild of the Basin marketing team and the town council." Gram shook her head, but her dancing eyes contradicted any apparent disapproval. "First annual Santa Ski and Snowboarding Event. It's going to be held on Christmas Eve.

"We have to do something to compete with the Silver Valley's Jingle Run." Gram got a devilish look in her eye. "Hah! They think people wearing battery-operated lights around their necks as they slide down their slope can compete with us." She leaned forward toward Tara, her body language indicating she was about to share something terribly exciting.

"Our Santa's going to ski down the main run with a pack of toys on his back. At the bottom of the run, he'll jump into a horse-drawn sleigh that will pull him to the ski lodge and the Christmas party of the season! Roaring fire. Christmas tree loaded with real gifts underneath. Christmas carols. Dancing, for the young people who like that sort of thing." Gram shook her head.

As far as Tara knew, Gram had never liked dancing.

"At the end of the evening, Santa will hand out gift prizes donated by local merchants. The grand prize is a season pass to the Basin." Gram wrinkled her nose. "Guess who insisted on that?" She shrugged as if to say, *What can you do?*

"Grandpa donated a night's free lodging here at Echo Bay. I'm giving away my one of my pies."

Tara cocked a brow and couldn't help teasing. "And the secret recipe, too?"

"Ha! They wish." Gram winked. "No one outside the family's getting any of my top-secret pie recipes. I already told you, not even my Copper Creek cookbook."

The event sounded like fun, and very good business for the Basin. But no way Tara would be going, especially on Christmas Eve. Just being in Echo Bay gave her frazzled nerves. She planned to spend the night before Christmas cuddled in front of a roaring fire with her grandparents as they waited for Saint Nick.

"People are supposed to wear their best Christmas sweaters, or Santa hats, maybe jingle bells, or reindeer antlers. Even necklaces with lights if they want." Gram chuckled. "We're throwing a Santa suit contest. Did I tell you Jim Dickson is going to play Santa? You remember him? Big guy, round belly. And he's gone completely white-haired—"

"And for people who don't board or ski?" Tara cocked a brow.

"They get to stay back here at Echo Bay Resort and cook dinner for the few lingering guests." Gram winked at Tara.

"Uh-huh. Right." Tara's stomach growled. She glanced at her watch and then out the window, where the snow looked like it was falling harder.

"It appears the snow's delayed your dressing man." Tara frowned in consternation. "What aren't you telling me about this guy, Gram? Why are you so eager for me to meet him?"

As if on cue, the bells over the lobby doors jingled. Tara couldn't see the newcomer from where she sat. But she felt the cold breeze that blew all the way across the lobby into the dining room.

"That's got to be your man. No one else is crazy enough to be out in this weather." Tara flew from her seat and rushed around the corner into the lobby to get her first look at him.

A tall, dark, snow-covered stranger stood in the doorway under the mistletoe, head down, tamping the snow off his boots on the rubber mat. He wore an AFI beanie, a navy jacket, and tight black jeans that showed off powerful skier's thighs. He held a twelve-bottle case of Copper Creek salad dressing in his arms. If he wasn't the dressing man, he was doing a darn good imitation.

Tara held in an appreciative sigh. She liked her men tall with broad shoulders. This guy fit the bill in spades.

And then in a twinkling, she got an idea. She got a brilliant, wonderful, evil idea. She'd stop Gram's matchmaking in its tracks and give them all a laugh. She shrugged. Blame it on him. The man *was* standing under the mistletoe.

She unbuttoned her blouse a button, fluffed her hair, bit her lips, and sidled up to him way too far into his intimate, personal space. She hoped Gram was watching. She'd be mortified.

Wearing a flirty, teasing grin, she brushed against him. She touched his sleeve, ran her fingers up his arm, and squeezed, feeling a firm bicep beneath all that coat. She leaned into him on tiptoes, staring into his chest, whispering in her best sultry voice, "How about a kiss to warm you up, dressing man?"

Then she reached to cup his face, looking up, up, six feet four up, into the deep brown eyes of Ryan Sanders.

He froze beneath her touch, looking as surprised as she was.

Her heart stopped. Her mouth fell open. Their gazes locked. For just a second, she felt as if she were looking into the eyes of the young Ryan, the one she'd loved and planned to marry and spend the rest of her life with.

Embarrassed, she jumped out of mistletoe territory as if scorched, sure her face was flaming. "I'll take that."

Reacting with pure survival instinct and shock, she wrenched the dressing out of his arms before he could speak. It was heavier than she'd thought, but she had to keep up the charade.

She turned, and strutting with hips swinging like a runway model, carried the carton to the kitchen where she dumped the dressing on the counter and started shaking.

Ryan stared after her. What did he do now? Even in his wildest imagination, he'd never pictured meeting Tara again like *this*. He'd been bamboozled, duped, and taken by surprise. How had everyone kept Tara's visit a secret from him?

Margie stared at him from the dining room entrance. He hesitated a second too long. She converged on him, effectively blocking his escape as she took his arm and patted it. He was almost certain she looked pleased with herself.

"I'm sorry about that." Margie shook her head. "You know Tara. She likes to tease." She paused. "You all right?"

"Fine." He didn't feel all right. He felt sucker punched.

Margie smiled timidly at him. "You're covered in snow." She called to Stormy. "Get the boy a cup of coffee. He looks like he could use some warming up."

"I'm fine. I've got to go." He tried to turn toward the door.

"Nonsense. You wouldn't leave before you've filled an old lady in on what's up in town. Plus I have a new fry sauce using the dressing for you to try." Margie grabbed his arm and led him to his usual booth. "You must be starving after fighting this weather."

She called to Kathleen in the kitchen. "A cheeseburger, heavy on the pickles, and an extra helping of fries with our new sauce."

Kathleen poked her head out. "Already on it."

Margie slid in across the table from him. "On the house tonight. For helping us out. We can't send you out into this storm on an empty stomach. You don't have an ounce of fat on you. Heaven forbid you get stuck in a drift and starve to death before morning." She chuckled in the small, merry, self-deprecating way she had. "I won't have that on my conscience."

He had no idea what to say. He was still feeling Tara's breasts brushing against his arm and hearing her breathy *dressing man* in his ear. He was stunned, simply stunned she still had the power to rock his socks with a simple touch and a come-hither look. He'd assumed what they'd had together as kids had been hormonally driven, not mature, lasting stuff. That's what he'd told his wounded psyche when he made himself forget her. Now he wasn't so sure.

Margie reached across the table and patted his gloved hand. "I don't want Tara's presence to chase you off. Harry and I enjoy having you around." She smiled, looking so kindly and grandmotherly there was no way to cross her. "Understand?"

He nodded, wondering how Margie had managed this ambush without giving herself away. How long had everyone but him known Tara was coming for Christmas?

Before he could ask, Stormy arrived with his coffee.

Margie patted his hand again and smiled brighter. "Sugar?"

CHAPTER THREE

In the kitchen, Tara steadied herself against the counter across from the grill as she watched Kathleen cook. What had happened out there? Why did she feel as flustered as the sixteen-year-old she'd been fifteen years ago when she fell for Ryan the first time around?

Cooing in his ear certainly wasn't what she'd imagined she'd say to him when she saw him again. And she'd run through every possible scenario throughout the years they'd been apart. Or so she'd thought until a few minutes ago.

Kathleen handed Tara her bleu cheese burger, then plopped two patties on the grill for Ryan's double cheeseburger.

Tara took a bite of her burger more out of politeness than hunger, eating on autopilot. And because it gave her something to do with her trembling hands. She should have headed off to her room. But that seemed so cowardly, and besides, she couldn't make her wooden legs move.

She didn't believe in Santa Claus and she refused to believe in one true love for everyone. Because if she did, she'd have to accept that quite possibly Ryan had been hers and she'd blown her chance with him when she'd been too young to realize what she was throwing away in favor of her career. Falling for Ryan had simply been a matter of proximity and naïveté. That was the lie she'd told herself since their split. And right now, as shaken as she felt, it sounded hollow.

A timer dinged. Kathleen pulled the fries up. She slid the bun on a plate, topped it with the patties and condiments, and set the bun top beside it. She shook the fries and dumped them on the plate with a little salt. Then she hummed as she set a cup of the new fry sauce next to it.

Ryan is the guy behind the cookbook. The implications turned her stomach into a tightly balled knot.

Kathleen held the plate out to Tara. "Take the man his burger. He's in his usual booth."

Usual booth? Tara stared at the plate and then at Kathleen. "I can't."

"You can." Kathleen's voice was tender. "You're a strong woman. You can face Ryan Sanders any day. You have nothing to be embarrassed about. I know you can. I've seen you do it before. It's time to let go of the awkwardness between you. Go out there and make a joke of it."

Tara reluctantly set her own plate on the counter, grabbed Ryan's burger and headed for the dining room to prove a point to herself. She could face Ryan like a mature woman.

Gram slid out of the booth and hurried off as Tara approached, leaving Ryan by himself, sipping a cup of black coffee. Ryan looked up at her with a wary expression.

She couldn't blame him for being cautious. "You ordered a double cheeseburger?"

"Margie ordered one for me." His tone was neutral, his expression masked.

"Good enough." She took that as an invitation and slid in across from him as she slipped the burger in front of him. She took a deep breath. *Here goes nothing.* Maybe Kathleen was right. If she made light of the situation...

"Besides its kiss-inducing powers, mistletoe obviously has little-known hallucinogenic properties." She paused, wondering exactly how to set him straight. "Forgive me, under its influence I thought you were someone else."

In the old days, he would have grinned and laughed at her lame apology. Instead, he looked surprised. *What does he expect from me?*

"You called me dressing man. You knew who I was." He tilted his head, ignoring his food. His eyes flashed and he sounded almost angry. "You weren't trying to pull my chain?"

"I had no idea *you* were the dressing man." Being so near him was unnerving and surreal. "Obviously you weren't expecting me, either." She tried to smile and put a tease in her voice. But she fell short, she was sure. "Are you so hard up for a date these days you've stooped to letting Gram fix you up?"

He stared at her a minute as if he couldn't believe what she'd just said and didn't deserve an answer.

When she couldn't stand it anymore, she broke the awkward silence between them. "Don't even try telling me you were simply delivering dressing." She was still trying to keep things light and cordial. "I know exactly what you're up to—you're behind the cookbook."

He shook his head. "Great job, detective. You found me out. Only everyone in the area and all the tourists know that dark little secret." There was more wariness than humor in his voice. He paused. "Talk about hard up. *You* hit on me, thinking I was a total stranger—"

She could tell he was trying hard to be jokey. "Hit on you? *Please.*" She rolled her eyes for effect and to hide her nerves. Her pulse was racing dangerously. "I wasn't hitting on *you*, per se. I was scaring off some poor bumbling fool who'd had the misfortune of stumbling into the Echo Bay matchmaker's lair. I was doing a favor for a stranger, since it's Christmastime. As it turns out, I was doing *you* a favor."

His expression made his skepticism perfectly clear. "In that case, apology accepted."

She studied him unabashedly, drinking in the sight of him as if she'd been thirsting for it for years.

He still had the same intense eyes. The same dark stubble and strong chin. His face had filled out, which made him look like a man, not a boy, and more attractive, not less.

He hadn't removed his coat and beanie. She hoped he was sweating under all those layers of clothes. But perversely, she wanted to see his hair. Maybe he no longer had any, or maybe he had a ponytail down his back. Either way, she wanted to see it. As if fulfilling her wish, he pulled his beanie off, revealing the same sexy, lush head of hair she'd loved to run her fingers through way back when.

She curled her fingers into a fist in her lap, hoping she was wrong and he wasn't making a play for Echo Bay.

Across the table, Ryan watched her.

"You're working for Copper Creek now?" She kept her tone polite, hopefully sounding as if she was simply making small talk, not prying. But she was dying for details.

He continued staring at her, watching her in a way that made her feel under the microscope. "I'm vice-president at the plant."

Vice-president? She should have been impressed, and relieved. Even Ryan wouldn't throw away a high-powered, high-paying position like that.

"Stop by and see the plant while you're here." He cleared his throat. "Check us out so you know we're not some big, evil corporation out to steal your grandma's secret recipes. Take a tour when you come. The bottling machine's a thrill a minute to watch."

She hesitated, not jumping right in to accept his offer, wondering why he'd issued such a half-hearted, impersonal invitation. Was he thinking they'd simply sweep their past away and go on as casual strangers?

"It's not much out of your way," he continued. "The plant's on the near side of town, only fifteen minutes from here on good roads, a little longer in the winter depending on the weather. Driving into work this week has taken me about double because of the snow."

"What?" Her mouth went dry as a terrible new thought occurred to her. Ryan hadn't run out from town on this errand. This wasn't going to be the sole meeting with him this visit. "Don't tell me you're the mysterious new resident number twenty-four? The one Grandpa changed the sign for?"

He nodded. "Yeah. Go figure. I guess I've arrived. After all these years, Harry finally added me to the sign. I bought the Tucker cabin."

Seeing Ryan again, finding out he was working in town, and now that he was living *right next door* in the cabin they'd talked about living in together someday was just too much for her. Yes, he'd always loved the Tucker place, but it had been an unspoken agreement between them that they keep their distance. Time had not healed their wounds. There were many beautiful pieces of property around the lake. He had to buy the land right next to hers?

"You bought the property right next to my grand-parents' resort?" Had he forgotten about the joint plans they'd had for the place? She couldn't keep the surprise out of her voice. But what she really felt was fear and shock.

"I've always wanted the Tucker place," he said. "When it became available, I had to snap it up. If I didn't, I might never get another chance at it. I'm a good neighbor. I swear." He shot her a half-smile.

Tara couldn't take any more surprises. She scooted to the edge of the booth, eager to escape. "Eat your cheeseburger and fries before they get cold. Gram and Kathleen are dying for your opinion of their new sauce."

He caught her hand as she stood, preventing her from running off. His hand felt too warm and intimate over her icy one. She hoped he couldn't feel her pulse leaping in her wrist. "It's good seeing you."

"Yeah, you too." But she was just being polite. Seeing him again was stirring up a maelstrom of emotions. She shook off his grip and made her departure.

As she walked past the pie case, she noticed the last slice of Gram's famous lemon meringue carefully set aside as if waiting for someone special. Since it was Ryan's favorite, she pretty much knew for whom. She loved lemon meringue, too. Not as much as Ryan did. But she suddenly needed something sweet to take the edge off the bitter taste in her mouth, and this slice was plated and ready to take. She grabbed it from the case and got a fork from the drawer, ready to head back to her room with them. As she headed toward the stairs, she turned over her shoulder for a final glimpse of Ryan. He had the gall to be unabashedly staring after her with a look she couldn't read. Mindlessly, she took a bite of pie.

Ryan's golden retriever Blondie popped out of her Dogloo and met him as he stepped out of his SUV into the carport, still reeling from his encounter with Tara. Blondie wagged her tail and barked her happy bark.

Glad someone loves me.

"Hey, girl! Hey." He knelt to let her off her tether, scratch her ears, and give her some loving, still picturing Tara's eyes as she ate his slice of pie.

"Miss me?" He pulled a bite of hamburger patty wrapped in a napkin from his pocket. "A little something for you." He unwrapped it and fed it to Blondie as he rubbed behind her ears with his free hand.

"Gotta love a girl who doesn't give me grief." He gave her a pat. "Let's get you some real food." As he stood, man's best friend took off for the cabin door, her nails clicking on the concrete carport floor as she ran.

"Hey, Blondie! Wait for me, girl." Ryan froze as a memory bubbled up. *Blondie.*

As a kid, he'd teased Tara, calling her blondie, an immature and ineffective way of flirting. She'd been a regular towhead. Her hair was a darker shade of blonde now, a result of growing up and living in a city without sun. She'd highlighted it, he could tell. The sun streaks in it now were professionally done, not the result of a season on the lake.

But her eyes were still the same snapping green. She always claimed they were blue, blue with yellow flecks around the centers that mysteriously appeared at puberty. He remembered how mad she'd been when she got her learner's permit and the guy at the DMV refused to list her eye color as blue, putting down green instead.

"Blue and yellow makes green. You're unique," he'd told her.

"Like a freak," she'd said.

"Like beautiful," he'd told her, meaning it with all his heart.

She'd blushed.

That Tara, the one I could comfort, died with Chad.

Blondie barked at him to come.

Damn! Without realizing it, I named the dog after her.

He wondered if it was too late to call the dog something else.

He cursed the bad luck that brought Tara back just now as he was making inroads with Harry. Although, to be honest, it was more likely Margie's conniving that had brought her to Echo Bay for Christmas. It was pretty clear Margie wanted them to kiss and make up.

He took a deep breath as a sense of foreboding washed over him. Tara would only cause trouble between him and the old man, just as she always had. And Chad wasn't around to champion him this time. And if Ryan wasn't careful, Tara would crush his heart again, too.

Tara curled up in front of the river-rock fireplace in the private living quarters, hoping the warmth from the crackling fire would overwhelm the cold shock she felt from the day's events.

She stared vacantly at the laptop in her lap, upset with her grandmother for tricking her into talking to Ryan. For setting them both up and keeping secrets. She knew her grandmother meant well, but she should have told Tara that Ryan was back and given her the choice of whether to see him again or not.

Gram sat on the sofa opposite the fireplace, bathed in a warm holiday glow the firelight cast on the polished open-log walls. She felt her grandmother watching her.

Gram took off her glasses and rubbed her eyes. It was only seven, but in another half hour, she'd head to bed so she could catch a few hours rest before Harry went to bed and his earth-shaking snoring began. "Working?"

"Puttering," Tara answered, not looking up for fear of giving her feelings away.

"Something wrong?" Gram put her glasses back on.

She couldn't fool Gram. Tara raised her gaze to meet her grandmother's. "You shouldn't have tricked me into seeing Ryan, Gram."

Gram hedged. "I didn't *exactly* trick you. I told you the dressing man was coming."

Tara shot her an arch look.

Gram looked sheepish. "Okay, you're right. I pulled one over on you and it wasn't fair of me. I'm sorry." She paused. "I'd just like to see the two of you make peace."

Tara softened. "I know you do. But if we do, it'll be in our own time and on our own terms."

Gram nodded. "Point taken."

From his well-worn recliner, Harry watched a basketball game on the HDTV her mother had given him for his birthday. He hooted at a three-pointer. His chair sat at a ninety-degree angle to the sofa, with the TV across from it.

Tara glanced at her grandfather. He looked happy as he watched his game, but old. Very old. And he had the volume up too loud.

"Harry! Turn that down." Gram shook her head at him and frowned.

"What? I'm trying to watch the game."

"And I'm trying to talk to our granddaughter without yelling." She handed him his TV Ears. He scowled, but put them on and turned the volume down.

Gram smiled at Tara, changing topics. "I'm glad you could shut the office down and come here for a few weeks. Especially with your parents off on that Christmas cruise. I didn't like the thought of you being without family for the holidays."

Her parents had invited Tara along. She could have been on that cruise, too, avoiding the painful memories of this sad anniversary. But she was trying to do the right thing and help her grandparents. They weren't making it easy, though.

"Me too. Fortunately, there's not much going on in the brand and marketing consulting business this time of year. Everyone's waiting for next year's budget." She could afford to close the office until after New Year's. Then it was hit-it-hard time.

Gram started to chuckle. "You sure scared Ryan today. You should have seen the look on his face when you greeted him like that!"

Gram's gentle laugh was contagious. Even though she still felt embarrassed and confused, Tara couldn't help smiling just a little. "Yeah? He did look kind of stunned, like one of Grandpa's stuffed deer heads." Tara pointed a finger at Gram. "It's your fault, you know. You hung the mistletoe." She paused. "I was trying to teach you a lesson about playing matchmaker. You're not mad at me?"

Gram chuckled some more. "Well, I didn't raise your mother to raise a brazen hussy, but I could tell you were only teasing. So I guess that's okay."

"Then I guess I'll forgive you for not telling me he's the dressing man and conveniently not mentioning he's the new resident Grandpa modified the sign for."

Her grandmother winced.

"Yes, I noticed the sign," Tara continued. "You can't believe I wouldn't?"

Gram shrugged and had the sense to look guilty.

"You've kept him an awful secret. Why haven't you mentioned him?"

"We know how you feel about him, dear." Gram's voice was soft. She looked thoughtful and concerned. She paused. "We didn't want his return to keep you away from Echo Bay."

"Oh, Gram! Ryan wouldn't keep me away from you and Grandpa." But even as she spoke the words, Tara knew she was lying. "How long has he been back?"

Gram bit her lip and squinted in thought, looking upward. "Oh, late this summer or early this fall. Maybe three, four months now."

How in the world did Gram keep that a secret for so long? Tara wondered.

"What's he doing here?" Tara hoped she sounded casual, like she was just asking about idle gossip. "Why'd he come back now?"

"I couldn't say. You'll have to ask him." Gram smiled innocently, giving Tara the impression she knew more than she was saying.

"Give the boy a chance, Tara," Gram continued in an almost pleading tone. "He's grown up and matured. Bob Hopkins thinks the world of him at Copper Creek. Bob said Ryan's already made production improvements that have saved them nearly a hundred thousand dollars. Did some things his own son Charlie would never think of. Bob may spoil that son of his, but he's never overlooked his shortcomings.

"Ryan's been a good neighbor to us, too. He helps Harry around the resort and takes him out fishing in that new bass boat of his. And then there's my cookbook, that was his idea." Gram stared at her, watching Tara closely.

Gram looked so pleased about the cookbook. Tara couldn't bring herself to say anything against Ryan just then. "He told me he bought the old Tucker place."

Ryan had always liked it for its view, claiming if he ever bought it, he'd build a wrap-around deck on it and live out there.

"It's tiny. Maybe nine hundred square feet tops."
Tara had always said that if they bought it, they'd have
to add on when they had children. Tara tried not to
think about Ryan fixing the cabin up for a future family. She knew he was still single, but not whether he was
involved with someone. "I suppose it's big enough for a
bachelor."

Gram nodded. "Plenty of room for him right now.
As far as I know, he's not seeing anyone." She took off
her glasses and rubbed her eyes. "Don't worry about
the cabin. Ryan has big plans for it. He's fixing it up."

"You mean building a deck around it?"

Gram smiled but didn't answer.

"He's been helping Grandpa?"

Harry didn't even flinch at the mention of his name.
He was too involved in his game, or maybe he simply
couldn't hear her.

Gram shot a glance in the direction of her husband
and nodded. "Grandpa appreciates it, too."

Tara's frown deepened. For as long as she could remember, Harry had been kind-hearted, but independent. He helped others, not the other way around.

Gram yawned again. "Time for bed." She rose slowly
to her feet. She'd never been known for her fleetness of
foot, but she seemed particularly stiff and slow now.

She walked over to Tara and ruffled her hair like
she had when Tara was little.

Tara looked up at her grandmother. "You've forgiv-
en Ryan?"

Tara didn't have to explain. Gram knew what she
meant.

"What's there to forgive? What happened to Chad was an accident. Nobody's fault. You both did all you could to save him. Grandpa and I know that."

Gram paused as if measuring her words. "Ryan lost his best friend...and a big part of himself when Chad died. Don't be too hard on him." She kissed her fingers, then tapped them on the top of Tara's head, transferring the kiss. "'Night, kiddo."

If only Gram knew. It *was* Ryan's fault. And *hers*. If they all hadn't drunk too much. If he and Tara hadn't been fighting so Chad had to step in and try to calm them down. If they hadn't all started arguing and screaming at each other. If they all hadn't headed down the slope angry and distracted just as a storm kicked up. None of this would have happened.

She watched Gram walk slowly and stiffly toward the bedroom. How much longer could Gram and Grandpa keep working and holding on? They should have retired years ago. They *would* have if Chad hadn't died. Or if she'd married Ryan.

Tara swallowed a lump in her throat, seeing clearly what her decisions had cost them. "Gram!" she called on impulse.

Gram paused at the doorway that led through the kitchen back to the bedroom and cocked her head.

"Would you like some help with the pies tomorrow?"

Gram smiled and nodded. "I'd love some."

"You're usually in the kitchen at four, right?" Tara grimaced, dreading getting up in the middle of the night. She wasn't an early morning person.

"I am. But you can come down at six," Gram said, taking pity on her. "I'll have all the prep work done by then. There will still be plenty of pies to bake at six."

"Thanks, Gram. You're an old softie, you know that." Tara wasn't going to argue with two more hours of sleep.

Gram turned to leave.

"You'll teach me how to make your famous Christmas pie?" Tara called after her.

Gram chuckled and waved behind her back. "I'll think about it."

"You better," Tara told her. "You're going to have to pass the secrets down to someone, and I'm a better cook than Mom."

Margie smiled as she got ready for bed. Things had gone pretty well today, all things considered. They might not even pull her matchmaker's license over this one. She chuckled.

Yes, it had been risky, very risky, arranging for Tara and Ryan to meet like that. But what was a grandma to do?

They'd avoided each other for ten years, each beating themselves up over Chad's death. They had to learn that life was a lot like the salad dressing Ryan delivered for her—a little bitter like the vinegar and sour cream, a little sweet like the sugar, and with a blend of herbs to spice things up. Individual ingredients, like individual times and events, might be too bitter or too sweet on their own, but mix them up, take them as a whole, and you have an excellent, tasty dressing. Or life.

Oh, Margie would love for those two kids to get back together. She'd always believed they belonged with each other. Anyone with eyes and a heartbeat could see that. But it would be enough for her old heart if they'd just forgive each other.

That's why she'd put Tara in room ten. Tara had to come to terms with her feelings about that mountain, too. And ten had a prime view of Ryan's cabin. Seeing that cabin every time she looked out the window would keep Ryan fresh in Tara's mind.

Margie chuckled again. People thought she was getting forgetful and maybe a touch senile. But she was just wily enough to use their impression to her advantage.

She sighed. She couldn't help dreaming of great-grandchildren running around the resort. How she'd love that!

CHAPTER FOUR

Six a.m. Too early to be up, dressed, and ready for pie-baking action in Tara's sleepy opinion.

Her night had been terrible.

She may as well have been visited by the Ghost of Christmas Present for all the rest she'd gotten, for all the visions dancing in her head all night long. And the visions that haunted her were anything but sugarplums.

She had a bad feeling remembering the way Gram spoke so fondly of Ryan. He seemed to be taking root into her grandparents' good graces like holly bushes in the forest.

She'd thought about it all night. She was going to stop by and pay him a visit at his office. She needed to talk with him.

She sighed and pulled on a sweatshirt and jeans, then went to the window and paused. Moonlight filtered in through a crack in the curtains. The storm had passed.

Her heart raced.

When she'd been young, the moonlight streaming in intoxicated her. Clear, cold skies after a storm meant snowboarding heaven. Fresh powder from the day before. Clear visibility. Boarding down the mountain would be like flying without wings.

With Ryan flying beside her, life was perfect. She could almost feel the nipping bite of the breeze in her face. See him as they raced down the runs, throwing powder in their wakes. Feel his arms around her as he hugged her at the bottom of the run. Taste his warm tongue in her mouth as their frozen lips met...

She shook her head. Useless thinking.

Heart pounding in her ears, she threw open the curtains.

A host of stars shone overhead. A nearly half waxing moon hung over the mountain, lighting the lake to liquid silver, and silhouetting the strong, unforgiving mountain. She could see the ski runs, silent and crisp.

Suddenly claustrophobic, she tugged open the window and inhaled deeply. The frigid air burned her lungs, but smelled perfect, familiar and clean.

Oh, Chad! You'd love this. Why aren't you here?

Tara found Gram in the kitchen, working on pies. Mel, the muscled, middle-aged breakfast short-order cook had just arrived.

He greeted her with a cup of coffee. "Hey, kid, good to see you back." His gaze ran over her. "Looks like you could use some caffeine to get you going."

She gave him a hug. "Gotta love a man who encourages my bad habits."

He laughed. "Go help your grandma before she finishes on her own."

"Hey!" Tara gave her grandmother an accusing look. "I thought I was supposed to be helping. Or am I just here for KP?"

Margie smiled and wiped her flour-dusted hands on her apron. "I have the shells made for the lemon meringue. You can get busy on the filling."

As Tara cracked and separated eggs for the meringue, she heard the hum of an engine outside and the distinctive scrape and swish of snow being plowed. She knew better than to think the county plow had reached them yet. She wondered which neighbor had come to plow them out.

Mel went to the window. "Looks like Ryan's out early with the plow." He stood there a minute. "Huh, appears he's going on by and won't be in for breakfast today. Guess we'll try the ranch dressing omelet on him another day." He wiped his hands on his apron and went back to work.

Tara turned to Gram, who ignored her questioning look. Just how much time did Ryan spend at the lodge? Tara was getting a funny feeling that he practically lived here.

A few minutes past seven, as Tara pulled the last perfectly browned meringue-topped pie from the oven,

the young new waitress named Sarah called through
the pass-through window into the kitchen, "Does anyone know when Ryan will be in today? I have a customer who says he said he'd help him wax his board. Oh,
and he wants Ryan's opinion on which kind of goggle
lenses are best for sunny weather. He says Ryan has
some in the gift shop he was going to show him."

Tara whipped around to stare at Sarah as Mel answered her. "Looks like he went straight to Copper
Creek this morning. He should be back here by six tonight, like he always is."

As Sarah bounced off to deliver the news, Tara's
grandpa drifted into the kitchen wearing his coat and
Seahawks stocking cap, killing the question on Tara's
lips. Just how deep was Ryan's involvement in all
things Echo Bay?

The breakfast rush had begun. Mel and Gram were
scrambling eggs and popping toast at an alarming rate.

Barely taking his eyes off the grill, Mel handed Harry a plate of bacon and eggs.

"Pour me a thermos of coffee, Tara. I like a little
cream, one packet of sugar." Harry looked out the window and squinted. "Looks like the storm's gone."

"It's going to be a pretty day." Gram slid another
round of toast into the industrial-size toaster and began buttering the batch that had just come out.

Tara got the feeling Gram was staying busy partly
to avoid her.

Gram slapped two slices on the plate Grandpa held.
"Good thing. You haven't been to the bank all week.
We need change and small bills. Now you can go to

town and make the deposits after you finish plowing the lot."

Grandpa scowled. "Too much snow. Going to take me all morning into the afternoon to plow the lot. By the time I get done, there won't be time to get to town and back before it gets dark."

Tara frowned, a sense of unease dawning on her. Since when had it taken Grandpa all day to plow the lot with his little Bobcat? And when had he become so afraid of driving in the dark?

Gram looked anxious. "Now Harry, you missed going on Monday—"

Harry turned around and snapped at her. "I'll get there when I get there, woman."

Tara held her breath. This was her opportunity. She looked out the window. Ryan the happy plower had cut a single swath through the parking lot to the main road and beyond. Once she hit the highway, the roads should be in good shape. She knew how to drive in this stuff. She'd done fine yesterday in the teeth of the storm. "I'll go the bank for you, Grandpa."

Ryan sat in his office, head bent over plans he was making to improve the second production line when Beth, his office assistant, tapped on the door.

"You have a visitor!"

Ryan wondered why Beth sing-songed the announcement. "Do I have an appointment I forgot about?" Beth always kept him honest.

"A drop-in. But I think you should see her. She's waiting in the lobby." Beth winked at him and disappeared.

Her?

For just a second, his heart pounded. No, he shook his head. No way Tara would drop by. He ran his fingers through his hair, made sure his shirt was tucked in, and grabbed the sports coat he kept for emergency business meetings from the hook in the corner.

He pushed through the glass door separating the offices and the plant from the public lobby to find Tara sitting in one of the guest chairs, leafing through a Copper Creek brochure.

She wore skinny jeans stuffed into faux-fur-rimmed boots, a fashionable black jacket, and scarf and matching knit cap. Hearing him enter, she looked up from the brochure. She was still Tara and still so damn beautiful.

His breath caught. His heart suddenly decided to act as if he'd just gone into a full-out sprint and it needed to pump at one hundred and sixty beats per minute. "What are you doing here? Something wrong?"

"Pessimist? Should there be? Maybe I misheard, but I thought you invited me for a tour?" She stood and shrugged. "I guess I should have called first."

Her impromptu visit would have made him way too happy if he hadn't detected an edge to her voice. "No need to call. We run a casual operation."

Ryan found the rosy flush in Tara's cheeks sexy as hell. "Come back this way. We need hairnets and white coats if we're going to get an up-close look at the production lines. We'll drop by my office first and pick some up." He indicated the door he'd just come through.

They went into his office.

Tara unzipped her coat. Beneath it she wore a tight pink sweater that showed off her curves.

"Take your coat?" he asked.

"Thanks, I'll just keep it on. I haven't warmed up yet. I'm afraid I've lost my tolerance for the cold. It rarely dips below freezing in Seattle."

It took all his effort not to simply stare at her. What did she want?

"It's not just you," he said. "Fifteen degrees is hard to tolerate."

An ad for the Santa Ski was pinned to the bulletin board just inside his office door.

Tara paused and studied it. "There are ads for that thing *everywhere*."

"It's big news here."

"Copper Creek's a huge sponsor, I see." Her tone was neutral. "Grandpa and Gram donated a prize to it, too. I suppose you're going?"

He laughed. "The whole town's going."

"I'll take that as a yes." She stared up at him with those penetrating green eyes of hers.

"I have to. The whole ski patrol will be there—"

"You joined the ski patrol?" She suddenly looked almost frightened.

"Yeah, of course." He couldn't understand why she sounded so surprised. He'd been a member of ski patrol since he was twelve. "You going?"

"No. I'm spending the evening with Gram and Grandpa."

He couldn't let her miss the event of the season. "You should come! Just for a few hours. I'm sure Harry and Margie would want you to. With the snow we've been getting, the boarding will be fantastic. You'll enjoy it, believe me."

She paled.

He stopped short and swallowed hard as a horrible realization began to dawn on him. "Tara, you still board and ski?"

"No." She shook her head. "I vowed never to go up on the mountain again and I've kept my word."

She'd been a natural, a talented snowboarder and skier. It was a love and passion they'd always shared. He couldn't believe she'd given it up.

"You're kidding?" He could tell from her expression the moment he spoke that he shouldn't have.

"I haven't been up since..."

He knew since when and what.

"I haven't been up on *any* mountain. I don't have the stomach for it anymore." She trailed off.

There were two possibilities why she hadn't been boarding, neither one of them good. Either she was too scared to get back up on the mountain or she was punishing herself for living when Chad wasn't. He swallowed a lump in his throat at the thought.

Right then and there, he vowed to get her back up on the mountain and onto her board. He owed her that much. Maybe giving her one of her passions back would atone in a small way for all the hurt he'd caused her. In the meantime, he knew enough to drop the subject.

"We each have our own way of dealing with grief." He spoke softly.

Tara was studying him intently.

He gave her a curious look. "What's on your mind?"

"I'm not really here for a tour." She hesitated. "Can we speak someplace private?"

He got a bad feeling from her tone. "This office is as private as we get." He closed the door. "Have a seat." He indicated a chair for her to take before leaning against his desk in front of her.

She took the chair he offered, tilted her head and stared directly at him. "Why are you back, Ryan?" Her tone was soft.

The question caught him off guard. "This is home."

Her intense look didn't waver. "You mean working for pimply-faced Charlie Hopkins is your dream?"

"Sshhh, this is his place." He laughed, trying to lighten the mood. He remembered how he used to tease her about Charlie liking her. They'd both called Charlie names behind his back. He lowered his voice. "No one's called Charlie pimply-face for years. And I don't work for Charlie. I work for Bob—"

"And we both know Bob's going to leave Charlie the business."

He couldn't refute that. He didn't try.

"Stay long enough and eventually you *will* be working for Charlie."

He didn't reply. Better to wait for her to explain herself.

They stared at each other.

When she finally spoke, her tone was pleading. "Don't *do* this, Ryan. Don't make me be the bad guy in this situation. *Please.* It's pretty obvious you've resurrected your old dream of owning Echo Bay. And that you're hoping Grandpa will sell the resort to you." She paused, looking like she was cautiously measuring her words, hoping to soften something there was no easy way to say.

He held his tongue, even though his heart pounded in his ears, and braced for bad news as he waited for her to continue.

"Please don't misconstrue what I'm about to say as vindictive." She paused again. "Grandpa isn't going to sell the lodge to you." She took a deep breath and spoke in a rush. "He won't part with it during his lifetime. And he insists he's leaving it to me as my inheritance. It's important to him to leave me his legacy.

"Ten years ago, I swore I'd sell the minute I inherited. Since then I've come to realize how important it is to keep it in the family. In any case, that's all a long way in the future." She paused, looking like she was trying to stay composed. "A lot of dreams were shattered that Christmas Eve ten years ago on the mountain. We've all had to move on and adjust. Let this aspiration of yours go, Ryan. Your obsession with owning the lodge will only hurt you. You don't owe it to Chad to keep his dream alive. It died with him. Let it stay there."

He opened his mouth to speak, but she cut him off.

"Don't bother denying it. I've already been to the bank and the local cash and carry. Everywhere I went people were eager to catch me up on all you've been doing for my grandparents. To tell me how much Gram and Grandpa love you and how you've been helping them out like a grandson since you've been back.

"And I appreciate it. I really do. Just don't expect more out of it than gratitude.

"I know you have the means, now, too. Ross at the bank said your grandparents left you a nice little nest egg in their will." She paused again. "I'm sorry about your loss. I liked your grandparents."

Ryan was too stunned to reply.

"Grandpa's past *getting* old. He *is* old. Even in the short time I've been back I've seen the change in him. He's slowed way down. If he slows down much more, he won't be able to run Echo Bay at all." She stopped herself, looking as if she'd almost said too much. "He'll have to retire soon. He should have years ago.

"I know how your mind works. It's like the Tucker place all over again. You think this is your opportunity to come back and convince Grandpa to sell Echo Bay to you." She stared him directly in the eye, still pleading with him.

He refused to flinch.

"Am I right?"

He shrugged.

She waved her hand. "It doesn't matter. You can deny it if you like, but I can read you, Ryan. Over the past months, I've made it clear to my grandparents that they can leave the lodge to me with confidence. I'll do my best by it.

"If you make a play for it, I'll discourage Grandpa from taking any offer you make. I'm sorry. I'm only doing what I think is best for everyone, my family especially."

He went cold. He knew she'd be trouble, but he hadn't imagined she'd be so direct. "What's your plan for the place? Are you going to come back and run the resort?"

She frowned at him. "I didn't say that."

"If you're not going to run it, then who is?"

"That's none of your business. But believe me, I'm doing what I think is best for everyone—Gram, Grandpa, and you."

He ran his hand through his hair and popped up to a full stand.

At his sudden movement, Tara looked startled. She stood, too, and tossed her purse over her shoulder like she was ready to run.

He stood tall. He didn't like himself for doing it, but he used his full height to intimidate her. "You're going to hire someone to run it, aren't you?" He had a hard time keeping his voice under control.

"Just let it go, Ryan." She pulled her purse tighter against her body.

"You're mistaken. I'm the best thing for Echo Bay. And I'm following *my* dream, not Chad's. Since when do you give a damn about me, anyway?"

Her face contorted with pain and disbelief. She shook her head. "I have exciting, sound plans for Echo

Bay, plans that will give my grandparents the comfortable, secure retirement they deserve."

"I have plans for Echo Bay, too, Tara. You want to farm the resort out to some faceless corporate hotel management company, no doubt. I love that place. I want to live there and run it in person. Treat guests special. Be a vital member of the community. Keep Harry's legacy alive. Whose plans do you think he's going to like better?"

She shrugged. "I'm his granddaughter. He knows I have Echo Bay's best interests at heart.

"My faceless, and you may as well add soulless, hotel management company has the expertise and experience to put Echo Bay Resort on the map and make sure it stays in business for years and years to come. That's what my grandparents want. They've already agreed to meet with them." After firing that salvo, she turned to leave and walk away.

"I'm not giving up on my dreams," he said to her back, stunned that Harry would agree to meet with a hotel management company and not tell him.

She paused, and spoke without turning to face him. "Suit yourself."

He kept his tone as calm as he could. "Tell everyone I'll be at the lodge around six to give the board-waxing clinic I promised."

She walked out, softly closing the door behind her.

He turned and banged his fist on the desk. No damn way he was giving up on what he'd always wanted. She couldn't order him around like an obedient bird dog. He'd have to convince Harry that Tara was wrong.

CHAPTER FIVE

Tara couldn't believe how stubborn and deluded Ryan was.

It was his and Chad's crazy, immutable plans for running Echo Bay that had driven her and Ryan apart and gotten them into this predicament. Those same dreams were also at least partly to blame for Chad's death. The night Chad died she and Ryan had been fighting over Ryan's plan to live at the lodge after their wedding. They'd been fighting for *weeks* before, ever since Ryan laid down the law. He wouldn't even listen to her side.

He and Chad had a semester of college left. Tara and Ryan had set a date for a June wedding after Ryan's graduation. Tara was only a junior. She still had her senior year to go.

Ryan had decided they'd spend the summer after the wedding together at the lodge. Then Tara would head back to school for her final year while he remained at the lodge to help Chad learn the business and build up sweat equity to eventually buy it from Harry. After Tara graduated, she'd come live at the lodge with Ryan.

Things came to a head that Christmas Eve when Tara accused Ryan of loving Echo Bay more than he loved her. She wanted him to move to the university with her and find a job there until she graduated. And then she wanted to go out into the world, live in Seattle, live somewhere she could pursue her marketing career. With his degree in food science, Ryan could work practically anywhere. She promised him that after a few years, they'd reevaluate. Maybe then they'd move to Echo Bay.

In the here and now, Tara believed it was in Ryan's best interests to find another plan for his life. If she had the opportunity to sit on Santa's lap this year, she'd ask Santa to make Ryan see sense and give up his obsession with Echo Bay Resort.

Tara caught a glimpse of her reflection in a storefront window. She looked horrible—upset, harried, and worried. She needed something to warm her up. Or maybe cool her down. She couldn't decide which.

What she really longed for was a nice, hot cup of cocoa, a shoulder to cry on, and someone she could innocently pump for local gossip without being too obvious. Her stomach growled, reminding her to make up her mind.

She doubted anywhere here could come up with a frothed cup of hot chocolate as good as the coffee shops in Seattle served. Topped with heavy whipped cream and crumbled peppermint candy. The old-fashioned automatic cocoa machine at the lodge was fun and had been great when she was a kid. But it just wasn't cutting it any more. There were only two ways to go now—very modern machines or K-Cups like she made in her machine at home, or totally upscale frothed affairs.

She really needed comfort now, of both chocolate and friends. And probably a sandwich. As of last summer, the Mountain View Café had had an old hot chocolate machine the same vintage as the lodge's. Their hot chocolate wouldn't be as rich and tasty as Tara craved, but it would be homey and familiar. And her friend Laurel worked there with her husband, whose father owned the place. Tara just hoped she'd be on shift.

Unfortunately, Tara hated the café's perfect view of the mountain. It felt as if the Ghost of Christmas Past was haunting her, chasing her all over town. That stupid mountain rose large and majestic in the café's front picture windows. But there was nothing for it. The mountain couldn't scare her away from her comfort drink of choice.

As Tara approached the aptly named Mountain View Café she was struck by how shiny and upscale it looked on the outside. Since her last visit, the old brick building had been scrubbed and refinished so that the bricks looked new. The glass in the picture windows was modern triple-pane. The door not only had a fresh coat of paint, but was new, too. Last summer, Laurel had mentioned something about plans for giving the place a facelift. But Tara hadn't expected such a pleasant transformation. Don was a notorious cheapskate. Which is why Tara had expected nothing grander than a new coat of paint.

A fresh fir wreath decorated with bright red Christmas balls hung on the door and a bell jingled when she let herself in and looked around for Laurel or her father-in-law Don, who'd owned and run the place for as long as Tara had been alive.

Inside the café was another surprise. The Mountain View had been around since the forties. It had its heyday as a fifties soda fountain. Had fallen prey to the garish colors and wild patterns of the sixties and seventies and been dying a slow, sad decaying death since. At least, it had been the last time Tara had been in town.

Now it sparkled and hummed, the perfect picture of updated retro. The fixtures gleamed. The paint was fresh. Pots of poinsettias wrapped in green and red foil sat on every table. A jukebox wrapped with a holiday bow played Christmas carols. And a garland decorated with exquisite old-world-style, mouth-blown, glittered Christmas ornaments ran the length of each wall of the café. The aromas of Christmas filled the room.

Cinnamon and coffee. Nutmeg. Ham sizzling on a grill. Meatloaf and gravy.

Tara looked around and strained to see past the long counter in the front to the kitchen beyond. But she didn't see Don anywhere. And there was no sign of Laurel.

The café was sparsely populated with locals, none that she knew. She used to know practically everyone in town. But in recent years it had grown so much she couldn't keep up. She looked around once more for Laurel.

It was quiet, and quite possible Laurel, or whichever waitress was on duty, was taking a break. Being a resort town, its rushes came at odd times compared to the rest of the world. In the morning about half an hour before the Basin ski resort opened. At around five in the afternoon when day skiing ended. And again at around eleven at night when the slopes closed. In between was usually peaceful and when you found the locals out and about.

The Mountain View had always been a "seat yourself" kind of place. Tara figured that hadn't changed with the décor. She slid into a corner booth away from the window and crossed her fingers that Ryan wouldn't decide he needed a sandwich, too, as she admired the vast variety of the ornaments overhead. They must have cost a small fortune. Tara knew quality when she saw it, and by her estimation each ornament had to have a price tag of ten dollars and up. And the garlands were covered with them. At a quick guess there were thousands of dollars of ornaments hanging in the once dingy café.

Tara was so occupied with calculating the cost of the ornaments she didn't hear the waitress approach.

"Oh my gosh! Tara, is that really you? I didn't see you come in. You should have let me know you were coming to town today! I didn't expect to see you for a few more days, at least until I could get out to the lodge. I know how you hate coming to town when there's a chance you'll run into you-know-who."

"Laurel! So good to see you." Tara popped out of her booth and tried to give Laurel a gentle teepee hug. "I would have, but this trip was supposed to just be a quick, spur-of-the-moment visit to the bank on lodge business. I wasn't sure I'd have time to stop by. Luckily, I finished my business quickly and thought I'd surprise you."

Laurel pulled Tara close against the large baby bump that came between them, complete with a tiny baby kick to Tara's abdomen.

"Hey! Take it easy, slugger. The newest member of the Walker clan doesn't like me. Either that or baby's protecting mama. I think you have a soccer player in there."

Laurel rubbed her belly as if to calm the baby inside her. "That was a kick of joy."

"Uh-huh. Sure." Tara shot her a skeptical look. "It recognized me from the womb, did it?"

"It recognizes the sound of Mommy's happy voice."

Tara shook her head and laughed. Laurel hadn't changed at all from the days the young incarnations of themselves waitressed together at the lodge back when Tara was sixteen and Laurel was a much more mature and experienced waitress at the ripe old age of eighteen.

Tara took Laurel in. "You look fabulous. Very glow-y."

"Isn't glow-y a euphemism for blimp? Because that's the way I feel." Laurel laughed and rubbed her belly again. "A belly like Santa, like a bowl full of jelly."

"No way. That tummy of yours is taut and all baby. No jelly about it. You may feel big, but you certainly don't look it. You look radiant. Turn around." Tara made a spinning motion with her finger.

Laurel hesitated.

"Seriously. Spin!" Tara watched her old friend do a self-conscious three-sixty.

"See? I am so not blowing smoke. From the back you are as svelte and lean as ever. No one would ever guess you're preggo. Serious. You are no blimp, girl."

Laurel shook her head again and they both laughed.

"Remind me—when's the little Walker due?" Tara had a hard time not staring at Laurel's baby bump with envy. There was a time when Tara had thought she and Ryan would live happily ever after and she'd sport her own baby bumps over the years. She'd thought she was long past that, but the twin-headed beast of biology and mothering instinct reared its heads at the most inconvenient and surprising times.

"Mid-January, and it can't come a minute too soon." Laurel looked Tara over and for just a second Tara felt pretentious dressed in her designer jeans and boots. "Now, *you* look fabulous. Really and truly terrific."

Tara shook her head. "Stop it. I look like Rudolph with his nose so bright. I've lost my tolerance to the cold. I could use a cup of the famous Mountain View hot cocoa and one of Don's notorious grilled ham and cheese sandwiches to warm me up. Maybe then I'll begin to look human again." She gazed pointedly around the café. "Where is he? I'd like to say hello."

"That could be a problem," Laurel said. "He's semi-retired now and snowbirding it in Arizona. He'll be back for the baby's birth, though. You'll have to put up with Donny's cooking."

"Donny's working here? He's cooking! Why didn't you tell me?"

"I wanted to surprise you." Laurel beamed.

"But I thought—"

Laurel interrupted her. "I know. I know. You and everyone else. Even Donny thought he had other dreams. But he's Don's son, and when it came down to it, after Don's heart attack last August, he gave running the place a try and now he loves it."

Tara arched a brow as if she didn't believe it. She *couldn't* believe it. As long as she'd known him Donny talked of owning a ski shop. He short-ordered for his dad during high school and beyond under duress and because it was expected. But he was always looking for his angle to escape the family biz.

"Seriously. I'm not kidding." Laurel laughed again. "Wait until you taste his cooking. He's better than Don."

"Donny always could cook. But better than his dad? I'll believe that when I taste it. Is he in the kitchen now? I bet he looks cute in his apron."

Laurel laughed. Like normal teenage girls, they'd been obsessed with cute guys when they were young.

"He doesn't just look cute. He looks hot in that apron." Laurel winked. "I'll put your order in."

"Send him out to say hello when he gets a chance."

"Will do. I'll be right back with your hot chocolate and then we can chat."

Yes, a nice, long chat to catch up and find out how much damage Ryan had already done was exactly what Tara needed.

Ten minutes later, Tara was sipping decadent hot cocoa. Real hot cocoa made from scratch by boiling cocoa and water, adding hot whole milk and vanilla. Laurel had served it with a large, square, freshly made marshmallow on top drizzled with gourmet fudge sauce, not the stuff from a can like Don used to use.

Okay, so add "made from scratch" to the list of options for updating a menu. And the grilled ham sandwich?

No more cheap bread and American cheese like in the Don days. This one was made from thick slices of gourmet, fresh-baked pugliese bread sliced by hand— easy enough to tell by the slightly uneven slices—and some kind of herbed white cheddar. The fries were hand cut, too. The new Mountain View Café rivaled anything in Seattle.

Her cell phone buzzed. A text from Cheryl Jones, the rep from Northwest Resort Management Services Corporation, verifying that Monday the twentieth would work for their meeting.

With as many times as Harry had postponed, Tara didn't blame her one bit for checking. Tara sent her a reply saying the meeting was still on just as Laurel returned and slipped into the booth across from her.

"So, what do you think?" Laurel said. "Am I right? Donny can out-cook his dad."

Tara made a face conceding defeat. "You have me. I didn't think it was possible. But this food is heavenly. Ambrosia for the winter wanderer's soul." Tara grinned. "Did you hear that, Donny?" she yelled toward the kitchen. "I just said your food is better than your dad's."

Donny popped his head out of the kitchen. "Better than the old man's? Of course it is. Hey, Tara! Welcome back, stranger. Laurel said you were out there, but I thought she was having one of her pregnancy-related hallucinations."

"Oh, shut up!" Laurel laughed. "Pregnant women don't hallucinate. Now get back in the kitchen where you belong so Tara and I can talk."

Donny laughed, too. He looked genuinely happy. "See you later, Tara. Come see us again when I'm not on shift." He ducked back out of sight.

"He does look cute in that apron," Tara teased.

"Yeah, he does. That's the way I like my men— aproned and in the kitchen."

They grinned at each other.

Tara pointed at her sandwich. "Tell me about this and the hot chocolate. Who are your suppliers?"

"Oh, you want me to brag, do you?"

"I do."

"All the ingredients are made right here in town. That's our theme, our brand. Everything local. Made from ingredients you can't get anywhere else. So when people come to the Basin to ski or board, they simply have to stop here to get their food fix.

"The bread's from Nelson's Bakery. The cheese from the Basin Cheese Factory that opened last spring."

"Really?" The town was growing and upscaling even faster than Tara had known or imagined. "The marshmallows?"

"From a little candy shop just down the street, Taylor's. Along with the fudge sauce. Isn't it yummy? Made from real butter and cream and deep, dark chocolate. It's almost impossible to resist. If I hadn't already gained my weekly allotment I'd be pigging out on it every day."

"Wow! I'm impressed." Tara wasn't using hyperbole. She really was. "You and Donny have taken the café to a new level. It's homey, yet upscale.

"Can I hire you as consultants if Gram and Grandpa ever want to revamp the lodge menu?" She was only half joking.

Laurel squirmed and pursed her mouth to the side as if she was guilty of something. And stalling, definitely stalling. There was something she didn't want to say.

"What?" Tara laughed again.

Laurel took a deep breath. "It's not *our* expertise you need. We had help. From an old friend with a lot of experience in the food business."

Tara's pulse quickened, and not in a good way. A sense of dread came over her as she suspected whom the help was.

"Oh, Tara, I hate to do this to you. I was trying *so* hard not to bring up his name." She took another deep breath. "Our expert is Ryan."

The hot cup of cocoa felt suddenly cold in Tara's hand. Everything went cold. *Ryan!* She should have known. Suddenly she could see Ryan and his "homey touch" fingerprints everywhere.

Laurel gave her a sympathetic look. "I'm sorry."

"Don't be," Tara said. "Hey, I asked." For it, she could have added.

"I wish you two..." Laurel rushed on. "I wish you two could just let bygones be bygones and put the past behind you."

Tara let out a heavy sigh. No one seemed to understand how complicated the situation was, and Tara was in no mood to bring up her battle with Ryan over the lodge.

Laurel reached across and squeezed Tara's hand. "Hey, kid. You may not like it, but he's back in town now, for good. At least, that's the way he's talking." She gave Tara a sympathetic look.

"He's the town's prodigal son. Everyone loves him. He's as popular now as he was when he was Basin High's star athlete and the best skier and snowboarder in town."

This town loved its athletes, and none more than Ryan.

"You're going to have to learn to get along with Ryan," Laurel said. "'Tis the season."

"Peace to men of goodwill," Tara said.

"Something like that." Laurel gave Tara's hand another squeeze and released it. "Oh, come on. Ryan's not that bad. There was a time you used to think he was pretty hot when he strolled into the lodge in his letterman's jacket.

"Remember how I used to play lookout for you and let you know when he was coming? Donny still hasn't forgiven me for using him as a source to track Ryan's movements for you."

Tara couldn't help smiling, slightly at least, at the memory. "Yeah, well, I was young and naïve. I did a lot of stupid things back then, like trailing after Ryan and Chad like a lovesick puppy. Turns out Grandpa had the right idea trying to keep us apart. Oil and vinegar, that's what we really are."

Laurel gave her a look that said she didn't believe her. Tara ignored it. She didn't feel like talking about the past anymore. Instead, she changed the subject and circled the room with her hand. "So all of this—the décor, the decorations—this doesn't look like Ryan at all. Please tell me this is you."

Laurel grinned. "Mine and a talented interior designer."

Tara arched a brow. "I love the old-world-style Christmas decorations."

"Good. Those are all my idea."

"They're gorgeous."

"And cheap."

"Cheap?" Tara couldn't believe that. "You have to be kidding. Have you come into a fortune I don't know about? I've seen ornaments like these in catalogues. They start at ten dollars for the small ones and go up from there. You have a mint's worth here."

Laurel grinned. "Sure. Retail they're pricey. But not at the new factory outlet here in town. Old European Christmas moved their headquarters here last summer. They opened up a factory outlet store after Thanksgiving. It will be open through Christmas Eve and then closed until next Thanksgiving. They're selling the ornaments wholesale to everyone. These ornaments only cost two to three dollars apiece. Everyone in town has them."

"I want some!" Tara said. "I must have them. They'll look great on the lodge Christmas tree and Gram will love them. Give me directions?"

"I will, but they aren't open today. They open at noon and close at six three days a week." Laurel's eyes lit up. "Hey, want to make a shopping date? A girl's day before I have this kiddo?"

"Love to."

"Good. I'll talk to Donny about getting an afternoon off."

CHAPTER SIX

Twice a week since ski season opened, Ryan had been giving a ski and board-waxing workshop in the lodge gift shop. He not only waxed boards, he made minor repairs to bindings and equipment. Fit people for helmets. Gave advice about snow conditions on the mountain and the best runs. Recommended instructors for those who wanted lessons. Calmed nerves. Just generally talked skiing and snowboarding with anyone who showed up and wanted to talk.

Since starting the workshops, sales at the lodge's gift shop had increased fifty percent compared to last year at the same time. Harry was the king of fishing and hunting advice, and Ryan was his skiing equivalent. People recognized passion when they saw it, and Ryan had passion in spades. And because he'd practi-

cally grown up on the mountain and was on the ski patrol, people trusted him. He never mentioned Chad's
accident, but he was adamant in his advice to respect
the mountain, never take chances, and to watch the
weather. It was his way of doing penance for his part in
Chad's death.

Everyone in Echo Bay and town, all the old-timers
at least, knew about Chad's fatal accident on the mountain. But none of them brought it up.

Ryan's work at the gift shop was partly therapeutic
and partly an investment in his future, if he could ever
wrest the lodge away from Tara's clutching hands and
her stupid property management company. Could this
wonderful property management company hire someone to do the workshops and hand-sell the goods as effectively as someone who genuinely loved the place like
he did? Why didn't Tara believe that he owning the
lodge was his dream and he wasn't living Chad's life, he
was trying to live his? That this wasn't a dark obsession, as she seemed to think?

Somehow, he'd have to make her see the truth.

Ryan would never work for her property management company. No amount of money could entice him.

He was still stinging from his interview with Tara
earlier and not keen on running into her again, especially so soon. If he hadn't already promised several
guests he'd be by to help them, he would have kept
driving and headed directly home. But Margie would be
waiting for him with a slice of lemon pie—assuming
Tara hadn't eaten that, too. And the stubborn, perverse

part of him refused to let Tara scare him off from doing something he loved.

She could choose to hang onto the guilt from the past, but he wasn't going to let it drag him down with her.

He turned into the lodge parking lot and pulled into a spot. Harry had managed to get the lot plowed, but he hadn't done a great job of it. Every time Harry plowed, the lot got noticeably smaller.

As Ryan walked toward the lodge, he was hoping for a small Christmas miracle—that Tara would be locked away in her room doing whatever it was she did there.

Tara stood in the lodge's great room by the river-rock fireplace staring at the gaping hole where the Christmas tree should have been. Weeks ago. And by gaping hole, she actually meant sofas and chessboard table that had to be moved to make way for the traditional Christmas tree in its traditional spot. Where it had been every year since Tara's birth.

And should have been now, not only for festive, family holiday reasons, but for business purposes. Guests came to the lodge to enjoy the winter holiday atmosphere. Without the tree, where was the atmosphere?

Gram and Grandpa were slipping, really slipping. A property management company would have had the tree up the day after Thanksgiving. Tara herself would have taken care of it immediately if Ryan and his antics hadn't distracted her.

She stood studying the spot with Harry, Gram, Stormy, and Kathleen looking on with her.

"You should have ordered one months ago, Grand-pa," Tara said. "Ordered exactly to your specifications and had it delivered and ready to go. It's too late now. And the tree you need is too big to just pick up at a lo-cal lot. Maybe the tree farm—"

"Too expensive," Harry said. "Way too expensive. You know that, Tara. Have you forgotten your child-hood? We go out in the forest and cut one ourselves."

Tara stared at her grandfather and sighed. In his younger days he was strong and fit enough to carry a tree the size of Canada on his back if he needed. These days with his arthritis acting up and his bad back, he'd be lucky to carry a sapling. She opened her mouth to say something, but Gram cut her off with a look.

"We were waiting for you this year, Tara," Gram said so sweetly maple sugar wouldn't melt in her mouth.

Yeah, Tara bet they were. They needed her brawn, such as it was.

She looked at Gram. "Have you at least gotten the forest service permit?" Permits were cheap and sold out quickly. The forest service only issued so many. They didn't want the forests clear cut.

Before either Harry or Margie could answer, the front door swung open and a cold burst of air washed in. Standing just inside the doorway, looking very much as he had the night before, and even more like he had when Tara had been in love with him, stood Ryan.

Tara glanced at the old-fashioned clock on the fire-place mantel. Ryan was right on time. He had just enough time to grab a quick burger before that board-waxing workshop of his.

Ryan took off his hat and shook the snow off it. "Hey, all. Are you having a convention without me?" Ryan came over to join them and stare at the sofa and other furniture as if he knew what was going on.

"We're discussing the plans for getting the tree," Harry yelled to him, even though by then Ryan was within easy hearing distance. "Have you gotten the permit yet?"

Tara went cold, and it wasn't because the door was still open letting a cold December wind in, either.

"Picked it up before Thanksgiving." Ryan pulled off his gloves, stuffed them into his pocket, turned his back to the nearby fire that was roaring in the fireplace, and put his hands behind him to warm them. "Wouldn't have mattered anyway. Rick promised to hold one out for us. Pays to have old baseball buddies in the forest service."

"Rick Dempsey?" Tara asked, wondering what excuse Gram and her grandpa had used to put off getting the tree for so long.

"The very one," Ryan said.

"Good, good." Harry nodded.

"But, Grandpa," Tara protested, "how are we going to haul a tree from the forest to the lodge?"

"We'll use the Bobcat." Harry smiled at Ryan. "You're still coming with us Saturday to help us cut it?"

What! Tara clenched her teeth so hard she thought she might crack a tooth.

Gram clasped her hands in front of her in a gesture that meant she was pleased. "Oh, good. It'll be like old times when you and Chad and Tara were kids and Harry took you into the forest to get our tree."

Yeah, old times. Great. Isn't that what kept me away at Christmas all these years?

"And you'll help us get the ornaments down from the attic, too?" Gram said.

Tara couldn't stand it any longer. "We don't need his help." She didn't want to relive old times, certainly not with Ryan. Just his presence was pushing her to places she didn't want to go.

Everyone in the semicircle gaped at her.

She swallowed hard. "I can get the boxes of ornaments down by myself." She bit her lip. "I'd like the time alone." She paused, trying to maintain control of her emotions. "I haven't seen them since..."

Gram looked at her sadly and exchanged a quick, worried look with Harry. Ryan remained silent, but his Adam's apple bobbed.

"Now that I've come back, I'd like to start fresh with new traditions, too. I'd like to buy some new ornaments for the tree at Old European."

"You've been talking to Laurel." Ryan's tone was surprisingly sympathetic.

Harry cleared his throat and looked like he didn't know what to say.

"They're my treat, Grandpa. Part of my Christmas gift to you." Tara never knew what to get them anyway. Facing the old decorations, the ones she and Chad used to put on the tree, in the attic on her own was one thing. The silly old school crafts they'd made over the years. The old favorite wooden and felt ornaments. The ornament Ryan had given her that final year. Seeing them on the tree throughout the season was another.

"Laurel promised to go ornament shopping with me." The fact that Ryan so easily read her and figured out she'd had a chat with Laurel only made Tara shakier.

Tara put her hands on her hips, as if defying anyone to challenge her plan.

"Now that that's settled," Gram said, "Ryan, have you eaten? I saved you a piece of lemon pie."

Ryan shot Tara a quick glance as if to confirm the pie still existed—in someplace other than her stomach. She rolled her eyes. Just because she'd eaten his pie once didn't make her a pie thief for life.

"Your usual?" Kathleen asked as she turned toward the kitchen.

As Ryan nodded, Stormy took his arm and led him to his usual booth. Tara was really worried. Ryan had seamlessly inserted himself into a time-honored family tradition.

Tara shot Ryan's retreating back another look. What else had he done? What else was he up to? She felt a stab of jealousy and pushed back the thought that he was trying to take Chad's place. That he was acting like a better grandchild than she was.

She bit her lip and turned toward the stairs to disappear into her room. She didn't want to be part of the Ryan-fest. Halfway there, she stopped short. Maybe it was better to face the enemy head on in his own camp.

She was going to go to that workshop of his and rattle his cage in the way he was rattling hers.

The ski and board-waxing workshop had been Ryan's idea from the beginning. He'd convinced Harry to give him space in the shop building behind the lodge. Too many guests arrived at the lodge with their boards and skis unprepared for the unique and changing snow conditions at the Basin.

Some were once a year skiers and boarders. Some newbies and beginners. And diehards. All seemed to be busy living fast-paced, modern lives. So busy they rushed out of town without a thought toward general equipment maintenance. Yes, there were ski and board shops in town, but an eager skier or boarder ready to hit the slopes would hate to have to stop and wait for his equipment to be waxed. So Ryan suggested the workshop. He inspected, waxed, and cleaned a few boards and skis, put edges on, recommended repairs, talked about the conditions on the mountain, answered questions, and just generally enjoyed himself.

He'd set up his equipment in the back of the unheated shop. Harry had come in earlier and turned on the space heaters so the place was cozy. In spots, at least. And well lit. Margie had decorated the place for Christmas with fir bows, Christmas balls, and a large wreath on the door.

Ryan set up an iPod and speakers and turned on a selection of Christmas music for atmosphere. The workshop smelled of fir, tools, wax, cleaner, outdoors, and irons—Christmas and the slopes. What could better? And what could be worse?

He inhaled deeply and unzipped the snowboard bag he'd brought with him. As he pulled an old, never-used snowboard from its case, he wondered why he tormented himself with it. What possessed him to keep the girlie thing with its bright pink, purple, blue, and green stripes? *The Ghost of Christmas Past*, he thought.

He set the board on his vises, ready to use for demonstration purposes.

I really should give this to some girl who can't afford one. Donate it to the Santa Ski. Let them find a good home for it.

And yet he knew he wouldn't. It was Tara's. Or, rather, it had been intended to be. He still remembered her eyeing it at the ski shop in town, hinting that was what she wanted for Christmas.

Hell, he'd had no money. He was a broke college kid. So he'd made a deal to work at the shop waxing and repairing boards over Thanksgiving and Christmas break to pay for the thing. He'd worked his ass off, too. Long hours, so many that the payment of the board hadn't even amounted to minimum wage. But that was where he'd learned his waxing technique. So maybe he should be grateful.

He'd planned to give it to her that night, the Christmas Eve Chad died. For obvious reasons, he never had. He should have traded it for something else all those years ago. But he'd had too much pride. Old Man Wilkes had ribbed him about it at the shop so often,

Ryan couldn't face returning it. And he'd been a fool. He'd held out hope...

Now it was just old technology. Good for demos. And a laugh at his naïve younger self. *True love never dies. Right.*

Like him, it had no bindings. It was perfect for demonstrations.

He set his waxing iron out and turned it on. He was arranging his assortment of waxes and cleaners as the first guests arrived with a cold gust as they opened the door. He looked up and smiled at the newcomers, a young teenage boy, thirteen or fourteen, came in with his parents. He was carrying a snowboard.

Ryan smiled at him and waved him in. "Welcome, welcome. Come on in. You brought a board to work on—excellent! Bring it on up."

Two more young men came in with a young woman. They were eighteen, nineteen, twenty maybe. One of the guys carried a board. The three laughed and teased and jostled each other. The trio reminded him of Chad, Tara, and him in younger, happier days.

A few more attendees straggled in as it approached six. He chatted with them, one eye on the door. A few minutes after, when it appeared no one else was coming, Ryan decided to start.

He hadn't realized how tense he was, worrying against the odds that Tara would show up. As if that would happen. He was pretty sure Tara considered this place a little shop of horrors. Besides, she knew how to wax and edge and make general repairs. He'd taught her himself.

But you never knew. She was unpredictable. She might get up the nerve to come in just to torment him.

"Let's get started," he said and rubbed his hands together. He patted the board in front of him. "I'm going to be demonstrating the process and technique on this board. It's never been used, just waxed and re-waxed dozens of times. Maybe one day, if it gets lucky, it will get a shot at the slopes."

Just then the door to the shop opened and Tara stepped in. She glanced at the board before locking eyes with him. His mouth went dry. He couldn't read the exact emotion in her eyes, but he was pretty sure it wasn't joy. More like shock. She had to recognize the board. She carried a tray with a coffee pot and cups that suddenly rattled in her hands.

Margie's fingerprints were all over Tara's sudden arrival bearing hot beverages. Bringing the coffee was Margie's job.

Ryan cleared his throat and tried to ignore Tara as she set the tray on a nearby table, took a seat at the back of the class, and crossed her legs and arms. Could she be any more closed to him? Why didn't she just drop off the coffee and run?

She might have been trying to rattle him, as she had the coffee, to scare him off. But what she'd really succeeded in doing was issuing a challenge. There was no way he was backing down or bumbling his workshop.

And since she was here, he may as well seize this opportunity to get his message across—he was here to stay. She could like it or lump it. Or she could believe him when he said this was his dream and cooperate. And come back to him.

He hated to admit it, but he'd take her back, even with all their sad past between them.

He picked up a spray bottle and showed it to his audience. "I use this citric acid cleaner. It's eco-friendly and biodegradable. Gentle on the board. Back in the bad old days, we used to use a caustic cleaner. Harmful on the skin, the health, and the environment. These days, we've moved on." He stared right at Tara, issuing his challenge: *It's time we move on, too.*

He sprayed Tara's board. "It's important to completely cover the surface of the board with the cleaner. This will get all the old wax off. As well as diesel from the snowcats that groom the slopes. Sap, it gets that out, too. This stuff gets out pretty much everything but old grudges."

Tara stared back at him. *Good, message received.*

"Impurities. Everything. We want this board stripped bare." *Like his soul.* He kept his gaze aimed at Tara.

Her cool returning stare matched the temperature in the already cool room. At least, that was the way it felt to Ryan.

"At this point we're not trying to make the board look pretty. We're trying to make a clean surface so the new wax will hold."

Tara barely blinked. Couldn't she tell he was apologizing? Or trying to? Or at least pleading a case to let bygones be bygones and start fresh?

"Now we use a Scotch-Brite pad and rub the surface of the board to get the wax up. Some boards are harder than others to clean. This one's pretty clean to start with."

The board was clean. Their relationship was complicated and messy as hell. He ran the pad along the board, trying not to take his frustrations out on it.

He stepped back and stared at the board, meeting Tara's eye. "I'm satisfied this board is pretty clean. But I'm going to go over it another time with a paper towel." He grabbed one from a roll nearby, ran it over the board, and held it up for the class to see. "Not bad, but there was still a bit of dirt. Seems like there's always something under the surface."

As he tossed the paper towel away, he took a deep breath. *Stay calm.*

Which was practically impossible with Tara watching him with those assessing eyes. He grabbed his heat gun. "Next we're going to heat the board up to open the pores." *Like we should be opening up a dialogue and a new relationship so we can heal.* "So the wax will really soak in.

"Now the board's nice and warm." *But not as hot as Tara looks.* "Which is just the way you want it."

Ryan grabbed a block of wax. "This is a cold-weather wax, perfect for average December temperatures as the Basin. It'll be harder to scrape off, but worth the trouble for the smooth, fast ride it will give us."

Tara's cheeks were flushed. Which gave Ryan an involuntary thought of a ride he'd like to take with Tara. In the bedroom.

"Now we melt the wax onto the board. I like to melt it down the middle of the board. This looks like about enough to cover. You don't want too much or you'll be waiting forever for it to dry and scraping it off late into the night."

He set down the wax and picked up his iron. "I like to iron in a good, long stroke. Then go back side to side along the board, making sure the wax covers the entire surface. You might have to make a few passes at it." He looked Tara directly in the eye. Yeah, he'd like to make a pass at her, but only if he thought there was a chance of succeeding. He smiled at her. She stared calmly back at him, unreadable.

"Finish up with long, horizontal strokes." He lifted his iron and set it down on the bench next to the board. "And now we let the wax harden."

Ryan couldn't figure out why Tara hadn't abandoned the workshop yet. Or why she'd fixed herself up since he'd seen her in the lobby and suddenly looked so damn hot.

Was she trolling for a teenager? He was the only other single guy in the room under fifty. And the rest of the guys over twenty were all married. Yet there she sat in her perfect, figure-hugging, long sweater with a deep V-neck and skintight black leggings. Knee-high boots with stiletto heels—boots that didn't belong anywhere near snow.

Her lips were pink and glossy, her eyes made up to look bright and sexy in varying shades of pink. And her cheeks and cleavage sparkled and caught the light, like she'd powdered them with holiday glimmer dust. She looked ready for a Christmas party. The joke was on her. This was no party. Or maybe the joke was on him—he still desired her. And worse, he was probably still in love with her. He wasn't sure he'd ever been out of love.

She sat with her legs crossed, bouncing one foot like she did when she was nervous.

He fielded a few questions as the wax dried and called up several volunteers with their boards, helping them clean and apply the wax while his demo board dried. He expected Tara to hightail it out. But she stayed, sitting silently in the back row.

Fifteen minutes passed. Ryan tested the board. The wax was dry and he was ready for the next skirmish.

"While the other boards are drying, I'm going to demonstrate the next step." He grabbed his triangular Plexiglas wax scraper and demonstrated how to use the notched edge to clean the wax off the edges. Then he looked around the room. "This next part takes elbow grease. I need a volunteer to help me scrape."

Six teenage boys raised their hands. Ryan ignored them.

"Tara! Great. Thanks for volunteering." He started toward her.

She looked shocked and about to bolt. "I didn't volunteer."

"Sure you did. You showed up, didn't you?" He quickened his pace and grabbed her by one crossed arm before she could escape.

"I taught Tara how to wax her board years ago. Let's see if she still remembers how to do it." Ignoring the wild look in her eyes, he practically dragged her to the front of the classroom.

"No. I really can't." She was shaking her head.

He thrust the tri scraper into her hands. "Of course you can. It will come back to you." He grinned at the crowd. "Come on, people. Give her a little encouragement."

She was still shaking her head as the group applauded.

"I'll help you out." Ryan positioned himself behind her, which was probably a mistake. He got a whiff of her perfume. She was hot and bothered. Definitely heated up.

He put his arms around her and clasped her hand, holding the scraper in his, then guided all hands to the board. "A lot of people don't wax the tip and tail. But I believe in doing a complete job. Waxing the entire board makes it look extra nice."

In his arms, Tara was stiff as a board herself.

"Start at the tip and always pull the wax with the scraper. Never push."

"I believe you've been pushing this whole time, Ryan," she muttered to him.

He ignored her and smiled at his audience. "A nice, long stroke is what you want. Firm pressure. Enough to get the wax up, but not damage the board."

Even as an unwilling captive, she felt good in his arms. He nodded to the other boys in the room, the guys he'd helped apply wax. "Come up here and grab a scraper and start on your boards. They should be dry by now, too."

He slid his arm around Tara's waist and pulled her toward the other end of the board. "When you're done with the tip, move to the tail."

He could use a little tail. With Tara in his arms, he felt like a desperate man. All he wanted for Christmas right now was Tara, willingly. She was fighting him at every step. Even now, resisting his efforts to help her clean the board.

As he guided the scraper in her hands, applying pressure and helping her pull the wax off the board, he realized she was trembling. And it wasn't from desire.

Something splashed on the sleeve of his sweater. What the—

He looked down at her just as a tear slid down her cheek. *She's crying?*

"This is my board." Her voice was soft and vulnerable, almost cracking.

"I believe it's still mine," he said without accusing. "You refused it. Maybe rightly so. I was being a jerk back then—"

She looked up at him, her chin trembling. With a sudden movement, she let go of the scraper, pushed his arms away, wrenched free of his grip, and ran from the room.

Leaving Ryan to feel the cold blast from the open door and the sting of her public rejection. Everyone was staring at him. *What did I do now?*

He forced a smile. "Apparently, not everyone appreciates the pleasure of waxing." He picked up his scraper. "Anyone else feel like quitting?"

No one moved.

"Good," Ryan said. "I thought not. Let's get on with the job. Then we can have refreshments. Wax off..."

CHAPTER SEVEN

Tara ran out into the cold and wiped a tear away with a flip of her hand. *Damn Ryan for using my board and bringing up memories best left forgotten.*

But even as she cursed him, she realized her anger was misplaced. It wasn't really Ryan she was railing at—it was the situation and herself. Chad had died ten years ago. She should have moved on and made something of her life, found happiness again. Rediscovered the joy of the holidays and enjoyed them like Chad would have wanted her to. Like Ryan had seemed to.

She envied Ryan, even as the thought made her unaccountably sad. *I'm stuck in my holiday misery.*

Back in the safety of Seattle, with its urban environment that felt light years away from Echo Bay, she'd even imagined she had healed. The truth was, though, maybe she'd only hidden.

That snowboard had felt good beneath her fingers, like youth and life and fun. Waxing it in Ryan's strong, warm arms, with the feel of his body next to hers and the smell of his cologne surrounding her reminded her how much she'd missed him. Since Ryan, men had pretty much come and gone in her life. There'd never been anyone she wanted to get serious with and she had to ask herself why.

Not that she really wanted to examine herself for the answer.

Ryan's workshop, and now the cold air stinging her cheeks, felt like a visit from the Ghost of Christmas Past, raising memories of being young and flying down the slopes chasing Ryan and Chad. Why was it that those two always beat her? She believed it was their bigger body mass—gravity working on all that weight to pull them down the hill at top speed. Ryan and Chad had always maintained they were handicapped by greater wind resistance, and it was their superior skill that made them faster than Tara. They'd all laughed and ribbed Tara about being a tail chaser. Tail-chasing Tara. Though there'd really only ever been one tail she'd chased. And that had been Ryan's.

The thought of beating Ryan in a race down the hill almost brought a grin to her lips. Just to prove her point and make a small revenge. Though she had to admit, he had the advantage of a whole lot of practice on her.

She'd given up snowboarding as penance for her part in Chad's death. Not because she'd suddenly lost her love of snow and slopes. Not even because she was afraid. She was, though not as terrified as she'd been right after Chad died. She was even more frightened now by her reaction to being in Ryan's arms.

She should have been furious with Ryan. Instead, she felt furiously determined. She didn't want to end up like Ebenezer Scrooge, an old person regretting an entire lifetime, repenting at the last minute. She still had time to make good Christmas memories. Starting now.

If she could avoid a visit from the Ghost of Christmas Future, that would only be a good thing. That ghost had always scared her more than the two other ghosts combined. More so now, as she applied the situation to her current state and life.

Ryan's workshop had solidified what Tara had known deep down—this community was built around a few seasonal activities. Hunting in the fall. Fishing and water sports in the summer. And skiing and snowboarding in the winter and early spring.

If she was going to continue her grandparents' legacy and honor her brother's life and memory the way he would have wanted her to, she was going to have to get back up on the mountain. If she wasn't willing to do that, she may as well pack up and leave Echo Bay and Christmas to heartache.

She stepped into the lodge and up the stairs to her room, where she dropped onto the bed and stared past the open curtains of her room to the lights sparkling on the ski runs on the mountain.

She was trembling as she grabbed her laptop and ordered a pass to the mountain before she overthought things and lost her nerve. She was getting back on the slopes as soon as possible. As a tribute to Chad. Yes, he'd like that. Rather than fearing the slopes, before she left for Seattle after Christmas, she'd ski the last run he had. And maybe leave a memorial on the run Chad had loved best.

She frowned. She needed boots and bindings. And a board. Ryan had the perfect one. But there was fat chance he'd sell it to her.

The next morning, the lodge was softly lit with Christmas lights down the banister and around the windows as Tara came downstairs dressed in athletic thermal pants, a body-fitting long-sleeve base layer top, a sky-blue fleece pullover, wool socks, and boots. Functional boots. If she was going out in the woods to look for a tree, she was going to be warm while fighting the raging storm of emotions and desire Ryan raised inside her.

She paused on the landing to stare down at the spot where the tree should have been. With their permit, they could only get a twelve-footer, maximum. The two-story space called out for an even larger tree. Wrestling in even a ten- or twelve-foot tree would be a challenge.

Next year would be so much easier on her grandparents, provided they accepted the hotel management company's terms. The hotel management team would simply order one delivered. They'd hire a decorator to come in to decorate it and the rest of the lodge in the most current Christmas theme. Easy-peasy. No muss, no fuss. And, well, any other rhyming cliché Tara could think of.

This having to traipse through the woods in the fog and cold and the latest layer of snow that had accumulated overnight was bogus and frustrating. Even if it had been tradition—way back during Tara's childhood. Life should be simpler.

Speaking of the smell of the forest, the aroma of fresh fir and pine boughs, pinecones, coffee, and cinnamon floated up to her. Along with the sound of dishes clanking, the pleasant white noise of happy holiday chatter, and der Bingle, as Harry called Bing Crosby, singing "Christmas in Killarney."

Yeah, all the folks were home in Killarney in Bing's world. And the same was true here in Echo Bay with one "folk" Tara really wished would head to Hawaii or someplace far away. She'd much rather Ryan sing "Mele Kalikimaka" on a beach in Maui this year than "White Christmas" here. One less Ghost of Christmas Past to deal with would make *her* holiday brighter.

Gram's choice of music was certainly homey and familiar. And stuck in 1950. Or, to put it another way, middle of the last century. Time to get something a little more contemporary.

It was just before eight, but the sun barely skimmed the eastern horizon, lighting up the lodge lobby in shafts of light filtered through evergreen trees in a way that was magical.

Carter Kennedy was making an artful arrangement of newspaper and kindling in the massive stone fireplace in the lobby, just as he'd done every day for the last thirty years.

Carter operated in his own world on his own time. That was what his mama had always said. However, ever since Harry had given him the job of keeper of the lodge fire way back when Carter was a junior in high school, Carter had kept fire time faithfully. He lit a fire every morning at eight and every evening at seven. Precisely. Coming to the lodge from his parents' cabin just up the road through rain and sleet and dark of night and morning. He was more reliable than the mail service. He chopped kindling and cleaned and maintained the fireplace, too.

Tara came down the stairs and admired his work. "That's the making of a beautiful fire, Carter. You are the master."

Carter grunted as he kneeled on the hearth and worked a bellow to fan the small flame he'd started. When Carter was working, he was all focus.

Tara waited while the flame took hold. Carter set the bellows down and fed kindling piece by piece into the growing flames. Finally he looked up and his face lit up. "Tara!"

He pushed up to his feet slowly and caught her in a bear hug. "Back for Christmas? I knew you'd come. Didn't I tell Harry you couldn't keep away forever? Not our Tara."

She laughed. "You knew better than I did, Carter. There was a time when I wasn't sure I was ever coming back for Christmas."

Tara glanced across the room to the breakfast counter. Harry's usual chair was empty. "Have you seen Grandpa this morning?"

Carter shook his head. "Nope. Haven't seen him yet."

Tara frowned. Her grandfather was always up at the crack of dawn. The crack of dawn came late this time of year, like right now at eight. Harry should definitely have been up having his coffee and dreaming of fishing season in the spring.

A piece of kindling popped, startling both her and Carter.

"The fire," Carter said.

"Oh, yes, sorry to disturb your work." Tara patted Carter on the back. "Don't mind me. You'd better get back to it. The guests are expecting a crackling blaze this morning."

She left Carter and wandered toward the kitchen looking for Harry, just as Rick Dempsey came in for his morning cup of coffee before making his rounds of the woods for the forest service. He stomped the snow off his boots on the mat inside the door and looked up to see her. "Well, if it isn't the prodigal granddaughter."

"Nice to see you, too, Ranger Rick." Tara delighted in teasing him. She'd read *Ranger Rick Magazine* as a kid. Her mom's idea. This Ranger Rick looked nothing like a cartoon raccoon. Rick had actually grown into an attractive man with a tease in his eyes. She used to think Rick was okay, maybe even idolized him a bit when they were young and he hung around with Chad and Ryan.

Rick laughed. "Going Christmas tree hunting today, I hear. Better bundle up. A cold front moved in overnight."

Yeah, she knew. It was called Ryan and his waxing clinic.

"We got probably another five inches. The forest service roads are going to be a bear. Ryan's truck won't make it far up the mountain, if at all. Even with siped tires and four-wheel drive."

So Ryan had been talking to Rick. It seemed everyone knew Tara's business. "Grandpa said we'll take the Bobcat."

"Huh," Rick said. "Hope you have some hand and toe warmers. It'll be a cold ride."

Didn't she know it.

"There's a nice little glen I told Ryan about. I've been keeping my eye on it all fall as I make my rounds. It has four or five decent trees. Nice size, pretty decent shape to them, healthy. I told Ryan about them. Even marked a few with yellow forest service do-not-cut-diseased-tree ribbons to keep the would-be tree thieves away."

Tara cocked a brow. "How thoughtful. But do you really think that's going to fool a savvy tree-hunter?" She winked at him. "Which tree did you mark for yourself and what kind of ribbon did you put on it? Protected species?"

Rick's laugh boomed as he pulled his stocking cap off and tucked it in his pocket. "Every job has its perks. I never wait until the last minute. I got mine last week. It's already up and decorated."

"How very efficient of you," Tara said. "Speaking of those perfect trees you mentioned—you wouldn't have had a hand in shaping them, would you?"

Rick shook his head. "You really think I'd use my forest-service-issue saw for something like that?"

"Do you want the truth, or a well-polished lie?" She grinned at him.

They walked toward the breakfast counter past booths bustling with guests filling up on ham and eggs, waffles, or breakfast scrambles before hitting the slopes for the day. Stormy came out of the kitchen, loaded up with plates of eggs and pancakes that smelled suspiciously of gingerbread and were piled high with freshly whipped cream. Since when did the lodge serve anything besides the standard commercial-mix pancakes?

Stormy set one plate in an empty space on the counter. "From your grandma," she said to Tara. "She said you need to eat before you go out in the cold looking for a tree. You're too skinny. You don't have enough meat on your bones to fend off hypothermia."

Tara shook her head. "Eat, Santa, eat!"

Stormy smiled. "Margie's words, not mine." Stormy breezed past to deliver the other plates.

"Tell her I have to catch a man before I can fatten up."

Stormy was obviously busy, so Tara went around behind the counter as Rick took the last available seat. She grabbed the coffee pot and a cup. "Coffee? On the house."

"I never refuse free coffee."

"How's Bob doing these days? He hasn't retired, has he?" Tara poured a cup for Rick and then went the length of the counter refilling coffee cups. When she was finished, she grabbed a mug and poured herself a cup before taking a bite of eggs and tasting the lovely, dark pancakes before her. Gingerbread. Definitely gingerbread. What as next? Eggnog waffles?

Ranger Bob had been her favorite ranger when she was a kid. He'd once rescued her when a scavenging brown bear had gotten between her and the lodge. The bear, that scoundrel, had been looking for garbage, knocking over cans and foraging when she'd happened upon it as she came back from an early morning run.

Bob had always asserted the bear wouldn't have hurt her, but you never can tell with wild bears. Then there was the time he'd rescued two treed bear cubs.

"Bob, retire? Never," Rick said as Tara returned to his end of the counter. "But he's more of an office guy now than he used to be. His knees aren't up to the forest terrain."

Rick eyed the pie case, which Gram had already stocked with fresh pumpkin, apple, pecan, and apple-cranberry pies.

"I suppose you'd like pie, too," Tara said. "Still an apple pie man?"

Rick laughed as she cut him a slice and placed it in front of him as the door flew open again and a cold December wind kissed her cheeks. Her heart pounded as she looked up expecting to see Ryan.

Rick caught her expression. "Expecting someone?" His tone made it clear he was razzing her. He knew very well who she was looking for.

She hated that she was so obvious and everyone seemed to know her business. Just like in the old days.

But the newcomer wasn't Ryan. Instead, an attractive blue-eyed man in a ski beanie and The Mountain Bread Company jacket dusted himself off with one hand as he balanced a plastic delivery tray filled with gourmet breads in the other. Tara didn't recognize him, but then she didn't recognize a lot of people these days.

Tara excused herself and went to greet him. Deliverymen usually came in the side delivery entrance to the kitchen. And anyway, what had happened to the steadfast, gummy, generic white-bread delivery guy?

"May I help you?"

"You are?" he said with a certain amount of hesitance.

Tara held out her hand. "Tara. I'm Margie and Harry's granddaughter."

"Ah," he smiled. "Keith Scott. I brought Margie's first order by. Ryan told me Margie wanted it in time for the lunch crowd. She has some new sandwich recipes she wants to use it for."

No doubt using Ryan's salad dressing for that cookbook Gram was so pleased about. Gingerbread pancakes. Gourmet sourdough and pugliese bread. All Ryan's idea.

As Tara directed Keith to the kitchen, she noticed he wasn't wearing a ring. Automatic ring checks came naturally to a single woman. She noticed Stormy shooting the new bread man a look and doing the ring-check thing, too.

As she watched the bread man head to the kitchen, the bell over the door jingled again. She turned around to see who'd just arrived, only to find herself staring directly into Ryan's broad chest. Since that embarrassing display her first night back, she'd recognize that coat anywhere. She looked up, into his intense gaze.

Staring into Ryan's eyes had once been like gazing into a flattering mirror. Now the reflection of herself there was less complimentary. Or maybe it was just that his opinion of her was masked. Still, she found herself mesmerized. Why hadn't he gotten old and fat, like he had in her fantasies? Why did he still have to be the Ryan that made her heart race, despite its better judgment?

"You make a habit of hanging out beneath the mistletoe so you can kiss all the men who come in?" He pointed to the offending foliage above her head.

She was standing so close she could smell his cologne and see the shadow of dark stubble on his cheeks. One tiny slip and she'd be in his arms. It went against all reason, but she had to restrain herself from reaching out and caressing his jaw and cheeks, pink from the cold. From taking advantage of that mistletoe and kissing him, warming up his blue lips and icy heart. What was it about this man that made her insides turn to mush and her good sense abandon her?

Once, he'd been her strongest ally. Now she wasn't sure what he was, friend or foe.

Tara stepped back out of mistletoe range and re-minded herself to take that stupid mistletoe down and throw it in Carter's fire when he wasn't looking. "No more than you make a habit of standing beneath it as you come in and brush off. I hope this isn't your new method of picking up women. And you're late."

Ryan glanced at his watch. "By whose time? I'm five minutes early by mine."

"Your watch must be off."

"It's an atomic watch. You're the one who's always setting her watch ahead so she won't be late."

She ignored him, even though he was right. And she was even later. She still had to finish her breakfast.

"Ready to go?" Ryan said as he looked around. "Where's Harry?"

"That's the question of the day." Tara walked back to the counter and grabbed her plate of breakfast. "I was just going to ask Gram."

She left him to chat with Rick as she went to the kitchen, eating her pancakes on the way, and trying to calm the restless, lusty urges Ryan stirred in her.

Gram was elbow deep in flour and dough as she fin-ished the last of the morning pies, looking like she was Mrs. Claus in the midst of a baking rampage. She even had flour on her nose. She was icing her famous frosted apple-raisin pie. "Ah, Tara, there you are. Good, you're eating your breakfast. What do you think of the new pancakes?"

"Delicious." Tara watched Margie with suspicion. Gram seemed just a little too nonchalant. Like she had another holiday surprise up her sleeve. Gram was beginning to remind her of an advent calendar—you never knew what surprise the door of the day was going to reveal. "Ryan's here. We're ready to go. Where's Grandpa?"

Gram swirled the pie on her open hand as she ran the knife along it, smoothing the icing without looking up at Tara. "Grandpa's down in the back today, sweetie. He told me to tell you the keys to the Bobcat are on their regular hook and to have fun."

Tara stared at her grandmother. Yes, Harry's bad back was notorious for acting up. When Harry didn't want to do something and needed an excuse to get out of it. Most of the time it healed pretty quickly when the fish started biting. But this felt more like one of her grandmother's setups. She decided to call her bluff. "Maybe I should check in on him before we go—"

"Oh, no need. He's sleeping. Leave him be. The keys are on the rack. Have fun, sweetie, and tell Ryan to drive safely."

"Wait a minute   what makes you think I'm going to let Ryan drive the Bobcat?"

"Oh, let the boy drive, Tara. He has more experience on these snowy roads than you do." Gram tried to brush her nose off with her wrist and simply succeeded in adding more flour. At least it gave a new meaning to powdering her nose. "There's a thermos of coffee over there for you. Don't forget it."

CHAPTER EIGHT

The Bobcat compact utility vehicle was an open-air two-seater reminiscent of a small Jeep. Harry had equipped it with a brush guard, a seventy-two-inch snowplow blade, a gun boot, a powered lift rear cargo box, a plastic canopy, and all-terrain tires. And then he'd declared he'd spent enough money on it and refused to buy the canvas cab that would have made it just that much warm and cozier on cold winter days.

Ryan backed it out of the garage and waited for Tara to climb in. He handed her a lap blanket to snuggle under. "This will be fun. Like a sleigh ride."

Tara shot him a sideways glance. "It would be more fun if I got to drive." It still irritated her that Harry trusted Ryan more than her with his prized Bobcat.

Ryan lowered the blade and plowed their way out of the driveway and up the main road. Rick had been right. A good five to six fresh inches of snow had fallen overnight. But the sun was shining now. It carried no warmth, a lot like Tara's relationship with Ryan, but did light up the world into a beautiful winter wonderland of frost and snow and sparkle. The world was almost bright enough to lift the darkest spirits, like hers. Tara was feeling set up. Again.

There were few cars on the road. They puttered along, plowing as they went in silence.

Finally, Tara couldn't take the dead quiet any longer. "What do you know about Keith the bread man?"

"Excuse me?"

He wasn't fooling anyone with his innocent act. Especially her. And she knew he wasn't hard of hearing.

"The new bread man at the lodge, the one who stopped by with a selection of breads for Gram to try out for her cookbook."

"Oh, that Keith."

"Yeah, wiseass, that Keith." She stared at him with her "pin him to the wall" gaze.

Sadly, he seemed unfazed by it.

"We studied food science together. When I decided to move back to Echo Bay I convinced him the area was ripe for a fine bakery. After all, nothing goes with a gourmet salad like a delicious hunk of bread."

Tara studied him. "So you *are* to blame. I knew it. You with your nefarious plan to use the addictive powers of freshly baked bread in your quest for world domination. Or at least, to take over the lodge."

"All I did was make the introductions."

She rolled her eyes. "I'll thank you to stop sending new deliverymen my way."

Ryan gave her a sidelong look. "I don't recall sending anyone *your* way, least of all unsuspecting deliverymen. Who knows what you might do to them beneath the mistletoe. I recommended Keith to friends who could put his goods to good use."

Friends. Even though she was game for a fight with him, that was a low blow. Like using her board for his waxing clinic. "What about those gingerbread pancakes Kathleen has suddenly put on the menu?"

"I might have mentioned something about mixing things up a bit with a seasonal menu. I am a decorated food science expert who works for a successful food company. There are people who pay good money for my help." His tone was light, almost teasing.

Uh-huh, she thought. Though he was right. And maybe she should have thanked him, would have thanked him for helping her grandparents, if he hadn't had ulterior motives.

Ryan turned off the main road onto a tiny forest service cow path barely wide enough for the Bobcat.

Tara spent the next ten minutes jouncing and dodging low-hanging brush that seemed determined to slap at her through the Bobcat's brush cage. At last, Ryan pulled into an open meadow. Tara spotted Rick's ribboned stand of Christmas trees on the far side of the meadow.

Ryan lifted the plow blade and took the Bobcat off road to the edge of the small stand of trees. "Here we are."

He jumped out and headed for them without either helping her out or waiting for her.

Not to be outdone, or left behind, Tara threw off the lap robe and jumped out after him. He was already standing with his hands on his hips surveying the first tree by the time she reached him.

The sight of him—broad shoulders, confident, wide stance, narrow waist evident even beneath his coat—nearly took her breath away. The way he looked sent her heart racing. *Lust is a fickle thing. If this is just lust and not something more.*

The whisper of the breeze in the trees carried the scent of pine and Christmas. Small wisps of blowing snow swirled throughout the forest to the tune of snow sliding off branches as firs and pines shed their heavy white burden. The crisp air deep in her lungs felt invigorating in a way she'd forgotten.

And the glade, this glade, so familiar. She bit her lip and looked around her as realization dawned. The old familiar trees had grown taller, and new ones had sprung up. Snow covered the landscape, but the landmarks of years ago the slope of the hills, the breathtaking view of the mountain and lake beyond, that big, old boulder where she and Ryan used to sit and neck— were still evident.

Déjà vu is an unsettling, unjust, sneaky, perverse emotion. She gaped at Ryan and was transported, involuntarily feeling like the young, hot, in-love Tara of over ten years ago. The Tara who'd had fire running in her veins rather than cold, competent ice.

That last Christmas, this is where Ryan took me to look for a tree.

Chad had bailed on them, saying he had to work. So Ryan and Tara had gone for the tree alone. Here, in this very glen. Tara gave Gram points for wiliness and cunning. The woman should join the CIA. This was a very clever setup. Gram had even involved Ranger Rick.

Tara came up behind Ryan, clenching her fists to resist the urge to put her arms around him. This wasn't old times. This was now.

"I like this one," he said without looking at her.

"You know the drill," she said. "We can't pick the very first tree we see. This is a no-regrets operation. We have to judge them all."

He shrugged and the games began. They circled the little glade, eyeing the trees Rick had marked for them as seriously as if they were in charge of procuring the White House Christmas tree.

"I like this one." Ryan had stopped in front of one that Tara judged to be about eight feet tall and pulled out his tape measure.

Very smart, Ryan. She gave him mental Boy Scout points for being prepared. She had a tape measure in her pocket, too. Never trust the eye when judging heights.

Tara came over to inspect it, standing just behind him and peering over his shoulder. Was he kidding? Or simply goading her?

"You're crazy. See that hole? Unacceptable. From where it will sit in the lodge, the tree will be viewed from every angle." She pointed to the offending lack of branches. "Don't bother measuring it."

Ryan cocked his head and pursed his lips. "I like it. It's not such a bad little tree. You can fill it with ornaments. With a little love—"

"And Linus's blanket. Who are you? Charlie Brown? And what have you done with the real Ryan?" She shook her head.

"Well, I'm not going for a shiny aluminum Christmas tree if that's what you mean."

"Keep looking." She moved on to another tree in the stand. "This one would be nice if the trunk wasn't crooked."

The next one looked too dry. Another was too flat on one side. She'd soon rejected all of Rick's trees. She was beginning to wonder if Rick had somehow set them up, too. "What was Rick thinking?"

"I see you haven't lost your exacting standards." His tone wasn't exactly complimentary, though it did have a tease to it. "With a little love and attention, any of these will do. Their imperfections are the beauty of them. They're real, not manufactured like trees from farms that city people get. And that's what our guests want."

Our *guests? A slip of the tongue?* She let the comment slide and turned her back to him as she put her hands on her hips and looked up at the tree, trying to see what Ryan saw in it. "I'm not exacting, just discriminating. The Christmas tree is the focal point of the Christmas décor—"

A wad of snow struck her in the back of the shoulder. "Ouch!"

She spun around to face Ryan as she brushed the remnants of a snowball off her coat. He innocently had his back to her as if someone else had chucked that snowball at her.

She reacted without thinking—reached down, scooped a handful of snow, packed it into the most compact snowball she could form, and let if fly using her fastball snap. Back in the day, she could pitch a softball fifty miles an hour. Yeah, she meant to show him.

The snowball hit Ryan square between the shoulder blades. He let out an *oomph!* then jolted dramatically and threw his arms in the air, looking like a character in a video game. He was such a ham.

She started laughing.

He spun around. "Hey! What was that for?"

"What was that for?" She wasn't usually a violent woman, but she *had* been aching to lash out at him since she'd arrived. A little harmless, all-in-good-fun physical violence felt good. "Me? You fired the first shot." She pointed to the remnants of snow on her coat. "I was just defending myself. But if you must know, that was for that stupid cookbook you're encouraging Gram to make."

"What are you talking about? Why would I throw a snowball at you?"

Back in their adolescent days, teasing her, throwing snowballs at her, tickling her, and dumping her in the lake had been his way of flirting. Maybe he hadn't learned a new technique. She shrugged. "Why would you bring me to this particular part of the forest?" She pelted him with another snowball and grinned.

He ducked, and in a twinkling, made a snowball and returned fire. Ryan had played baseball in high school and had quite the arm on him. He hit her square in the chest. On purpose. Ryan had always had an obsession with her breasts. "That's for coming back and causing trouble for me at work."

"Bastard!" She whomped him with another snowball. "That's for suggesting gingerbread pancakes!" Tara ducked behind a dry tree for cover while she made more ammo.

Ryan tore out after her. She made a good run for it, but he caught her in the thigh with a shot that stung as she darted between trees.

"That's for interrupting my board-waxing workshop."

She fired back. "That's for stealing my ideas for the lodge before I could implement them."

Ryan turned sideways and took the hit to his shoulder, still charging after her with a handful of snow. Ryan had always been fast—faster than her, anyway. And as sure footed as a mountain goat.

She ran and slipped. He caught her around the waist from behind, kindly arresting her fall before stuffing snow down her collar as she twisted to get away. Ryan could always outmuscle her. He didn't let go. She only managed to twist herself around until she faced him in his arms beneath a towering white pine.

Ryan pulled her into the well free of snow beneath the tree. Into its sheltering protection out of the breeze.

One minute she was staring into Ryan's eyes, and the next the world just suddenly stopped. The cold. The smell of fresh pines and forest. The deep blue sky peeking through the branches above. And Ryan's arms around her. The fire of desire was still pounding through her, her senses heightened by adrenaline and fresh air. And Ryan. It was nearly Christmas again and so much like when they were still in love. She was re-called to that time where being in his arms made her breath catch and her heart race. To that very first time he'd kissed her. In the forest. In *this* forest.

Ryan's lips angled downward toward hers. Against all reason and logic, she tilted her head and went up on her toes until his mouth met her lightly parted lips.

The first time he'd kissed her, he'd been a boy, ten-tative and gently awkward, though she'd sworn he was the best kisser ever and had sighed for weeks just re-membering his lips on her. This Ryan was grown up and confident. He kissed her fiercely, his mouth hard and insistent on hers as he cupped her butt and pulled her hips into his. He danced her backward until he pressed her up against the rough bark of the pine and cupped her head so she couldn't escape his kiss.

At that moment, escape was the last thing on her mind. She slid her arms around his neck and met his tongue with hers. Kissing Ryan, she hadn't forgotten what he liked and he hadn't forgotten what turned her on. He still knew exactly how to take her breath away. He bent his knees and pressed against his until she felt his desire pulsing through his jeans and hers.

A breeze stirred the branches overhead, but they were safely cocooned beneath that big, old pine as Ryan slid his gloved hands beneath her coat, up her fleece pullover, and clasped her around her waist. If his touch, just glove to fleece, could make her burn, what would his bare hand on her skin do to her?

As she reached to pull Ryan's glove off, she heard a whoosh, snow sliding off limbs. She opened her eyes and looked up as an avalanche from the limbs above crashed toward them. She struggled to pull away from Ryan's kiss and warn him. But he held his mouth firmly to hers as she watched in horror as a big, cold pile of the white stuff doused them.

She and Ryan broke apart, sputtering, standing in a snow pile that covered the tops of their boots and slid down to their socks and over their collars. It covered their shoulders and hats and hair.

Ryan blinked to get it out of his lashes as he wiped his eyes. "Now that's what I call a cold shower."

Yeah, and Tara was coming back to her senses as she spit snow out of her mouth. "I never eat December snow. It's not ripe yet." She dusted Ryan's shoulders off, not looking him in the eye. "I always wait for January."

As kids, they'd watched *A Charlie Brown Christmas* together every year. She was sure he got the reference.

Stupid, stupid branches that couldn't hold their weight. She looked back at Ryan, who had pulled his hat off and was slapping it against his thighs to clear it of snow. Her heart caught again. They'd been so good together. And so terrible.

Brought to her senses by a snow-covered pine. He looked up and caught her watching him. "What?"

"You, covered in snow. I tried to warn you..." She started laughing. She couldn't help herself. The whole situation—Gram's matchmaking, throwing snowballs like kids, kissing Ryan like a horny teenager—was ridiculous.

"You should see yourself." He dusted her shoulders and took a step into her. "Your lips are turning blue."

No doubt they were. Her lips turned blue easily.

He leaned down as if to kiss her again and warm up those icy lips of hers.

She sidestepped out of the way, hating herself. But she was confused and didn't trust herself not to do something they both might later regret.

Ryan frowned slightly, looking hurt. He covered it quickly and masked his expression. "You know I didn't throw a snowball at you, right?"

She swallowed hard and tried to get the light mood back. "Did too."

He shook his head. "Not to start with. That was just a smaller pine tree dumping on you."

She nodded. He was right. He had to be. "Something about this forest doesn't like me."

"Maybe because you're here to cut down one of its children," Ryan said.

"Maybe. But only to make it a star of the Christmas season. Good intentions should count for something." As Tara pulled off her knit hat and dusted it off, she hoped he understood what she was saying.

Ryan gave her shoulders a squeeze, then slid his gloved hands down her coat sleeves, pausing to hold her hand when he reached the end of her sleeves. "Yeah, I suppose."

She couldn't look Ryan in the eye, so she looked past him, right at the most gorgeous, most perfect tree in the forest.

"There it is, Ry! Look! Behind you. There's our tree. Get out your tape measure."

Ryan frowned ever so slightly, an expression of determination crossing his face before he turned to look over his shoulder. "Looks like a contender. I'll grab the saw."

At least they agreed on something.

She made her way to the tree and watched while Ryan measured it.

"Eleven feet, two inches." He recoiled the tape measure and turned to her for confirmation. "This is the one, then?"

"Perfect! It's definitely the one." Tara stood by their tree, wondering what life would have been like if she'd stood by her man all those years ago.

"Stand back." Ryan shook the snow from the tree and retrieved the saw from where he'd dropped it before their snowball fight.

She smiled at him as he returned and held the saw out to her. "Want to do the honors?"

She shook her head. "I think I've done enough cutting for a while."

Which was certainly true. Besides, she knew what tree cutting involved. Crouching beneath a tree and working up a cold sweat with the handsaw. "You cut. I'll hold the tree up."

She grabbed the tree trunk. Ryan went into a crouch, sawing with one hand and hanging onto the tree with the other. Such a show of confidence in her.

And such a nice view of his very fine butt. She had to resist the urge to reach out and cup it. Yeah, what would Ryan think of that? That would put her on the naughty list for sure.

She grinned, knowing what would help her avoid temptation. "Make sure you saw nice and straight. That's key."

The tree stopped jiggling. Ryan had paused midslice. She pictured him rolling his eyes. He hated bossy advice.

"Yeah, I didn't know that. Thanks for the tip." He started sawing again.

That should keep him out of the mood. Oh, I'm bad, she thought, still watching his ass.

Ten minutes of luscious booty viewing later, Ryan sliced through the tree. It took another five to drag it to the Bobcat, even with her help. Or, Ryan might have said, despite it. And another ten to lash it onto the Bobcat so it wouldn't fall off as they jounced on home.

By the time they started back, they were both shivering and cold to the core. Ryan tucked the lap blanket around Tara again and cranked up the heat. Which did little more than melt the snow in Tara's hair and make her look like a wet dog. Or so she imagined.

Neither of them spoke. What was there to say? That the kiss had been a mistake?

That wasn't exactly true, but Tara couldn't see a way forward for them. They still had opposing views on what was best for each other and the lodge. And she still wasn't comfortable with Christmas and wouldn't be until she faced the mountain again.

As Ryan negotiated the Bobcat along the cow path again, Tara decided the mood was still civil enough between them to bring up another sensitive topic. "I'd like to buy my snowboard from you."

"What?" Ryan glanced at her. "Why?" He looked suspicious.

She bit her lip. "I'm going to take up boarding again. At least give it a try while I'm here. And I hear—actually, saw with my own eyes—how well waxed and ready to go it is. I was hoping you'd give me a deal on it. In return, I promise to give it back to you if the boarding thing doesn't work out for me."

Ryan frowned, obviously suspicious of her and wondering whether she was serious. "You're serious?"

"I already bought a pass. Which means I need to go up on the mountain at least four times just to break even on my investment."

He took a deep breath and kept his eyes on the road. "I'd hate to lose my best demonstration board."

"Come on, Ryan. That board deserves its chance on the slopes. Let me dirty it up for you so you can give it a real cleaning at the next workshop."

She couldn't believe she was pleading with him. She had no idea why it was so important to her to have *that* board, the last Christmas present Ryan had ever bought for her. Even though she'd never actually received it. In some weird way, it felt like by taking it off his hands, she was making amends for past hurts.

"Okay," he said after a long pause. "That sounds reasonable. On one condition."

She dodged a branch and turned to stare at him. "Name it."

"You let me take you up on the slopes the first time."

Her mouth fell open at his audacity. Ryan kept staring at the road. She couldn't see his eyes and his face was a mask. What, exactly, was he asking? Was this a date? Or Ryan the ski patrol guy preventing a terror from taking to the slopes and endangering the lives of others?

She inhaled so deeply her lungs burned in the cold air.

He filled the silence and answered the question in her mind. "It's been a long time since you've been up on either the mountain, or a board. I have to be sure you'll be safe."

"Riding a board must be like riding a bike. You never forget."

"We'll see. My terms are non-negotiable. You want the board, you have to take a lesson from me."

Yeah, but what kind of lesson? She twisted her mouth to the side. She could tell from the tone of his voice he was serious. "Okay. Deal. If the price is right."

"Great. I'll make you an excellent deal—you can have the board for nothing." His tone didn't give his feelings away.

"No, I'll pay you for it. It's the least I can do."

He shook his head. "It's yours. It always was." His jaw was set. "Do you have boots and bindings?"

She didn't argue with him. She could tell it was futile. And she'd hurt him enough already. "Yes. No. Maybe. I think my old gear is still in the attic."

"You'll want new. New technology is much better than what we had ten years ago. I can help you with that. Digger runs the ski shop. He'll give you a deal. Anyway, I insist on checking your gear out before you go down the mountain."

"That's two conditions," she said. "You only get one."

"Safety isn't a condition. It's part of the first lesson."

He had her there.

He pulled the Bobcat onto the main road.

"Okay, fine. Deal. What happens if I find a board I like better at the shop?"

He shrugged. "That's up to you. I still get to take you out your first time back up on the slopes."

CHAPTER NINE

Back at the lodge, Ryan unloaded the tree from the Bobcat and put it in the workshop to dry out before he brought it into the lodge to decorate. He was still stunned from the magnitude of that kiss with Tara in the forest and the electric force of attraction that still sparked between them. He'd almost lost complete control. If not for that smart ass tree dumping a pile of snow on them...

He frowned. *Thanks a lot, Rick, buddy.*

Ryan had walked right into a trap and not even seen it coming. Until he'd parked the Bobcat and seen the view, he hadn't remembered that glen was the very place he'd first kissed Tara. How had Margie known? And his purported friend Rick was her conspirator. The woman was good.

But what did Tara think—that Ryan had set her up? He'd been as duped as she'd been.

Ryan put the tree in a bucket of water with a little sugar and headed into the lodge. Tara met him with a warm, dry pair of wool socks, and a steaming mug of hot coffee made just the way he liked it. He looked around, hamming it up as he mocked being perplexed. "Have I stepped into *The Donna Reed Show*?"

She smiled. "Maybe. Echo Bay has always been behind the times."

He held up the socks. "Did you knit these while I was out?"

"They're Harry's," she said. "He offered. Come on, come sit by the fire and warm up."

Oh, Ryan was warm. Way warmer than he should have been, in fact.

He slipped off his boots and took a seat in the chair Tara led him to. She took his coat and gloves and laid them on the hearth to dry out as he changed his socks. Carter had made a magnificent blaze. Ryan was warming up already. His brain was heating up too. He was suspicious and wary, especially after Tara had shut him down in the glen. The woman ran hot and cold, as if she couldn't make up her mind how she felt.

That kiss had made him realize, again, that much as he may have suppressed his desires, he wanted exactly two things in this life—Tara and the lodge. And since they went hand in hand, a package deal, he'd just have to convince Tara she should go hot—hot for him.

When Ryan looked up from his thoughts, Tara was studying him. And she had a twinkle in her eyes.

Where had that come from? And what was she up to? He should be grateful for small mercies. At least she wasn't quite looking at him as if he were the devil. But what was she thinking?

She cleared her throat. "While you were out, I took a peek in the attic." She paused. "Just to see if there's anything up there we can use for the tree. Garlands or glass balls, that kind of thing." She bit her lip. "I know what I said earlier about not needing your help. But I was wrong."

She glanced down at her feet before raising her eyes to look at him directly. "Those boxes look awfully heavy and unwieldy. I'm not sure little old me can handle them by myself. What I could really use is a big, strong man to help me. And with Harry being down in the back, he's in no shape." She looked up from beneath her lashes and smiled at Ryan.

It was clear she was playing him, teasing him. But she looked so damned vulnerable.

What was her game? He hesitated, mostly from shock. Most of those boxes were full of ornaments and practically as light as a cold, dry snow.

"Look, Ry. I don't want to face them alone. You're the only one who really understands. I know it's an imposition. If you have plans—"

"No plans. I'd be happy to help." Anything to be near her. Anything beat going back to his lonely cabin and trying to live down old memories.

She smiled very slightly and visibly relaxed. "Thanks, Ryan. I mean it."

He downed his coffee in almost a single gulp, scalding his tongue and nearly choking, but it was worth it. He didn't want Tara changing her mind or chickening out. "There's no time like the present." He stood. "After you."

He followed Tara to the attic, watching her pretty little ass as she climbed the stairs in front of him. It gave him the same ideas he'd had in the forest. Ideas he shouldn't entertain. Not yet.

Tara unlocked the door to the attic and climbed the stairs, stopping abruptly at the top on the edge of the room. He nearly collided with her, avoiding an accident only by putting his hands around her waist as he stopped. He leaned in and peered around her at the room he'd helped Harry organize earlier in the fall. Nothing scary there. Just shelves filled with neatly labeled boxes. Yet Tara seemed terrified.

Ryan flicked on the light and studied the room. He knew exactly where the Christmas ornaments were. And her old snowboard gear. And anything else she wanted.

Tara stalled, not making any move to enter the room.

"You okay?" he asked. "Hey, Tara, no worries. No fears. The bats aren't here this time of year."

Bats liked the attic. Tara had always been afraid of them.

She bit her lip. "Thanks. But you know it's not the bats that have me freaked. It's all the ghosts of the past hidden away on shelves up here."

He still had his hands firmly on her hips. She hadn't shaken them off and he liked them where they were. They felt like they belonged there. "Tell me where to start, Tara. You just stay here if you like, and I'll bring you whatever you ask for. You can sit on the steps and look at the contents."

The roof of the attic sloped to a peak in the middle with a round paned window at the center, letting the low winter sun in. If one wasn't facing fears, it was actually a pretty, homey place.

"Something innocuous. A box of Christmas balls, maybe?" Her voice trembled. "I want to see what we can use before we haul them all down three flights of stairs."

"Sure." He moved around her and studied the shelves until he found a box labeled *Christmas balls*. He pulled it off the shelf. When he turned back to her, Tara was sitting on the top step, just as he'd suggested.

He carried the box over and set it next to her.

She stared at it. "I'm sure you realize why my parents are on a cruise this year for Christmas."

The statement seemed to come out of nowhere.

Ryan stared at her. Yeah, he knew. Of course he knew. But he didn't answer aloud.

She kept her gaze fixed on the box. "With the ten-year anniversary..."

She traced a pattern on the box with her finger. "You've probably noticed that neither them nor I have been able to face a Christmas here since.

"Gram and Grandpa endure on, year after year, refusing to leave for the holidays. Saying Thanksgiving through Valentine's Day is a big, moneymaking time of year for them and they can't afford to leave.

"So we've been at a standstill, or maybe a standoff, all this time." She paused and looked around the room. "I had so many happy Christmases here as a kid. So, so many. It was the best childhood ever.

"Gram and Grandpa are getting older. They practically blackmailed me into coming and giving Christmas here one last try. For old time's sake.

"They mean well. They want me to think of those Christmases with my brother with love and joy, instead of sorrow. I owe it to him. I know it's what he'd want. I'm hoping that maybe I *can* recapture some of that joy." She bit her lip, looked at the floor, and shook her head. "You probably think I'm a coward. But really, Ryan, I'm the bravest of my family. Not that that's saying much."

He sat on the floor next to her, took her chin, and tipped her face up. "I don't think you're a coward at all."

"You're a terrible liar." She smiled, but there were tears in her eyes. "But I appreciate the sentiment." She took a deep breath and lifted the lid off the box beside her.

Ryan had been extraordinarily careful in his selection. He expected her to pop the lid off and breathe a sigh of relief at the boxes of red and green Christmas balls within. There shouldn't have been anything personal or sentimental in that box, nothing that you wouldn't find in any department, discount, or grocery store anywhere in the country during the holidays. But there was.

Sitting right on top of the boxes and tubes of ball ornaments was a hand-stitched, hand-embellished ski hat ornament with his name embroidered on it—by Tara's own hand.

Ryan cursed silently to himself. That hadn't been there when he'd put the boxes away. He'd swear to it. Now what would Tara think?

She pulled the little white and blue hat out of the box by its string and held it in front of her, watching it gently swing. "I haven't seen this in years."

"Nor have I. I swear, Tara. I have no idea how that got there."

Tara had given it to him for Christmas one year when she was in high school. She'd made a matching one for Chad. After Tara had called off their engagement and given back his ring, Ryan had returned the ornament, leaving it at the lodge for her. He'd been hurt and acting like an ass. He'd never known if she'd actually gotten it back or what had happened to it. Looked like the mystery was solved.

She turned to look at him. "Don't you?" There was no accusation in her tone.

She arched a brow. "I have a pretty good idea, like a grandmotherly Mrs. Claus figure who's writing a cookbook."

She returned her focus to the ornament in her fingers. "Look at this! I was really awful at embroidery." She shook her head, but she was smiling slightly.

"Chad's was worse, poor guy. But they were made with love." She laid the ornament flat in her hand.

Ryan swallowed hard, trying to get rid of the lump in his throat. She was exactly right. There *had* been so much love. So much history together. He'd loved her fiercely and she'd loved him back with equal intensity. There had to be a few embers still smoldering within her, however weakly. Tragedy or no, misunderstanding or not, how could a love like that just die?

She opened her mouth to say something, but nothing came out. She shook her head.

He put his arm around her, took the ornament from her, and replaced the decoration in the box. "Let me put this away and get another box to look at."

Tara smiled at him and laughed softly. "Are you kidding? They're all booby-trapped. You know that, right?"

"Then screw it!" He stood and held his hand out to her. "Let's go to town and buy new Christmas balls. We'll raid the dollar store and Walmart and buy them out if we have to. And while we're at it, we'll stop by the Alpine Shop and see about getting you set up to hit the slopes tomorrow. I'll get your board from Harry's shop."

Town bustled with shoppers, skiers, snowboarders, snowmobilers, and tourists darting around the sidewalks and streets. And Santa Ski fliers were pasted absolutely everywhere. The window of the Alpine Shop was practically wallpapered with them.

Yes, Tara was determined to face her fears and get back up on the slopes as a tribute to her brother. But the sight of hundreds of Christmas revelers skiing and boarding recklessly down the mountain high on wassail and wine and Christmas spirits was an event she still intended to avoid. The last thing she wanted to ever see again was another crash. She still didn't know how Ryan faced the Basin on ski patrol, knowing he could be called to assist in an accident like Chad's at any time.

Ryan held the door to the Alpine Shop open for her as he stomped the snow off his boots and held her board in his other arm. A Trans-Siberian Orchestra arrangement of Christmas carols blasted out of the shop at the volume of a rock concert.

Inside was an explosion of gear, garland, animated skiing Santa figures, and garish lights. And, yes, costumes for the Santa Ski—helmets with reindeer horns, ski poles covered with flashing LED Christmas lights, ho-ho-ho noisemakers, and holiday decals for helmets, boards, skis, you name it. The innocuously named Alpine Shop was a holiday shop of horrors in Tara's opinion. Long gone was the familiar, traditional Alpine Shop of her youth.

Digger Jameson, snowboarder and ski bum extraordinaire, popped up from where he'd been hiding behind the counter. Or, more likely, bending over to pick something up off the floor.

"Ryan, dude! Good to see you, man." Digger clasped Ryan's whole arm as the two shook hands.

It took Digger a long stare, a look of puzzlement, and Ryan's prompting—"You remember Tara"—before real recognition hit Digger. "Tara Clark! It's still Tara Clark, right?" Digger's gaze bounced between her and Ryan as he spoke over the music, looking like something didn't quite jibe.

She nodded confirmation. "Digger. Good to see you." She almost had to yell.

Ryan motioned for Digger to turn the music down.

Which Digger did, a notch, before grabbing Tara in a whole-arm handshake. "Christmas miracles will happen! I never thought I'd see you in a board shop again. Not here, anyways. A dedicated boarder like you, I never believed that nasty gossip that you gave it up. Once the pow is in your veins, it don't leave, I said. This is rad!"

He grinned and pointed an accusing finger at Tara. "I have you pegged. 'Fess up. You've been shreddin' the gnar on us elsewhere."

He arched a brow as if in question. "Thrown us over for Whistler in BC or I miss my guess. Just like Seattleites to head there and ignore the rest of us. Or maybe Crystal." His grin spread as he nodded, believing his own theories without giving Tara an in to protest.

Ryan shot Digger a quick look, warning him to back off that particular line of supposition, and glanced at Tara. She smiled to reassure him she was hanging in. Digger had never had social grace. She didn't hold his enthusiasm against him.

Digger ignored Ryan's visual warning. "Whoa! Wait a minute—is that an antique board you're carrying, dude? You can't be plannin' to cruise the pow on the Basin on that?" Digger finally released Tara's arm to inspect the board.

"Not without bindings and boots," Ryan said.

Digger shook his head. "I got better gear than this, man. I can give you a good pre-Christmas discount, too."

"No!"

Both men swung around to look at Tara with surprised expressions on their faces.

"I want that board, and no other." It was crazy, but that was exactly the way she felt. That board that Ryan had bought for her years ago symbolized how life was supposed to have carried on—happily, joyously. And by golly, she was going to carry on, on that very board. "Contrary to your theories, Digger, I have not been up on the slopes since my brother's death ten years ago."

She pointed to the board. "That board is ten years old, just the technology I was last comfortable with. It'll do. I'm only going up a few times, anyway."

Digger shook his head. "I can rent you some gear, Tara."

She shook her finger at the board. "That board. Young looking, twentysomething polka dots and all, I still like it.

"Ten years ago it was state of the art and I had my eye on it and was dying to ride it." She winced when she realized her word choice. "I dreamed day and night of riding that thing. Ryan bought me that board and hung onto it all these years." She gave him a shaky smile. "It's about time my dream came true. I'm riding the gnar on that board.

"Now, I'm open to reasonably priced, current technology boots and bindings. Providing you can get the bindings on the board and have it ready for us to pick up tomorrow morning on our way to the Basin. What do you say, Digger? Will you sell me some gear?"

Digger grinned. "I got just the boots for those petite feet of yours, Tara. Just the ones.

"But first, I'm all out of Santa suits." He gestured to a shelf behind the counter. "But I got some cool, sexy elf costumes that would look good on you for the Santa Ski. And Santa hat snowboard helmet covers. You can still do the Santa Ski in style..."

Twenty minutes later, they were back on the street again, sans elf costume, and Ryan was laughing and apologizing for Digger. "You have to deal with Digger on a certain level. He runs the best shop in town, and knows his stuff, but he can be a little insensitive. I'm sorry about that."

Tara waved her hand, dismissing Ryan's concern. "No problem. I had a good time." She peered into the Alpine Store bag she carried. "I still can't believe he sold me a Rudolph flashing red nose, though."

Ryan laughed. "He didn't exactly sell you the nose. He tossed it in for free."

"Yeah, only if I stepped up to the more expensive bindings."

"Those were the best deal, anyway," Ryan said. "And he threw in free installation, too."

"Yeah, dumb as he looks, the guy's a marketing genius." She shook her head. "I'm still not going to do the Santa Ski."

"No one says you have to." As they crossed the street to Ryan's car, he stepped out of the way of a snowmobiler barreling down the street. He beeped the car and opened the trunk for her. "But you might enjoy it."

Tara gave him a doubtful look and put her bag in.

"Where to now?" Ryan asked. "Walmart? The dollar store?"

Tara looked around her at the quaint, but decidedly upscale town filled with boutique shops that had sprung up since her girlhood. Dollar-store ornaments didn't exactly fit the new image. And besides, they were no fun to buy. "It's Saturday, right?"

Ryan gave her a puzzled look. "Yeah?"

She glanced at her watch. "And nearly noon. The ornament outlet store opens in ten. Laurel told me where it is. I say we head there and forget about boring Christmas balls. But we have to hurry or we'll miss all the good finds of the day. Word on the street is you have to be there when it opens to get the gems."

CHAPTER TEN

Ryan gave her a look of mock horror. "You mean Old European Ornaments? Oh, no, no, no. No red-blooded male goes into that store unless he's coerced. Forced. Arm-twisted. It's all glitter and decorating talk in there."

He shook his head, but there was a tease in his voice and just a hint of apprehension. "You should hear the horror stories from the guys at the plant. Women walk into that store and don't come out."

Tara arched a brow. "Ever? Sounds dangerous. You should get the sheriff to look into the disappearances."

Ryan grinned. "For hours. They don't come out for hours. And when they do, they're all sparkly and their wallets are empty."

"I see. Sounds like a mission for a man with guts and courage." Tara put her hands on her hips and shook her head at him, teasing him back. "You were willing to look at Christmas decorations at Walmart. What's the difference?"

"Walmart has plenty of other stuff to look at. Like guns and hunting equipment. Besides, we were just talking Christmas balls and maybe some dollar ornaments. But full-fledged, deep-into-Christmas-territory decorator shopping, I don't remember signing up for that."

Tara called his bluff, shrugged, and pulled out her cell phone. "If you're not secure enough about your manhood to come with me, I'll call Laurel and plead an ornament emergency. I'm sure *she'd* love to come."

Crazily, she wanted him to protest and stop her. Face the wilds and terrors of Old European Ornaments with her and ignore the consequences, even if it meant a good teasing from the guys at the plant. She had a flashback to the young her tormenting the young him, once she'd discovered her power over him. Teasing him, trying to get him to admit he wanted to spend time with her.

The memory was particularly warm and fuzzy and powerful and youthfully romantic at the same time. She'd been having such a surprisingly good time with Ryan. Mending fences. Putting the past to rest. Reliving ethereal emotions she hadn't felt in years. She didn't want it to end *just* yet.

She scanned her menu, stalling as she looked up Laurel's number, waiting for Ryan to react like the old, young Ryan. Her finger hovered above Laurel's number, just about ready to press it, when Ryan grabbed her arm.

"Let's not call it a day yet," he said, pulling the phone out of her hand. "I'll take you. I'd go anywhere with you, you know that.

"But be prepared to face the consequences. In this town, if a guy shows up at Old European with a woman, people are going to talk and make something out of it. No one will believe I'm just helping out an old friend."

His voice. The expression on his face. Her heart caught. He was the old Ryan, untainted by tragedy. And they were still in love. That was the way it felt to her, as if no time had passed at all.

Hope shone bright in his eyes.

She was filled with that ridiculous sort of joy that young women get when the right guy smiles at them. *Crazy.* This was Ryan.

She held her hand out for her phone. "Oh, that's ridiculous. Who will care or even see us together?" She gave him her most dazzling smile. "But I'm glad you're coming. I'll need some muscle to carry all the boxes and bags of goodies I plan on buying." She winked at him.

He slapped the phone back into her hand. "Trust me. This isn't the anonymous big city." Then he grinned. "Get in the car. We'll have to drive. I'm not carrying your packages, boxes, and bows for miles. As it is, we'll be lucky to find a spot in the lot."

Less than five minutes later they pulled into a hopping, busy parking lot that looked as if it belonged in the heart of urban holiday frenzy, not small-town

America. The Old European factory was a long, flat, boring industrial building in a small industrial park. The retail store was located in a two-story office building next to the factory at the end of the lot. Both buildings looked unremarkable and unexciting. Until Tara looked more closely at the windows of the office building and got a glimpse of sparkling decorated trees through the windows and glass doors.

"Look at the line!" Tara pointed to a long line of women that snaked along the sidewalk and out into the lot.

Ryan scanned it and tucked his head down as he drove her to the end of it. "Yeah. It's a popular place."

"See anyone you know?" She grinned at him. "Looks like a lot of tourists to me. There aren't enough people in this town to generate at crowd like that."

Ryan shook his head. "Get out and get in line. I'll park the car and join you."

She studied him. "I see fear in your eyes. You're not planning on bailing on me?"

He grinned.

"Ry!"

"I'll see you inside. Promise."

"Good. And I hope you're not planning to come incognito. If you show up in a ski mask to hide your identity, you'll scare the marauding hordes of ornament collectors." She playfully tapped his cheek and jumped out of the car to get in line.

Tara watched Ryan as he drove out of the lot and down the road, cruising for a spot. She had a ridiculous smile on her face. Positively *ridiculous*.

This day had been like something out of a dream. A Ghost of Christmas Present kind of feeling. Cutting Christmas trees with Ryan. Going to the Alpine Shop to get new bindings and boots. And now going ornament shopping with him.

It was what life could have been like, and somehow—for this moment, anyway—was. And it felt remarkably good and somehow right, like things should be. Which was also ridiculously scary. What was she thinking?

She wasn't. That was the problem. She was simply feeling. *Don't think; feel. Good advice or damning pabulum?*

Then again, what did it matter if Tara let go and enjoyed herself during the holidays for once? She'd only be here until a few days after Christmas. Making peace with Ryan could only be a good thing in her path in life. Help her let go of that part of the guilt of Chad's death—being at odds with his old friend, who'd been so important to her brother. Accepting the past. Yes, Chad would have wanted her to stop blaming Ryan and herself and be happy.

Maybe coming back to Echo Bay for Christmas had been exactly what she'd needed, after all. Take care of Gram and Grandpa. Get them settled. Make up for not being Chad. Stop blaming Ryan and herself for living. Christmas miracles could happen. At least they seemed to be on the horizon.

"Hey, look, there's the boss. Hey, Ryan!" A middle-aged woman several places ahead of Tara in line waved as Ryan came into view from down the street, jogging toward the line.

Again, that pesky, ridiculous sense of almost school-girl-crush joy assaulted Tara and she smiled. He was not only keeping his promise—he was jogging back! Without a ski mask to hide his identity.

His breath came out in puffs. Watching Ryan jog, Tara thought he looked athletic and attractive. In a word, *hot.* And from the looks of the faces on several of the women in line, Tara wasn't the only one who thought so.

"Ryan!" A few more women in line called to him as he nodded and jogged past.

The middle-aged woman caught Ryan as he slowed just before he got to Tara. The woman was dressed in a knit red and white scarf and hat and hideous, garish old Christmas sweater, jeans, and boots with fur popping over the top. "Hey, salad dressing boss man, what are *you* doing here?"

Ryan got a sheepish look on his face, as if he'd been caught red-handed somewhere he shouldn't be. Suddenly Tara appreciated his reluctance, and the courage it took for him to come with her. He was never going to hear the end of this once his buds at the dressing plant found out about his little excursion here.

Tara was so used to living in the big city where people were anonymous that it seemed ridiculous to think of running into someone he knew. But Ryan had been right. This was a small town where everyone knew everyone else *and* their business. And evidently, every salad dressing plant worker, worker's girlfriend or wife, every woman in town who wasn't working, was at the ornament factory looking to stock up on holiday spirit in ornament form.

"Hey, Carla," Ryan said.

Carla suddenly preened for him and pointed to her sweater. "I need a man's opinion, boss—what do you think of the new sweater?"

Tara inwardly shuddered. *Let's see you get out of this one gracefully, Ry.*

Ryan paused, ran his eyes over the outfit with a professional eye, pursed his lips, and grinned. "That is the butt ugliest sweater I have *ever* seen."

Carla blushed and laughed, obviously tickled and flattered. "I told you, girls," she said to a pair of women next to her.

"I'm gonna win the ugly sweater competition this year." She nodded and leaned in toward Ryan. "This is only my *second* ugliest sweater. You should see the one I'm wearing to the plant on Christmas Eve. I'm taking the prize, I'm telling you."

Ryan studied Carla's sweater again. "If you've got a sweater more tacky and hideous than that one, I believe you."

Carla laughed. "Hey, boss," she said. "What, may I ask, are *you* doing here? Shouldn't you be hitting the powder at the Basin today, getting ready for the Santa Ski? Bob said wild horses wouldn't keep you off the mountain on a Saturday, especially not a Saturday when the powder is perfect."

"The ski report said they got eight inches of fresh powder overnight," another woman chimed in. "My son took off at dawn to hit the slopes."

Ryan looked the tiniest bit sheepish again. "Don't worry. I'm ready for the Santa Ski. Count on it." He cleared his throat. "I'm going boarding tomorrow. Today I'm helping a friend get her tree ready." He flicked a glance at Tara, and what seemed like dozens of pairs of scrutinizing eyes turned her way.

Brows arched. Smiles formed. And scrutiny began. Good thing she was having a good hair day beneath her cute hat.

Ryan waved Tara to come stand next to him.

"Hey, wait! Is that Tara?" one of the women said. "Good to see you! I almost didn't recognize you in your winter gear. Seems like we only see you in the spring and summer."

Tara recognized her as a friend of Gram's. "It is indeed. So good to see you, too."

The other ladies called out greetings, introduced her to those she didn't know, and asked after her grandparents and Echo Bay Resort, making her feel right at home.

As for Ryan, he seemed to know everyone. Oh, this really *was* going to make life difficult for him. Shopping at the ornament factory outlet when he should have been on the slopes? When wild snowmobiles usually couldn't drag him down?

Ryan must have loved her grandparents very much to give up his precious Saturday to help them get their tree. Tara was touched again by his kindness toward them and her.

"So, what ornament are we looking for today?" Ryan asked the group at large. "What's the prize?"

"I've been looking for the great white wolf ornament since they opened for the season," Carla said. "They only put out a few each morning. And I swear they mix them into the bins and hide them just to make things interesting."

"Good marketing ploy," Ryan said. "Scarcity does drive up demand."

One of the women studied Tara as the others talked, looking as if she was trying to place her. "Wait! Now I remember—you came by the factory a few days ago to see Ryan." She glanced at Ryan and smiled, implying there was something going on between Tara and Ryan.

Fortunately, the doors to the shop opened at that very minute, sparing Tara from further scrutiny and having to answer any unwanted questions. So Ryan's protests hadn't been all bluff and tease.

He leaned into Tara and whispered in her ear. "Want to place any bets on whether they've already alerted my mom to this little outing?"

His mom had once been one of Tara's biggest fans. She'd been ready to welcome Tara with open arms into the family. Now, Tara guessed she was probably pretty much on the top of his mom's naughty list, *permanently*. For breaking Ryan's heart, shattering his dreams, and even to this present day being the obstacle to Ryan taking over the lodge.

"Oh, come on," Tara said. "I'm sure your mom knows I'm in town. How is she these days?"

"She's great. And, yeah, she knows you're here for the holidays. But not that we've had any contact other than the incident at the salad dressing plant. She thinks we're at war."

"Won't she be glad the lion's laid down with the lamb, then?" Even as Tara spoke she realized her poor choice of words and that she was being deliberately obtuse. His mom would not be happy about Ryan being out with Tara. She didn't trust Tara anymore. And who could blame her?

Ryan arched a brow in skepticism.

"Just tell her this is part of your diabolical plan to win the lodge," she said with a tease in her voice. "You have to be nice to me to get to Harry and Margie. I'm sure she'll understand."

Ryan laughed. "You're an evil woman."

She grinned back.

Thoughts of Ryan's unhappy mother quickly fled as the crowd surged forward and Tara found herself inside the factory outlet, facing Christmas in all its gorgeous finery right in the face.

Tara had been to some fabulous Christmas displays, some wonderful Christmas stores, and some terrific Christmas bazaars, but she'd never seen anything like this.

Every square inch of the store was decorated for Christmas and covered in ornaments. Themed Christmas trees stood in the corners, covered so heavily in hand-blown silver-lined glass, heavily glittered old-world-style ornaments and lights that the branches were barely visible. Wreaths ran the lengths of each wall and were similarly decked out.

Green and white divided cardboard ornament boxes in all sizes were stacked against the walls. And in the middle of the room, bins and bins and bins of the delicate ornaments, haphazardly thrown together, ran in aisles. Repeat customers who were familiar with the shopping process grabbed boxes and began digging through the bins.

In retail stores these ornaments were carefully hung on trees or sold in individual boxes, packaged carefully with tissue. Signs warned customers of the fragility of the decorations. Here there was none of the reverence as the throngs attacked the bins.

Tara's mouth fell open at the sight.

A clerk saw Tara staring and laughed. "First-timer, huh?"

Tara nodded with Ryan behind her. He was also watching the scene in amazement.

"Sure they can break," the clerk said. "But they're not as delicate as they look. The ornaments in the bins are four dollars apiece. The small ornaments in those few bins over there are two apiece. The specially boxed ornaments are priced as marked.

"Most of the ornaments in bins are perfect. Just overstocks or discontinued items. Some have slight flaws. A few do get broken, so examine your finds carefully before buying. We have a no-refund policy. If you see something you like on one of the trees, feel free to grab it. Every ornament in here is for sale." She grabbed two boxes and handed one each to Tara and Ryan. "Better get to it before all the good ones are gone." She leaned toward them and whispered something to Ryan before she winked and walked away.

Tara stared into her box with its cardboard dividers stuffed with tiny puffs of tissue paper to protect the ornaments once they were boxed. Why suddenly treat them like glass? The whole experience was horribly incongruous.

Ryan's eyes were wide as he scanned the store. "What are we looking for? Do we have a theme for the tree or does anything go?"

Tara had never seen so many old-fashioned ornaments in one place before. However she'd pictured the ornament store, it hadn't been like this. There was an infinite variety of figures available.

She rolled her eyes at Ryan and looked around the room for inspiration. "Anything goes? What kind of talk is that? That's craziness.

"The lodge is all homey woodsy-ness. Our mission today is to collect glittery pinecones in all colors, snowflakes, birds, animals, and fish," she said, trying to take it all in.

Ryan stepped over to the bin nearest them and pulled out a bright purple and orange tropical fish "Like this?" His eyes twinkled.

She shook her head. "No! Like trout and fish we have here. The kind Grandpa is always on the hunt for. No tropical fish or exotic animals. Only Northwesty wildlife. Now get serious. We have a lot of work to do."

Ryan put the fish back in the bin and saluted. "Okay, so do we work as a team or is it divide and conquer, every man for himself?"

Tara scanned the room. "I say we divide and conquer or we'll never get out of here. Just stick to the mission statement."

Almost before the words were out of her mouth, Ryan was off. Tara scanned the room again with almost childlike glee. *So this is what it's really like to be a kid in a candy store?*

She fought the crowd to the far row and bins and dug in. At first, she delicately picked up one ornament at a time and carefully considered it. But before long she became a jaded pro like the rest of the shoppers. She dove into the bins, sticking her arms in and gently pawing through, digging to the bottom, and bringing the stock on the bottom up to the top.

Deep down she wanted an elusive white wolf. Wouldn't that be the crowning glory for her tree? She'd always liked wolves. Well, except for meeting them alone in the woods. And as she dug through the bins, she was determined to find one.

She quickly filled her box with all manner of pinecones, snowflakes, and animals. But she'd scoured every inch of the shop. No white wolf. She grabbed another box and filled it just as quickly.

"Found one!" A woman at the bin next to her grinned from ear to ear as she held up a prized white wolf.

Curses, foiled again.

Someone applauded the find and everyone went back to their shopping and treasure hunting.

Once Tara looked up and spotted Ryan carefully holding up and inspecting a brown bear with a trout in its mouth. Something about the sight of him so seriously studying the ornaments made her smile. He caught her looking and grinned at her.

She refused to be embarrassed and winked back at him.

Tara filled two boxes, then three, four, and more as she quickly lost track of time. There were so many ornaments it was easy to fill the boxes. Too easy. But too hard on her wallet. And it was only with the greatest of will that she resisted the many temptations not on her list.

In almost every bin she looked through, the most adorable gingerbread boy and girl looked up at her, begging her to take them home. The gingerbread girl wore a bright red Santa jacket with sparkling white fur collar, and had zigzag frosting on her skirt. The boy wore a Santa hat and had shiny holly berry buttons.

She and the boys—Ryan and Chad—used to decorate gingerbread people together every year with Gram at the lodge while Grandpa carefully constructed their gingerbread house. Tara always carefully decorated hers, while the boys piled theirs high with as much frosting and candy as they could. Happy memories.

Tara held the gingerbread couple up and watched them glitter and sparkle in the light. *As much as I love you, you two are just too common. Where would I put you?*

She reluctantly set the gingerbreads back into the bin. She had way too many ornaments already.

"Hey, how's it going?"

She looked up to see Ryan smiling at her as he held a box of bird ornaments.

"I think Margie will like these." He held his box out to her. "What do you think?"

She peered into the box. "Gram will be thrilled. She loves birds." She made a funny pout. "No luck finding a white wolf, either?"

"Not yet." Glitter sparkled in Ryan's hair and eyelashes, and on his cheeks. It rested on his shoulders and ran down the sleeves of his coat.

Tara laughed at the sight of the glittery Ryan. "You should see yourself. You look like you were in an explosion in a glitter factory." She reached up and tried to brush the glitter out of his hair. But she only succeeded in adding more sparkle to him.

"Well, you look like you overdid it with the holiday glitter hairspray and the glitter powder and lotion. You are simply sparkling all over." He dusted her shoulder, grinning as he wiped glitter from his hands all over her coat.

"Hey, stop that." She pushed his hand away and patted his cheek playfully, leaving a handprint of glitter in her wake. "You're just trying to add more glitter to me."

He grabbed her hand. "Ditto to you, baby."

He was staring into her eyes. She was staring into his. For a moment she forgot herself and where they were, and it was only the two of them.

He brushed a strand of her hair away from her face and leaned into her. "You have glitter in your eyelashes." His gaze traced her face and came to rest on her lips. "And in your lipgloss."

The moment was mercifully shattered by a pushy lady. "Hey, get out of the way. Do your kissing elsewhere."

Kissing?

Yes, well, Tara supposed they had been on the verge. That seemed to be happening a lot today. And she couldn't even blame it on mistletoe.

"Sorry," Ryan said to the lady as they stepped back out of her way. He gave Tara an eye-roll and a conspiratorial look that made her grin.

Ryan changed the topic. "I've filled five boxes." He pointed to a stack on the counter. "How about you?"

"Eight."

"Do you think that's enough?"

"I think that's probably all I can afford."

"All right, then," Ryan said. "Let's check out."

CHAPTER ELEVEN

Ryan and Tara rode back to the lodge with Christmas music blaring. Tara had always loved hearing him sing. He had a nice, melodic singing voice. Tara's sucked. But they sang along as they rode home, and laughed over their experiences with Digger and Old European. It felt so good to laugh with Ryan again. She hadn't remembered missing all this so much.

"How upset will Laura be about you hanging out with me?" Tara couldn't help herself. The question popped out between Christmas carols. "Will she advise Santa to put coal in your stocking?"

Ryan kept his eyes on the road and shrugged. "Mom has never hated you."

Tara stared at him and shook her head. "Right."

"Seriously. Disparaged you. Been disappointed with you. Not liked you. But hated you? Never."

She smiled at him. "You sure know how to make a girl feel better."

He turned past the Echo Bay population sign and into the lodge parking lot just as more flakes of snow began falling. "The question is," he said as they hopped out of the car, "whether we need a hand-truck to haul all this loot in or not."

Boxes filled both the trunk and the backseat. Tara stared at them. "I'd say we need a sleigh. Grandpa keeps a sled in the shed."

"And a hand-truck. That'll do."

This time as they walked together into the lodge, Tara had an insane desire to actually pause and beg a kiss beneath the mistletoe. Was it her imagination or did Ryan eye it, too, as they walked by?

It was just after three-thirty in the afternoon. Dusk was falling outside. Inside was quiet—between dinner rushes and most of the guests still being on the mountain.

Gram was in the kitchen. She spied them from the pass-through window. "Ah, there you kids are! How was town?"

"Fine," Tara said. "I brought you and Grandpa back an early Christmas present. They're in the car. What smells so good in here?"

Kathleen popped out of the kitchen with a dishtowel in hand. "Our new secret recipe for the cookbook. Anyone want to try a bite?"

Oh, no! Tara thought.

"I'm game." Ryan rubbed his hands together as he headed for the kitchen.

For some reason, thoughts of the cookbook still irritated Tara, reminding her of the stakes at hand. She put a hand on Ryan to stop his forward progress. "Wait a minute, big boy. We can't keep that glass outside in freezing temperatures."

"You're right," he said. "Where does Harry keep the hand truck?"

Ryan not only brought in the ornaments, he hauled the tree in from the workshop, too. Tara had a very fine view of his butt and strong legs as he maneuvered beneath the tree, getting it braced and aligned within the stand while she called out directions.

"It's leaning to the left. A little to the right," she said.

Gram and Kathleen were still exclaiming over the ornaments, going through box after box. Gram held her hands in front of her in that position that meant she was pleased. Harry seemed to be at a loss for words, but he was smiling.

"This is wonderful, just wonderful," Gram said, picking up a bluebird and smiling. "Best Christmas present ever." Her gaze kept bouncing between Ryan beneath the tree and Tara.

Tara got the distinct feeling Gram had the wrong impression.

"We'll have a decorating party tonight," Margie said. "Invite all the staff and guests who want to participate. We'll serve hot chocolate and spiced eggnog."

She turned to Harry. "You can make your famous Tom and Jerrys." She clasped her hands in front of her again. "Tara, you remember how we used to roast hotdogs in the fireplace when you were little?"

"We'll get Carter to make a big blaze. I really am fond of a good blaze. And we'll roast marshmallows and hotdogs."

Ryan wiggled out from beneath the tree and stood. "I think that does it." He stood back to admire his work.

"You'll stay, of course," Margie said to Ryan.

Looking uncomfortable, he shot a quick glance at Tara and then focused his attention on Margie. "Thanks for the invitation, but I have to pass. I have to stop by home and feed Blondie, give her a little love and attention. And then I'm off to have dinner with my parents." He glanced at the clock. "In fact, I have to get moving or I'll be late and Mom will kill me. You know how she prizes punctuality."

Tara couldn't believe how incredibly disappointed she felt that he couldn't stay.

Laura and Kirk Sanders lived in the same modest bungalow cottage on the outskirts of town that they'd raised their four boys in. It may have been modest in size, but it was filled with love. And these days, it would have gone for nearly half a million on the open market, though they'd only paid sixty thousand for it in the first place. Moneyed people from outside were always looking for little houses to buy up and use as ski cabins, running up the prices and the taxes for the locals.

Strings of red and white Christmas lights ran along the roof lines and around the big evergreen tree in the front yard, and the old light-up Santa sat at the bottom of the front porch steps just as he had throughout Ryan's childhood.

It was homey and inviting and Ryan wished he could run the other way before his parents spotted him. His mother was going to give him hell. He was fifteen minutes late and even though he'd called, she was not going to be happy with the source of his lateness.

Man up.

"Hey, Ma, I'm home!" he called as he walked through the front door.

Laura came out of the kitchen wearing a holiday oven mitt and matching apron. "And about time, too. The prodigal son returns." Her gaze ran the length of him. "Looks like you still have your heart. At least it's not obviously ripped out of your chest."

"Leave the boy alone," his dad said as he popped out of his easy chair and set aside the iPad that he'd been playing games on. "Let him at least take his coat off before you begin grilling him."

"Hey, Dad." Ryan slid his coat off and hung it in the closet. "So you heard about my trip to Old European, I take it."

"Don't use that casual tone on me, Ryan Allen Sanders. Of course I heard. And even if I hadn't, I have eyes. You're covered in glitter."

Ryan looked down at himself. *Damn.* He'd showered to get rid of the evidence, too.

His mother shook her head. "Sally saw you and texted me all the events as they happened. So don't think you can keep anything from me. I know all."

"If you know all, then there's nothing more to tell you."

Laura arched a brow and gave him the penetrating Mom stare. "Except your side of the story."

His mother, the inquisitor. She was kind of cute in an irritating sort of way. But at least she cared.

"I was just helping Tara buy some ornaments for the lodge Christmas tree as a way to help out Margie and Harry. That's all. Nothing sinister in that. You know how much I care for those two." He kissed his mother on the cheek.

"Uh-huh, but here's the thing. I thought you and Tara were at odds?"

"You know the old saying, 'Keep your friends close and your enemies closer.'" He sniffed the air deeply. "Pot roast! My fave."

"And by close, you mean looking as if you want to kiss them?" his mother said.

"Who said I wanted to kiss Tara?"

Laura rolled her eyes. "You've wanted to kiss that girl since the first time you laid eyes on her when you were in elementary school. You never haven't wanted to kiss her, Ryan. And despite how she stomped on your heart and treated you like dirt, I don't see that that's changed. At least that's what I'm hearing and fearing."

"Ma, I appreciate your concern, but I'm a grown man. I can handle myself." *He hoped.* Because his mother was exactly spot on.

Laura stared at him. "So you tell me. I just don't want to see you get hurt again. You know I always liked Tara. But after Chad died, she changed."

"Maybe she's changed back."

She shook her head and looked at his dad for confirmation. "How in the world did I manage to raise such an optimist? I thought I raised you to be realistic.

"Once upon a time Tara changed as quickly as the weather on the mountain and froze your heart. Don't think that can't happen again.

"Maybe she's using the same 'keep your enemies close' philosophy and playing you?"

"When did you become such a cynic, Ma?"

Laura rested a hand on Ryan's arm. "I know well enough to leave my boys alone in love. Women set the tone for the household. Say anything that gets me crosswise of the girls in my sons' lives who might eventually become wives and I lose my boy forever.

"I'm not going to make that mistake with you, Ryan. I know you well enough to know you'll do what you'll do. So consider this a friendly mother's warning, and then I'm backing off. Proceed carefully. Enough said. Just remember, I'm always on *your* side."

Harry handed Tara a glass of his famous holiday cocktail, the 1950s favorite, a Tom and Jerry— whipped egg whites, cinnamon, hot water, brandy, and rum, topped with nutmeg. Carter had built a great blaze in the fireplace. Christmas music played over the sound system. The guests and staff were having a wonderful time decorating the tree and partying, as far as Tara could tell.

They'd gone through dozens of hotdogs, bags of marshmallows, and used all the roasting sticks Carter had meticulously whittled for the occasion.

Margie was handing around a tray of veggies and chips and dip. "Try a carrot stick or chip and be sure to dip it! The dip is our own secret recipe using Copper Creek Salad Dressing. If it passes muster, the recipe will be in a new cookbook in the spring. What do you think?"

Stormy had just hung the last ornament on the tree. She dusted her hands together to get the glitter off. "I think that's it."

Tara stepped back to appraise their handiwork and smiled. The tree looked as if it belonged in the Old European showroom, and that was a good thing. Barely a bit of branch showed through the happy concoction of holiday glitter and charm.

The tree was perfect—reminiscent of days gone by. But not Tara's specific days. No, this was a fresh look and a fresh start. Very classy and totally lodge-style at the same time.

She had only hung a few ornaments before stepping back to direct the decorating. The guests and staff had crowded her out anyway, and she was happy to watch them all having so much fun.

If only Ryan had been able to see and enjoy the fruits of their shopping excursion.

"It looks fantastic, everyone. You've all done a wonderful job." Tara admired the forest animals, snowflakes, and pinecones covering the tree's branches. "It has every forest animal Old European had available, except for that elusive white wolf. Ryan and I tried hard to find one. But they're rare prizes and we just struck out."

Margie set the tray down on a coffee table and came over to give Tara a hug. "It's gorgeous! Even without a white wolf. The best tree yet. We made some good memories today." She smiled at Tara in the sly way of hers that led Tara to believe she was speaking as much of Tara and Ryan making good memories together as the group before them. "Thank you for this early Christmas present. I haven't enjoyed a gift so much in years."

Kathleen came up beside them. "I'll say it's pretty—pretty Christmassy and perfect."

Stormy cried out. "Oh, no!"

They all turned to see Stormy looking perplexed. She pointed toward the far corner. "We missed two boxes."

Tara looked at the tree and frowned. "There's no room at the inn for them, that's for sure. Or on the branches, either. We've pretty much obscured our tree."

Stormy walked over and collected the boxes. "All sales final," she reminded Tara. "You'll just have to take them home with you." She paused as she picked up the boxes. "Oh, this one has a note with your name on it, Tara."

Gram and Kathleen glanced at each other before giving Tara a significant look.

"Wonder who that's from?" Gram grinned. "Looks like Ryan's handwriting to me."

Tara took the boxes from Stormy. It was indeed Ryan's handwriting. No way was she going to open that note in front of all the prying eyes in the room. "I'll just run these up to my room to get them out of the way for now. Be back in a sec."

Before anyone could stop her, Tara took the steps in record pace and dashed into her room. Once the door was safely closed behind her, she took a deep breath to steal her wildly pounding heart and calm her happy nerves.

What could Ryan possibly have to say in a note? That was so old school. Tara had always liked to string out her Christmas presents, slowly opening them to extend the pleasure. She set the boxes on her bed and pulled the lid off the first one, the one without the note. Inside was a collection of animals and fish.

She could take these home, but though they were pretty, they weren't her style. Too masculine and definitely not urban enough. Ryan! They'd look perfect on his tree. She'd give them to him in a kind of ornament exchange. It beat a cookie exchange anyway, and was a lot less fattening.

She pulled Ryan's note off the second box and read it. *To my beautiful, glittering companion in ornament shopping. Here's to new memories. Ryan.*

She removed the lid from the box and gasped. "A white wolf! Where..."

Then she remembered the shop clerk whispering in Ryan's ear and the way his face lit up in devilish delight. And the way he'd been suspiciously hovering around one of the trees.

Tara smiled. The white wolf wasn't the only ornament in the box. *He must have been watching me.*

The gingerbread boy and girl were nestled snuggly in tissue paper in the middle of the box, so close it looked almost as if they were holding hands.

Tara grabbed the white wolf to take down to the tree. She knew the perfect spot for it. At the door, she hesitated. She pulled her cell phone from her pocket and texted Ryan.

I've always loved gingerbread boys. And wolves ;-)

CHAPTER TWELVE

"Hey, Blondie, girl." Ryan couldn't hold down his smile as he patted Blondie and gave her her breakfast. "You be a good girl while I'm gone today."

The dog whined as if she recognized she'd be alone again. Blondie had a pretty good sense of when Ryan should be home for the weekend. She was smart enough to recognize she'd gotten the short stick regarding his attention for the past week or so.

For his part, Ryan couldn't wait to see Tara. If he dabbed a little cinnamon behind his ears would she gobble him up? He certainly hoped so. He could play a wolf as well as the next guy.

He washed his hands, grabbed his coat, and was off. Another five or six inches of snow covered the yard and roads. Ryan eyed his roof dubiously. The snow was stacking up. Fortunately it was light and dry. But if it piled up much deeper he was going to have to shovel the roof. It was pitched steeply enough that it shouldn't collapse, but he wasn't taking any chances.

The snow crunched beneath his feet as he got into his SUV. It was a perfect powder, which made him itch to get up on the slopes before the crowds turned it into crud. His only real hesitation was Tara—how would she react to the mountain? Unlike Ryan, she hadn't been back to the scene of Chad's death since the accident. She hadn't even been back on the mountain.

Grief was a funny, capricious thing, as he knew only too well. It could strike out of nowhere without any provocation. He and Tara had had such a good time yesterday. Ryan was hopeful. He just hoped the mountain didn't bring back up emotions and feelings that would ruin things between him and Tara. He had a careful plan to keep her in the new areas as far away as possible from anything that still remotely resembled the way it had been ten years ago. But there was still no telling how Tara would react. He texted her that he was on his way.

She was waiting for him on the front porch and looking like the most delicious of snow bunnies in her white beanie, coat, and scarf. She stuck out her thumb when she saw him pull up.

He laughed and leaned across the seat to open the door for her.

"Going to the Basin?" she said innocently.

"Hop in. I'll give you a ride. As long as Harry doesn't catch us."

She laughed and he was relieved to see she seemed at ease and not at all nervous.

"You big, secret-keeping guy! How long were we at Old European before you found that white wolf? All of five minutes, I bet," she said with a flirt and a bit of tease in her voice. "I bet that clerk told you where it was, didn't she?

"And yet you let me look and look and get totally frustrated, all the while keeping a straight face. Remind me not to play poker with you."

"You never play poker with me. You suck at it." He put the SUV in drive and headed toward town. "Hey, I wanted that wolf to be a surprise."

"And it was. A pleasant one. Now the proud wolf is hanging in the place of honor, the prime locale for all to see. Thank you. Now, what do you have in the way of Christmas music?"

In town, Digger had Tara's board waiting for them. Soon enough they were on the road to the Basin and Tara became quiet as they wound up the well-plowed mountain road in a stream of traffic. The morning was clear and beautiful, with no fog or breeze. As they climbed the winding road, Ryan could see for miles out across the lake and the forest. The trees along the road glistened and were weighted down with snow. It would have been perfect if he hadn't been worried about Tara. "You okay?"

She stared out the window. "I'd forgotten how gorgeous the view is from up here."

"Uh-huh," he said. "That doesn't answer my question."

"They've made the road wider."

"Yes," he said. "A few years ago."

"Progress. Life goes on and all that." She nodded. "It looks and feels different."

"Different enough?" he asked, knowing what she was referring to.

"For now." She seemed to relax a bit. "The snow looks perfect." She turned and smiled at him. "The kind that makes you tingle with anticipation. I'd forgotten that feeling, too. Do you feel it? Are you tingling?"

Oh, yeah, he was tingling. But it was mostly because Tara was sitting next to him and things were going better than he expected. He focused his attention on the road, which was so well sanded and plowed it wasn't slippery at all. Unlike his heart, which was on an extremely slippery slope.

"Yeah," he simply said.

"Who knew the look of snow is as powerful a memory jogger as smell is?" She turned to look out the window again.

He hoped it didn't jog *all* the memories. Just the good ones.

"I'm nervous," she said when they were nearly to the ski resort village parking lot. "Is boarding like riding a bike, do you think?"

"Do you mean do you ever forget how?" He thought about her question. "I have no personal experience. But from what I've seen, it comes back quickly. We get a lot of people on the slopes that haven't been up in years. Usually, in no time they're back in the game."

The resort village came into view. Ryan found himself holding his breath as he waited for Tara's reaction to it. He had to force himself to keep his eyes on the road and not stare at her. If she was going to break down, this was the dangerous moment. Make that the *first* dangerous moment.

"Wow! Look at that." Tara shook her head as they entered the village. "The A-frame rental cottages are all gone. Replaced with a fancy alpine hotel. And is that a shopping mall?"

"A small one," he said, relieved. She sounded like she was hanging in.

"This used to be just open land. It's really built up." She paused. "I saw all this on the Basin website, but experiencing it in person is something else."

As a perk of being a senior ski patrol member, Ryan had a permit to park in the reserved upper lot without paying a fee. The upper lot was closest to the runs, close enough there was no need to take a shuttle. He turned into the lot behind half a dozen other cars. "Getting the feel of being on the board should come right back to you. Just be prepared to be sore tomorrow."

She laughed. "Yeah, even though I go to the gym at home, boarding does tend to use muscles you didn't know you had."

Dangerous moment number two approached as The Basin Lodge came into view. Next to him, Tara stiffened, simply staring at it. Ryan gave her space and time to process, crossing his fingers she didn't crash and burn.

"It looks just like it does on their website and promo materials around town—different. Remodeled. Refurbished. Everything's different." The words faded away. Then she shook her head and laughed softly. "Who was the architect? He should be shot. He took away all the old character of the place."

Ryan breathed a sigh of relief. *Things are going to be okay.*

As soon as he parked, Tara hopped out of the SUV and stood in the fresh snow, looking around with an unreadable look on her face. He followed her out of the SUV and watched her.

"This lot is new, too."

He nodded again. That was part of the reason he'd decided to park here. Besides not having to pay. He'd carefully orchestrated everything to give her new, and hopefully pleasant experiences at the Basin.

She bent, scooped up a handful of snow, and sniffed it and then the air. "Yes, it still smells like fresh crispness up here. It's a smell you don't forget. That, at least, hasn't changed. Leave it to Mother Nature to remain constant in the face of progress."

She stared at the snow in her hand and blew on it, sending the fresh powder blowing away. This was an old Tara method for testing the snow conditions. "Perfect." Her smile was a little wistful.

Yes, the snow was perfect and so was the sight of her. He forced himself to look away and unload their gear.

"I have a ski-patrol-issued locker in the new addition to the lodge. We can store our valuables there."

"Ah, the perks of being on patrol." She grinned at him.

She seemed to be holding up well. He hoped that continued.

Tara trudged alongside Ryan, carrying her board and bag at her own insistence. Everything was different—more commercial and upscale. It didn't feel like home anymore, certainly not like the stuff of her childhood memories when the Basin catered to the local middle-class family crowd. Now it was a destination vacation spot. And she wasn't sure she liked it. On the other hand, to her relief, it didn't spark any old, anxious memories. It was as if the Basin was offering her a clean slate and a fresh start.

Ryan held the door to the lodge open for her. Inside the lodge was as different from the old lodge as it could be. Even the floor plan was different. A gigantic, obviously professionally decorated Christmas tree filled the center of the room. A large gas fireplace blazed as a group of Victorian-dressed carolers sang in front of it. Very pleasant, but very staged.

The large, cafeteria-style restaurant had been replaced with a modern café. Tara stared at the menu board and nearly gaped at the prices they charged for what she bet was basically a fancily renamed hamburger and fries. *Pomme frites*, indeed.

Part of it was impressive. After all, this is what she pictured for Echo Bay Resort, only on a much smaller scale. But surprisingly, there was still something unsettling and impersonal about it. Like a piece of Americana had disappeared. Like Christmas going commercial and being run by a large eastern syndicate.

Where were all the friendly people who used to greet her by name? No one even paid any attention to Ryan, and he was a regular and valued member of ski patrol.

She followed him as he wound through the lodge to a private bay of lockers. He stopped in front of one with his name on it. "Hand me your purse and whatever else you'd like to store."

They changed into their board boots, stashed their board bags, and attached their passes to their zipper pulls.

Ryan slammed the locker shut. "Shall we start with the bunny hill?"

"The bunny hill? Are you crazy? I haven't been on the bunny hill since I was four years old. Take me to a nice, gentle advanced beginner run and we'll go from there."

At the base of the lift, Tara strapped her boot into the forward snowboard binding.

Ryan was watching her. "You okay? Need me to check your binding?"

"Oh, shut up!" She laughed. "I still know how to get into my bindings, for heaven's sake."

"I take it that means you still know how to step and glide, too?"

She rolled her eyes. But as she watched the skiers and boarders hop onto the chair lift in turn, a wave of anxiety crashed over her. She found herself overthinking a process that had once been almost as natural as breathing. Slight crouch to the knees, angle one butt cheek on, and then the other.

The lift operator watched her hesitation, and of all the humiliation, slowed the chair down for her when it was her turn. Indignant, and relieved, she got into the chair without a problem as Ryan hopped on next to her, looking way too innocent. She hadn't seen it, but she was pretty certain he'd signaled the operator to slow that chair for her. She wasn't a little old lady. Not yet, anyway. And she may have been rusty, but she wasn't a novice.

I'll show that Ryan and pull his chain. Which is when she hatched a perfectly beautiful plan.

The chairs on the lift were new, too. She sat with her board dangling from one boot and turned to Ryan. "If you rock the chair, you're a dead man." It was an old joke from when she was little. She was still a bit afraid of heights.

He laughed. "Okay, small fry. I won't rock you out."

The view as they rose up the mountain had remained constant and true and as breathtaking as it had ever been. From up on the lift on the mountain she felt as if she could see forever and through time. She'd once told her brother that, and he'd confessed to feeling the same. She thought of him now and smiled to herself, picturing him somewhere in the heavens looking through time back at her. He'd be happy she was with Ryan. She knew he would.

From the lift she could see Canada, three different mountain ranges, three states, the large meandering lake, and Echo Bay. A kind of Christmas joy, a religious

sort of experience at viewing the beautiful world over-
came her and she almost broke out in carols. Next to
her, Ryan's presence felt warm and reassuring. She appreciated that he was giving her space and privacy.
There were no words to express the feelings the view
and the mountain and being with Ryan brought out in
her, and she'd rather not try.

The mountains, the lake, and the sky blended together on the horizon in varying shades of blue, bright
and brilliant to deep and muted.

I'm on top of the world. And I love it.

She felt like the complete opposite of the Grinch.
Everything she saw below her—the snow-covered evergreen trees they were gliding over, the skiers and
boarders sliding down the mountain, the tiny, busy
spot of town below, the cars winding their way up the
mountain from below—brought her great joy.

Getting off the chair lift is the next most frightening time for a beginner. Or someone who hasn't done it
for a while. Tara, however, had taken to it immediately
as a tiny four-year-old. Now, she suddenly felt another
stab of nerves as she angled sideways, ready to plant
her bound front foot forward to glide off the lift. The
fear stemmed from the humiliating thought of wiping
out before clearing the chairs. Which many people did.

Ryan reached over and squeezed her hand. A second
later, the chair positioned itself over the departure
spot. Tara planted her board, put her free back foot on
the stomp pad Digger had installed, free of charge, and
executed a semi wobbly J-turn down the small departure slope. But at least she hadn't fallen on her face.

Ryan glided to a perfect stop beside her.

"If you tell me that was very good, I'll clobber you." She winked at him.

"Still have those violent tendencies. I thought you'd outgrown them."

She laughed at him, seeing through him as he tried to divert her attention and encourage her. She felt hope pouring off him. *It's important to him that I regain my old love of the sport.*

It was so obvious in the way he was treating her, encouraging her, and guiding her away from any unpleasant memories of the past. It was touching, very touching.

Skiing and boarding were like air to Ryan, always had been. It was something they'd always shared. Any woman who wanted to spend her life with Ryan would have to either love it as much as he did, or be content to be a snow widow during the winter.

"This is a new run, isn't it?" she said, knowing it was and that Ryan had chosen it with care.

"Yeah," he said without elaborating. "We have quite a few new runs here at the Basin. It's expanded like crazy these last years." Then he grinned at her. "Follow me."

Stepping and gliding came back to her easily. She *hadn't* forgotten. But she made a show of stumbling along. "It really *has* been a while."

Ryan waited patiently as she "struggled" to the top between two runs. "Left or right? Left is a gentler slope. Right is more scenic and only slightly more difficult."

Decisions, decisions. In the spirit of my charade...
"Left. This time."

"All right, then. Strap in and we'll cut across."

Tara fell backwards into a sit with a plop into the soft powder and strapped her back foot into her bindings. Seattle got very little snow and when it did, it was usually wet and short-lived. Or quickly turned to concrete iciness. So she hadn't played or sat in snow in years. Cold, but it sure felt good.

Ryan sat next to her, strapped in, and leaned over to check her bindings. "Let's see what we have here."

A beanie covered his thick head of hair, but didn't quell the urge she had to reach out and stroke his head.

"You have to be kidding?" she said to him. "I know how to get into bindings."

"Sure, but these are newfangled bindings."

"Uh-huh. Which means poor helpless me can't figure them out?" She made a fist to resist the urge to reach out and stroke Ryan's hair like she used to.

"It never hurts to exercise caution and double check."

Ryan was not usually a fusser. Generally, he was pretty mellow. Which meant he was worried and didn't want anything to go wrong this first trip down. Tara wondered at his motivation. He probably figured he owed it to Chad to help Tara rediscover her love of boarding.

"Which means I get to check yours?" she said, teasing her.

"No way!" He stood on his board and grinned at her.

Standing up with your feet strapped to a snowboard can be a bit tricky at first. Tara, however, was a rusty pro. But she was intent on pulling one over on Ryan, with the idea of showing him he didn't have to worry about her. She leaned back on her hands and tried the old frog stand, failing, on purpose, and falling back on her butt.

Ryan immediately stepped in. "Let me." He offered her his hand and pulled her up.

She flashed him her best smile. "Thanks."

Ryan had always been gentlemanly and protective of her up on the slopes. Sometimes it was annoying. Sometimes she thought it was sweet.

All around them kids, mostly, were cruising down the hill on their boards. A couple of teenagers giggled next to them as a boy coached a pretty girl on how to get started.

Tara looked out on the view and the blue with her heart pounding. Anxiety welled up out of nowhere. She *would* do this. As she dusted the snow off her butt, Ryan leered at her. "Enjoying the show?"

He shrugged. "You always did know how to wiggle your ass."

"Shut up." She shook her head again.

"We'll take it slow," Ryan said. "Just push off gently and cut to the left-hand run. I'll be right behind you if you need me."

Situated between the two runs in a nice little hole sat a first-aid station hut. At a quick glance, Tara saw several inexperienced boarders who were trying to cross between runs having difficulty and sliding desperately close to the snow precipice above the first-aid station. *Ah, the perfect scenario.*

Tara pushed off and began cutting slowly down the slope in the general direction of the left run. She wobbled at first, and intentionally fell over into the powder, just to see what Ryan would do. He was right there to give her another hand up with a firm squeeze. Which felt good. Too good.

Back on her feet, Tara slid toward the run. The feel of the board beneath her feet and how to control it came right back. Her nerves faded away as a sense of exhilaration at performing a long-forgotten skill came back. She resisted her urge to control her speed and direction and let the slope carry her toward the first-aid station and that ledge that preceded it. She gained speed quickly and pulled away from Ryan.

"Tara, carve over!" he called to her.

She played helpless and let herself slide toward the station as Ryan boarded toward her.

"Tara, slow down! Dig your board edge in!"

As if he had to tell her. She knew exactly what to do and did the opposite.

"Tara!" Ryan was gaining on her.

But not fast enough. Even she could see that. If she let herself continue, she was going to end up as a pancake on the first-aid station's doorstep. Really, they should have put the station in a safer, more accessible spot.

Even as she slid, though, she relished the bracing fresh air on her face and the spray of the powder around her. The thing with boarding in powder is that speed is your friend. Slow too much and you dig into the snow, rather than gliding along the surface.

"Tara!"

Okay, time to end this charade. She leaned back on her heels, digging the board into the snow, and fell back onto her butt about fifteen feet from the precipice above the aid station.

Ryan glided to a stop next to her in a spray of powder.

"Good job, ski patrol," she said. "You got here quickly."

"Tara, don't tease. What were you thinking? Why didn't you fall down sooner if you couldn't control yourself?" He looked almost pale beneath his helmet and goggles. But maybe that was just the cold.

"If I'd had control, I would have used it." She called upon her meager acting skills and tried to sound upset and scared. And to look vulnerable.

Ryan pursed his lips and took a deep breath as he held his hand out to her. "I'll help you across to the run. I should have thought ahead. The run is much gentler than this crossing. You should be fine on it."

He pulled her to her feet, but didn't let go of her hands. Instead, he put his arms around her, looking as if he were about to dance with her. "I'll guide you. Just relax and let me lead. Boarding is all about relaxing. Just remember, boarding moves are just the same as everyday motions you make all the time, just on a moving board. They'll come back to you." His tone was soft, but firm, almost a command.

She stared into his worried eyes and nodded. There was something mesmerizing about Ryan's gaze and the concerned look on his face. About his desire to please her and help her rediscover love—of the slopes.

She did relax as he pushed off, or as much as was possible with Ryan's arms around her. His touch and the gentle, yet firm, way he held her brought back so many passionate memories. There was a time she never wanted to leave his arms, and she was coming danger-ously close to rekindling those feelings. She was sup-posed to be gaming him, and yet she felt he'd somehow gotten the upper hand.

Ryan was smooth on a board. He pointed them to-ward the run and guided her cleanly with his hands firmly around her waist. His gaze flicked between her and where they were headed. "How are you doing?"

"Heavenly," she said without thinking. She flashed him a wavering smile, as if she was trying to be brave. But in fact, she'd spoken the truth. On the mountain again in Ryan's arms on such a beautiful day in perfect powder was heaven. Why had she avoided this and de-nied herself all these years?

She clutched him tightly, as if for security, as if he was her big, strong hero. But really she held onto him as if grasping for the joy of the past.

He came to a stop at the top of the run. "Here we are." He stared into her eyes.

She stared into his. Neither of them let go of the other.

"Are you up for trying?" His tone was soft and full of encouragement. "You *can* do this."

She nodded. "Yes, of course I can." She reluctantly let go of him.

"I'll be right behind you this time. Promise."

"You'd better be."

He released her. She pushed off and it all came back to her, just like riding a bike.

CHAPTER THIRTEEN

Tara flew down the hill past all the beginner boarders and skiers. She flew past Santa Claus handing out candy canes to the children on the slopes. She sped along laughing with joy. With Ryan right behind her.

At the bottom of the run, she pulled to a perfect stop and grinned.

Ryan pulled up beside her. "You big, fat liar! Look at you board, as if there'd never been an interruption." Happiness tumbled through his voice.

Tara had the distinct impression he was hoping other interrupted things, one interrupted relationship in particular, came back with the same ease. The thought was both thrilling and frightening. She and Ryan lived in two different worlds, maybe they always had. And she wasn't certain there was any way of reconciling them, even after all these years.

She smiled at him. "That was too easy. Let's go again. On a more difficult run."

He shook his head. "Don't get cocky, kid. We'll go the right run this time and then we'll see about upping the difficulty points."

"Oh, come on," she said. "I think I'm ready for some tricks."

"I think you've already pulled one on me."

"I'm going to hit the trick park by the end of the day."

"We'll see about that."

The day slipped away all too quickly, and even though Tara was exhausted, she hated for it to end. She'd worked her way up to boarding the intermediate runs and even did a few easy tricks at the trick park. Then she'd watched Ryan show off for her.

She and Ryan had gotten along amazingly well. Tara felt as if that darn old hatchet was finally buried. If only a few inches deep.

Ryan stopped the SUV in front of Echo Bay Resort and popped the back so they could unload Tara's gear. They each hesitated in their seat.

"Come in and have dinner with me." Tara hoped she didn't sound too eager. Because she was, and she didn't want to scare Ryan away.

"On me," she said when he didn't answer right away. "Last I heard, Gram was intent on making her special mincemeat pie, and I'd lay money she saved a few slices for us."

"I'd love to, Tara."

She sensed a "but" coming. Unfortunately, she wasn't disappointed.

"But I'll have to take a rain check. I have to get home and feed my girl. She's been cooped up all day. She deserves a little time and attention and a nice romp outside before we hit the coldest temps of the day."

Tara was disappointed. Maybe she'd been wrong and Ryan wasn't as interested in her again as she thought he was. Losing out to a dog? Now that wasn't so great on her ego. She almost told him to go get Blondie and bring her over. But if he hadn't thought of that on his own, she wasn't going to push him.

"Another time, then. I'll hold you to it." She hopped out the SUV and helped Ryan unload her gear.

He set her board bag just inside the lodge door. They both ignored the mistletoe dangling over their heads. No matter how many times Tara removed it, that silly stuff always seemed to reappear as if by magic. Though she suspected Gram and a stepladder were the real culprits. Gram probably had a mistletoe man who made unending emergency deliveries on the sly.

Tara walked Ryan out. "I had a really great time tonight." *Sheesh, I sound like a junior high girl on her first date. Lame.*

Ryan smiled. "So did I. We'll do this again?"

He was sending really confusing signals.

She nodded. "Sure."

They stood facing each other and looking into each other's eyes. The day had seemed like a date. A good-bye kiss seemed appropriate, but they suddenly both seemed awkward. Tara couldn't figure out what had happened. They'd had no problem kissing out of the blue yesterday. But that had been reactionary. To kiss now would be purely intentional and a much bigger commitment.

"I'd better be going," he said.

She nodded. "See you tomorrow when you stop by for your morning coffee?"

"Yeah, if you can get up that early."

Tara watched him get into his vehicle and drive off toward his cabin, feeling a funny sense of unrequited love welling up. If this was a modern retelling of Dickens' *A Christmas Carol*, next one of the spirits would show her Ryan happily married to someone with a brood of merry children. They'd probably be riding snowmobiles and playing with that darn dog.

The thought of Ryan married to someone else made her not only unaccountably sad, but jealous to the extreme. Frowning, she went inside and sneaked up to her room with her gear, studiously avoiding Gram. Mercifully, Stormy and Kathleen had Sunday off and their weekend replacements didn't take an interest in Tara's love life or lack thereof.

In her room, Tara got out of her snowboard gear and changed into a sweater, skinny jeans, and fresh warm wool socks. As she set her gear in the corner, she spied the box of ornaments that she'd meant to give to Ryan when he dropped her off. She pulled back the curtain and looked across to Ryan's cabin. A light burned brightly in the window and she got an idea—a delightful, wonderful idea.

Ryan parked, grabbed his gear, and let himself into the cabin. Blondie attacked him instantly, nearly knocking him over. "Hey, here's a girl who's happy to see me!" He kneeled down and scratched her behind her ears.

Ryan was still confused about what had happened up on the mountain. On the one hand, he was delighted that Tara had taken to the slopes again with such ease, even though she'd punked him. Mission accomplished. He could stop blaming himself for killing a great joy of hers. One amend made.

On the other hand, he was completely confused and too hopeful. It certainly seemed that she'd been flirting with him; teasing and playing with him just like the old Tara. He wanted that old Tara back. He wanted her back in the body and mind of the current Tara. But he was wary, not wanting to push too hard or too fast. So he resorted to his dutiful dog owner excuse so he could think things through.

As he went to the cupboard for Blondie's food, he looked around his cabin. It was woefully lacking in Christmas spirit and decorations. All that ornament shopping yesterday had made him feel guilty. Or maybe inspired. He should have bought a few for himself and put up a small tree. If he could muster the heart for doing it all alone. Yeah, his mom would have helped him and dragged his dad along. But what Ryan really wanted was a special woman—like, say, Tara—to help him. At the very least a good buddy like Chad. And barring a miracle, he wasn't getting either one of those wishes.

He flipped on the TV. *It's a Wonderful Life* was playing. Yeah, Ryan wondered what his life would have been like if Chad hadn't died. But he wasn't going to get an angel like Charlie to show him. And he wasn't sure he could handle the could-have-beens if even he had.

For just a second Ryan wondered about fate. Maybe, if fate was fate and destiny was destiny, and unchangeable, he wouldn't be with Tara even if Chad had lived. Maybe she would have still headed off to the big city chasing her dream of career success and validation. Maybe he'd still be alone. The thought was depressing as hell.

He fed Blondie and took her out for the promised romp in the yard, built a nice fire in the fireplace, and headed in to take a shower, leaving the TV on. He'd just toweled off and slipped into a pair of jeans when someone pounded on his front door.

What now? Who could that be?

"Coming!" he yelled as Blondie barked up a storm. He grabbed a shirt and headed to the front door. Shirt still in hand, he grabbed Blondie's collar. "Calm down, girl."

He flung open the door with his free hand. Tara stood on his stoop with a bag of delicious-smelling food—fresh burgers, fries, and onion rings or he missed his guess—sitting atop two Old European

Christmas boxes. She wore skinny jeans and a stylish coat with a faux-fur collar and looked good enough to eat. "Tara?"

"You said you'd have dinner with me another time. Were you serious, or was feeding the dog your equivalent of 'I have to wash my hair'?"

Ryan's heart grew at least one size right that minute, and pounded out of control. Tara, on his doorstep, with food and Christmas decorations in her arms—that sounded like a wish come true to him. Funny, he hadn't seen a falling star when he'd wished.

Blondie barked and wagged her tail as he held her back from jumping all over Tara and stealing his dinner. Man's best friend was smelling the burgers, too.

Ryan stepped back, pulling Blondie with him. "No, I was washing my hair, too. Neither were excuses."

Tara ran her gaze the length of him, from his wet, tousled hair, down his bare chest to his bare feet. "Hmmm, you look like you're telling the truth. For the sake of our friendship, I think I'll choose to believe you. Has the dog been fed and played with?"

He nodded. "First thing."

"Good. And this must be the famous Blondie. Oh, she's a beaut, Ryan."

As Tara knelt to pet her, Ryan stepped between them. "Not with my dinner in your hands. I'm a starving man and Blondie doesn't share." He was telling the truth. He was starving for Tara.

Tara stood and grinned at him, or rather his chest where his nipples stood erect. "You must be freezing.

Do you always answer the door half naked?" She shut the door with her foot.

He glanced at the shirt in his hand. He'd almost forgotten he was holding it. And no, he wasn't cold. He was burning.

Tara walked to his small, round dining table and set her bag and boxes down. Ryan let go of Blondie and slipped his shirt on.

Blondie charged Tara, who seemed delighted as the dog jumped up on her. She leaned down to pet her and got a big, sloppy dog kiss for her trouble. She only laughed and cooed to the dog. Tara had always loved animals.

"She really is a doll," Tara said. "Grandpa swears golden retrievers are the best bird dogs. Do you use her for hunting?"

"A bit. But she's kind of spoiled." It warmed his heart to see Tara so happy with his dog. Maybe old angel Charlie was here granting his wish after all. It sure seemed like this was a glimpse into what Christmases could have been like.

"Oh, so you're like Gram, then—a dog spoiler. Grandpa blames her for the ruin of many a good hunting animal." She laughed, still scratching Blondie behind the ears and cooing to her. "Oh, you're a good girl. You're a beautiful girl."

Ryan wanted some of that loving attention for himself. He went to the cupboard and got two plates, two beer glasses, and some napkins and set the table while Tara played with the dog.

As he got the spread out, Tara stood, went to the sink, and washed up.

"Just what I was hoping for—burgers!" Ryan got two beers from the fridge, but rather than just popping the tops, he reached for a corkscrew. What could he say? The fruity Belgian-style beers Tara liked at the holidays were corked. He removed the cork and handed a beer to Tara.

"Cranberry lambic!" She grinned. "I do love a good fruity Christmas beer." She looked at the label. "Made locally."

"Yeah, by a friend of mine in town. He runs a little microbrewery. If you're interested, I'll take you there sometime." Okay, that was a half-assed way to ask a girl out.

But she didn't seem to mind. Tara raised her bottle to his. "To the holidays and new, happy memories."

He clinked with her, wishing for exactly the same thing—deliriously happy memories.

"Yum!" Tara licked the beer foam off her lips. "Nice and bubbly. Effervescent. That's what I love about lambic—it's the champagne of beers." She grinned at him again. "But I didn't peg you for a lambic man. I thought a nice holiday ale was more your style."

He shrugged. "And you'd be right. These two came in a mixed holiday pack. They're all I have left." Fortuitously, because Tara had always loved fruity drinks and holiday beer.

They sat down to eat and unwrapped their sloppy burgers.

"The *soon to be very famous* Copper Creek bleu cheese burger," Tara said.

Ryan's heart was in danger of growing another size. She was trying to please him. Maybe he should have been suspicious, given their rivalry, but he chose to take the gesture for what it was—very touching.

Tara broke off a piece of her burger and fed it to Blondie, who begged at her side.

"Hey! Now who's spoiling?" Ryan poured his beer into his glass.

Tara shrugged as she did the same. "What can I say? I'm a chip off Gram's block." As they both dug in, Tara looked around the cabin.

He could tell she was trying to hide her consternation. "You don't like my décor?"

She pursed her lips. "No, it's not that. It's just...well, there's a shocking lack of Christmas decorations. With all your jolliness around town and your enthusiasm for the Santa Ski, I sort of pegged you for a Christmas-loving guy. Looks like I came just in time."

Ryan nodded, wondering just how much he should say and whether he should come clean with Tara. "Looks like you did. I'm privately in danger of becoming old Scrooge."

He paused and worked up his nerve. "As for the Santa Ski, it wasn't my idea. But for as long as people will be drinking and skiing and boarding while making merry, I'll be there to watch over them and keep them safe." He looked down at his burger and then up at her. "I won't have another Christmas Eve tragedy on my hands. Not if I can help it."

Tara stared at him a moment before reaching across the table to squeeze his hand. He squeezed back, not wanting to ever let go.

Her eyes were misty, but she smiled. "I can't have you turning into Scrooge. After we eat, we'll get you a tree. Otherwise the extra ornaments I brought over from the lodge are just going to go to waste. And we can't have that.

"There must be a Christmas-worthy tree in your yard, one you can sacrifice to the Christmas cause." She squeezed his hand again.

Cutting a tree in the dark by flashlight was more challenging, but more fun than Tara could have imagined. So many of them looked long and distorted by shadow; ghostly reflected in the flashlight beam. Yet stunningly, eerily beautiful—even the most plain trees. And holes were practically impossible to see, both on the ground and in the tree.

Ryan caught her elbow on more than one occasion as she misstepped. "Hey, go easy. I can't have you turning your ankle so close to Christmas. What will people think if I have to carry you into the emergency room?"

She wasn't sure, but being in Ryan's arms sounded good to her. "These trees all look so deceptively small out here in the forest." She put her hands on her hips and studied the ones around her. "But none of them are under ten feet. We should have brought a ladder so we could top one."

Ryan shook his head. "No way, I'm not topping a big, healthy tree, not even for Christmas."

Blondie barked. They both turned and shone their lights on her as she raced around the woods on the edge of Ryan's property, freezing as if she was playing flashlight tag before a scraggly, but right-sized tree.

"That one looks good." Tara raced to it, as fast as she could in the dark without taking a tumble.

"You're crazy," Ryan said as he came up behind her.

"This little one is perfect." Tara shone her flashlight on it.

Ryan came up behind her and added his light to hers. The two beams melding together seemed symbolic. Tara smiled to herself. She'd been surprised by Ryan's place and the complete lack of anything Christmas in it. And she completely understood and admired his reason for supporting the Santa Ski. People would be up skiing and reveling whether he or Tara condoned it or not. Any warnings they could give would simply be shrugged off with a silent *That could never happen to me.* But life could change in an instant, as she knew only too well.

"Perfect? Are you the same woman who went Christmas tree cutting with me yesterday? Either someone body-snatched you or you've suddenly gone blind. That tree is an embarrassment to treehood."

Tara laughed. "I could say the same of you. What happened to the kind and compassionate Charlie Brown tree gatherer of yesterday that I went into the woods with? That man would have seen the possibilities in this little guy."

"Even the Peanuts gang couldn't make something out of this scraggly stick."

Blondie gave a happy bark and circled the tree. Tara laughed. "Yeah, we know you like it, girl." She paused, considering it. "Beggars can't be choosers. That little tree will fit into your cabin, and at this point, that's all that matters."

"And that it's not full of spiders."

Tara broke out laughing. Ryan referred to the time as teens they'd brought a tree in from the forest into his parents' house. When the tree warmed up, a batch of spiders hatched just as they were decorating it. Tara didn't stop screaming for a week, or so her brother liked to tease. She screamed until she cried, that was for sure.

"I don't see any spiders," she said.

"That's because it's dark."

She ignored his protests. "I'll hold the light. You chop it down."

"Wow, that's harsh," he said. "Just chop her down."

"Okay, then, gently saw her. Have you never read *The Little Christmas Tree*? It's every tree's goal to be a Christmas tree. Besides, this little tree is almost on life support. The big trees are hogging all the light and slowly strangling it. Unless you're planning to move and replant it, you'll be doing it a favor."

"It's a mercy killing then?"

She gave Ryan a gentle shove in the shoulder.

He laughed and handed her his light. "Mercy killing it is." He got down on his hands and knees and started sawing while Tara admired his butt.

Ryan had always been too easy on her eyes, even in the dark.

When he was finished, he carried the tree to the house while Tara carried the saw and Blondie trotted next to them. The tree had been sheltered by the big trees and was remarkably dry and free from snow.

They probably should have let it dry out overnight, and, given their past history, doused it with spider spray, but Tara was in the mood to decorate it now. She couldn't keep trumping up reasons to stop by Ryan's. And she was afraid he might lose the decorating mood.

"Do you have a stand?" she asked.

He shook his head. "No, but I have a bucket."

"That'll do."

CHAPTER FOURTEEN

It took Ryan fifteen minutes to locate the bucket, cut a base from some of his stash of kindling, and nail it to the bottom of the tree before he stuck it in the old metal bucket filled with sugar water. Tara directed him as he maneuvered it into a spot in front of his picture window just far enough from the blazing fire to be safe.

"Spin it half a turn." She eyed it. "No, no, not quite right. Give it another quarter-turn."

He complied.

"Again."

"Give up, Tara. This tree has no good side and I'm not about to play spin the tree all night." He let go of the tree and came over to stand beside her.

She couldn't help noticing how close he was, nearly shoulder to shoulder.

"Sure it does. See! You found it." She clapped and broke out laughing. Ryan was right. It was the worst tree ever. "It's just that its good side is pretty pathetic."

"Yeah, it is." He laughed, too.

She turned to him. "Do you have any lights?"

He arched a brow. "Why would I have lights?"

"I guess it's a good thing I threw a few strings in on a whim." As Tara went to get them, Ryan put some Christmas music on.

They strung the lights and hung the twenty or so ornaments she'd brought, and the tree still hadn't improved much.

Tara pursed her mouth off to the side as she inspected their handiwork. "I'm sorry. It's still sorry looking. It was supposed to add cheer to your place, not depress you.

"You don't have any construction paper or popcorn that we could string, do you? Something to fill it out a bit more?"

He shook his head no. "No need. I like it."

"Liar."

"Seriously." He put a hand on her shoulder as he stood behind her. "It may be a laughingstock of a tree, but we put it up together. It's already full of happy memories, and that's what counts."

Beside them, the fire crackled merrily, casting a warm glow on the tree. The ornaments, sparse as they were, caught the light and sparkled. And outside, snow lit up the scene out the picture window, making it look like a Currier and Ives Christmas card. Viewed in the right light...

"I'm just glad you're here and we're talking and laughing together again," he said. "There was a time I didn't think this would ever happen."

She turned around to face him. She'd felt the same. "I know," she said softly, feeling the weight of her guilt.

"It was my fault," they said in unison. And then, "No!"

Ryan shook his head. "I should have been the one who died that night. I was the hothead. If I could take it all back—"

Tara put a finger to his lips. "Don't talk like that. Don't say it. *No one* should have died that night.

"Ryan." She cupped his face in her hands. "Look at me. I'm sorry I blamed you. My grief counselors over the years have said what I felt was a means of transference. Because I couldn't blame Chad for being reckless. He was the victim. He was dead. Instead I blamed you and I blamed myself.

"Neither of us was at our best that night. But none of us could have predicted what would happen. Neither of us meant for it to happen. Or wished for it to happen. It was an accident. That's all. No one, not even Chad, was to blame."

She bit her lip and stared into Ryan's eyes. "I should have apologized years ago, but my heart was broken and I couldn't face you. This last few days together have helped me see the real you again.

"I'm so sorry. About everything. I certainly never meant to ruin Christmas for you. You didn't used to be like this." She gestured around the room. "You used to love Christmas. Chad wouldn't want this. He loved Christmas, too, and would have wanted us to enjoy it."

"Yeah, he did."

Ryan's lips were inches from hers. So tantalizing. And the look in his eyes as if he needed healing and she was the one to do it. She wanted to make everything better. She wanted to make *them* all better. She closed her eyes and leaned up to brush his lips with hers.

"Tara," he whispered as he wrapped his arms around her and pressed her tightly against him, pulling her into a full, deep kiss.

Some kisses are full of passion. Some of lust. Some of longing. Their kiss, this kiss, was full of need and healing. Yesterday in the forest had been pure passion. But this was a kiss to wash away the years of blame and hurt. This was absolution for her and him.

She put her arms around Ryan's neck as she leaned into him and kissed him back. She had to show him that she'd forgiven him as much as she needed to feel he no longer blamed her for the way their lives had gone.

The years fell away as he cupped the back of her head, kissing her with more experience and expertise than she remembered.

She trembled in his arms as she ran her fingers through the short hair at the base of his neck and lightly traced the outline of his ear. They fit together so well.

"Tara," he whispered, leaning his forehead against hers. The tone of his voice and the way he said her name spoke volumes and told her everything she needed to know.

"I've missed you." She tried to look into his eyes, but his were closed. "Ryan?"

"I'm just hanging onto the moment. I don't want this to be a dream or a misstep." His voice was ragged.

It was clear to Tara he was afraid of making that misstep, yet passion and desire shown in his voice. She needed Ryan, right there, right that minute. Ten years of pent-up desire for the communion of their bodies, for the forgiveness of hurts, for the intimacy was too much, and Tara was willing to risk all. She gently tugged his shirt free of the soft denim of his jeans and ran her hands over the strong muscles of his back until he shuddered beneath her touch.

His opened his eyes and they were questioning and hopeful. "Tara?"

She unbuttoned the top button of his shirt and kissed the hollow of his neck as she reached for the next button. The fire popped next to them and a jazz version of a popular romantic holiday song played. Outside, the snow continued to fall.

"Don't overthink it, just feel," she whispered back, giving him all the permission he needed.

"You're—"

"Totally prepared," she replied as she slid his shirt off his shoulders and it fell to the floor.

He ran his hands beneath her sweater, warm hands that felt good against the bare skin of her waist. As he kissed her with sudden urgency, he pulled her sweater off over her head and removed her bra.

She rid him of his undershirt, unfastened his jeans and slid them off his hips, kissing passionately in the process. She was lost in feel of his bare skin against hers. In the emotion crackling between them. In the connection she'd never felt with another man.

Her soul hummed with joy as she pulled Ryan down to the plush rug in front of the fire. It wasn't exactly the bearskin rug of fantasies, but it was good enough. In fact, it was perfect. The fire and Ryan felt hot on her skin as he braced over her, kissing and stroking her.

Her nipples budded as he stroked and caressed them. She wrapped her legs around him. "Now, Ryan, now."

He thrust into her and the world collapsed to a symphony of just the two of them. If joy and forgiveness could be expressed as physical pleasure, this was it.

If she'd been in her rational, thinking mode, she might have worried that they'd have forgotten how to move together after all these years. But she wasn't, and that definitely wasn't the case.

They moved in perfect union as her pleasure built and built as she rocked with him and their lips didn't part. He kissed her and thrust until she gasped and moaned into his kiss. Finally, she arched up as waves of pleasure crashed over her. He moaned, too, and they collapsed together, spent.

He finally broke the kiss and stared into her eyes. "I love you."

Maybe it shouldn't have been unexpected, but it was. She hesitated as her pulse raced and her spirits soared.

"It's all right," he said. "You don't have to respond in kind. I just thought you should know."

"No, that's not it." She had to make him understand. "It's just...I can't believe you still do, after everything and all the years."

He smiled and shrugged as he pulled a plush throw off the sofa next to them, threw it over them, and pulled her into the crook of his shoulder to cuddle.

The fire still blazed next to them, but she had to admit the side of her away from it was cool. His gesture was thoughtful.

"True love never dies—" He cut himself short as he realized what he was saying. "Sorry. I don't mean... Shit. I'm bungling this."

"No, you're not." She snuggled closer. "I love you, too. And that's not a platitude or an obligatory 'I love you.' I've loved you nearly all my life, Ryan."

He smiled and neither spoke as they listened to the Christmas music and the fire burning.

"As fantastic as this is," Ryan said at last, "this floor is getting hard." He leaned up on one elbow. "Come to bed with me. Spend the night."

She looked up at him and laughed. "Are you crazy? Harry will kill you if I don't come home tonight. Is that what you want?"

He laughed. "I'd be willing to brave it."

"The last thing you need so close to Christmas is to be on his naughty list." She stroked Ryan's cheek. "Seriously, Ry, I *have* to go back to the lodge." She paused, trying to put her feelings into words. "Right now, this is so beautiful and new again. I'd like some time to cherish it and keep it just between us.

"If Harry and Margie find out, and your mom, well, we don't need the pressure, do we?"

She studied him, but his expression was masked.

"No, you're right. Just between us." He grinned.

He looked happy. She was relieved. She just needed a little time to think things through. She hadn't come to his cabin expecting to seduce him, thinking he'd confess his undying love for her and that she'd admit her feelings.

She loved him. She really and truly did, and it seemed like a Christmas miracle. But even miracles had logistics, and she just wasn't sure how they were going to work them out. Right now, she didn't want to think about them.

"But I can ask you out, right? We can be seen in public together? This isn't a clandestine relationship?"

"You already took me snowboarding, so I'd say no, we're definitely not clandestine. We're just not letting the world in on how serious we are."

"So you'll go out with me?"

"Depends on what you have in mind."

He was grinning and studying her. "Come to the Christmas Eve Santa Ski with me."

"What!"

"Come on, Tara. I want to spend Christmas Eve with you and I'm on duty that night, for at least part of it. Come with me to the party. You've already braved the mountain. You can do it."

He was right. They were moving past the past, putting it behind them and making bright, shiny new Christmas memories. "Okay."

"Okay?"

"Sure."

He laughed. "Okay, it's a date."

She glanced at the clock on the mantel. "Oh, crud! Time slipped away from me. I didn't realize how late it's gotten. I have to go." She reached for her clothes.

"You don't have time for one more?" His eyes were devilish.

"Maybe one."

"Then I'll walk you home."

Ryan walked home from the lodge in the gently falling snow. He couldn't remember a December this snowy, ever. But he loved it. The snow lit up the night and matched the glow of his spirits.

Tara loves me. He couldn't push the thought away. It danced through his mind over and over again.

On his porch, he dusted the snow from his shoulders and shook off his hat as he stomped the snow out of his boots. Inside, his cabin was toasty warm and his new Christmas tree glowed.

The sight of it made him smile, not that he'd stopped grinning since making love with Tara. He'd probably sleep with a grin on his face.

He hung up his coat and hat and pulled off his boots before walking to his tree. The little thing was pathetic, but his grin grew at the selection of animal ornaments Tara had brought for him. And then he spotted an ornament he hadn't seen before. Tara must have hung it.

A shiny gingerbread boy snuggled into a branch. He grinned, thinking of her having the twin gingerbread girl on the tree at the lodge. The two should be together, hanging side by side forever...

And then Ryan got an idea, a wonderful, terrible, brilliant idea that made his heart race. He went to the bedroom and pulled open his sock drawer. Nestled beneath the socks and underwear, he found a small ring box. He carried it into the living room, sat beneath the tree, and opened the lid.

Tara's diamond engagement ring winked back at him, catching the multicolor lights of the tree. It wasn't a big ring, but it was what he could afford back then.

What did a guy do with an engagement ring a girl returned? He'd never had the heart to try to pawn it. Another woman would never want a castoff ring. And besides, there'd never been another woman he wanted to marry.

She deserved a bigger, better, more modern ring. But this one would make a nice placeholder, a perfect gift for Santa to pull out of his bag.

An entire proposal plan hatched right there. Santa would be handing out gifts at the Santa Ski party at The Basin Lodge. Ryan would wrap this one up and have Santa give it to Tara. And then he'd go down on one knee and propose. That would be the perfect new Christmas memory to erase, as much as possible, the old sad ones of the Basin. A new start.

His heart pounded away. *Maybe I'm jumping things, moving too fast...*

But he knew his heart. He'd waited for her for ten years. He couldn't let her get away now. And if she refused him? Well, it was better to know now, before he wasted any more of his life dreaming of a woman he couldn't have.

He reconsidered for just a second—was a public proposal the best plan?

Ah, hell. He'd have Santa give her the package and find a secluded corner for her to open it in.

She loves me. After all this time. She said yes once. Why would she say no now?

CHAPTER FIFTEEN

Tara woke in the morning with a smile on her face. And it was all because of Ryan. Last night had been wonderful. Just the sense of relief and forgiveness was a gift she'd badly needed, but add in the intimacy and she felt like she'd already had Christmas.

She stretched and sat up and then she remembered. *Today's the day Cheryl Jones from Northwest Resort Management Services is coming.*

There was so much to do before she arrived. Like making sure her grandparents were truly open to listening and that Harry would actually show up as promised. No mere down-in-the-back excuse was going to get him out of it.

Tara felt a pang of guilt when she thought about Ryan and his desire to buy the lodge. But she was also optimistic. If they got married someday, Ryan would own the lodge just like he'd always dreamed. She smiled at the thought. In the meantime, NRMS would make sure the lodge stayed profitable and provided a good income for her grandparents for the rest of their lives.

As she knew all too well, it was one thing to love Ryan. It was another to make the relationship work. And right now, she didn't have any kind of clear vision about how it might, other than if they took things one day at a time they stood a fighting chance.

Tara slid out of bed and went to the window. It was still snowing. The world looked lovely and Christmassy. But this had to be some kind of a record snow year. There was already a good four feet of snow outside. And that was where it wasn't piled up. The parking lot was getting smaller and smaller as Harry or Ryan plowed the snow and had to put it somewhere. The same was true with the winding lake road. But for now, Tara vowed to enjoy it.

She headed to the shower, humming "Jingle Bells."

Most of the gifts—in reality, prizes—for the Santa Ski were locked in the safe at The Basin main lodge. Even though it ran contrary to general measures of security, Ryan wasn't about to trust Tara's ring to that. He went directly to Jim Dickson to entrust it into his care.

"You sure about this?" Jim stared at the wrapped jewelry box with Tara's name on it in his hand.

"There's no one else I'd trust with it."

"Oh, you can trust me, sure enough. I'll lock it in the gun safe. No one will get it there. It's just..." Jim hesitated. "Are you sure a public marriage proposal is the best thing and is going to net you a genuine answer?

"I always wondered about boys who proposed on big screens at football games and the like. Put on the spot like that, what's a girl supposed to do? Look like a bitch by turning the poor guy down? I expect that often happens later in private."

Ryan shook his head. "Oh, this isn't really all that public, Jim. Not like that, anyway. All you have to do is hand her a small wrapped present. I'll corner her and make sure she opens it where there are no prying eyes."

"Still, everyone will want to know what's in it."

Ryan shrugged. "No reason she has to tell them if she doesn't want to. Tara knows how to evade questions when she wants to. I can even cover, saying I didn't know what to do with that damn ring after all these years and thought she should have it regardless."

Jim arched a brow. "Well, you seem to have an answer for everything." With his long white beard, curly white hair, and rotund belly, it felt almost as if Ryan was speaking with the real Santa. The committee had done a good job in picking Jim to be Santa this year. In fact, he probably had the job for life.

"The thing is, I can't make hers the first gift of Christmas. The people at the Basin would have my head for that. But I can work this in somewhere in the middle where it will be less conspicuous. I don't think any of the other merchants will have a problem with that."

"Sounds good to me." Ryan grinned.

Jim held out his hand for Ryan to shake. "Good luck, young man. I hope this is your Christmas."

Cheryl Jones from Northwest Resort Management Services Corp., NRMS, was personable, charming, and professional. Frankly, Tara was impressed with her as she sat down with her grandparents and Cheryl in Harry's private office.

"We've done a thorough analysis of Echo Bay's financial performance, assets, profit margins, and facilities. After inspecting them today, personally, I'm favorably inclined toward the lodge and its possibilities," Cheryl said.

"I'll have more information for you after I get back to the office and input my observations. But let me say, I do believe NRMS can be hugely valuable to you and our partnership profitable for all of us.

"First, let me give you a quick analysis of our fees and services." Cheryl glanced at Harry and Margie.

Tara studied them, too. Tara already knew about NRMS's services and fees, but she had butterflies in her stomach—would Cheryl think there was enough profit possibility to partner with Echo Bay Resort, and how high of a percentage would NRMS demand? The upper five percent of their range? Or was there enough profit potential to only take three percent?

Harry sat with his arms closed, not looking at all receptive to the idea of hiring NRMS. Margie looked only slightly more willing to think about things.

"My team will develop an annual strategic business plan, along with defined financial goals and performance measures, as well as quarterly performance reports. We'll also make a five-year property improvement plan. We want to upgrade this place and make it a destination resort." Cheryl smiled.

But Harry was on the verge of a scowl.

"We'll take over the daily operation of your property as well as sales and marketing, accounting, hiring, human resources, and guest services."

Harry was definitely scowling now. "And how much will that cost me?"

Cheryl remained unfazed by Harry's gruff nature. "I'm getting to that, Mr. Jansen. Our rates are very reasonable. We work for either a flat monthly retainer fee, or take a percentage of proceeds.

"In Echo Bay's case, I believe a percentage is to everyone's advantage, at least from what I've seen so far."

"And that percentage would be?" Harry seemed to cross his arms more tightly. His knuckles looked white.

"In your case, I have to admit they'd be at the upper end of our range—five percent."

Tara let out a breath she'd hardly been aware of holding. *Five percent.* Not good.

"Five percent!" Harry looked about ready to come out of his chair. "That's more profit than we make."

Cheryl didn't lose her smile. She laughed and held up a hand. "I understand, Mr. Jansen. But we intend to make you so much profit, that while we'll be taking our share, you'll be making more than you ever have before.

"We have years of experience in streamlining operations while maintaining the feel of the establishments we manage and improving them at the same time.

"You've done an excellent job of keeping this lodge running and homey. But just from a quick look around I can name half a dozen relatively inexpensive improvements that would return tenfold on your investment and pay for our services.

"And then there are elements in your operation that I've observed that can be quickly changed to cut costs and up your profit margin."

Margie leaned forward, looking at least somewhat interested. "Such as?"

"Well, for example—your fire-lighting man," Cheryl said. "I've never seen an establishment have a separate staff member purely for lighting one fireplace."

Tara stepped in. "You mean Carter? He's been doing that job for years, over twenty of them. He really doesn't cost much. And, though we'd never admit it publicly, keeping Carter employed is really a bit of charity. He's disabled and without this job, I don't have any idea who would hire him. He'd lose all his self-esteem. He takes so much pride in this job. And his services make us unique."

Cheryl's smile didn't slip, not in the slightest. It became clear to Tara that she was used to hearing such objections.

"Oh, we can keep the fire-lighting ceremony, if you will. We'll have another fulltime staff member do it. We can even outfit that person in a special uniform.

You see, we're not trying to change what's working here."

"But what about Carter?"

"By paying Carter, you're losing money. If you referred him to a charitable organization for employment, you could make a personal contribution toward work for him and write it off."

Laying Carter off didn't sound very charitable at all. Tara couldn't help frowning. Her two grandparents didn't look like they thought so, either.

"I'm sure we can work something out," Tara said. She'd never meant to put Carter's job on the line.

Cheryl nodded. "Of course we can. But I must be frank. Unless you're willing to make the changes we suggest, we can't guarantee we'll be able to work with you. You're working on a very thin profit margin. Even at five percent of proceeds, we'd be taking a risk by taking you on and working for the least money we possibly can. Unless we can quickly increase revenue, we could all be in trouble."

"What about staffing?" Margie asked. "Would you keep our staff on?"

Cheryl nodded. "All of them who perform up to our standards, absolutely!"

Even her gentle-mannered grandma frowned at that. Tara could almost read Gram's thoughts as she worried about Kathleen and Stormy and the others.

Tara had to head off any further questions. "I'm sure all of them will, Gram. Kathleen, Stormy, the maids, they're all topnotch."

Cheryl nodded. "And of course, we'd put them all through our training program and give them ample opportunity to prove themselves before making any judgments."

Thank you, Cheryl.

Tara cleared her throat. "Tell us about the new manager you'd bring in to run the place. I think Gram and Grandpa, as well as the community, would expect you to hire someone local, someone they knew they could trust." And, of course, Tara had the perfect candidate in mind.

Cheryl pursed her lips as if in thought. Finally, she nodded. "We like to support the community. We need their support. If you have any candidates in mind, we'd appreciate the recommendation. We'll certainly consider any viable applicant."

Tara had thought about it all morning. Ryan had the touch with the lodge. He'd be the perfect person to manage it. He'd hate watching anyone besides Harry run it. If they could swing a comparable salary to what he made at Copper Creek, she was sure he'd take the position. It seemed like a winning solution for everyone for the time being. "I was thinking Ryan Sanders would jump at the opportunity—"

"Jump!" Harry nearly jumped out of his chair. He pounded the desk in front of him, startling them all. "You're crazy, girl, if you think that. Ryan wants to own this place, not be told how to run it by outsiders who've never spent more than five hours in this place."

Ryan was apprehensive all day. Deciding to propose could do that to a guy, he supposed. But he also knew Tara, Harry, and Margie were meeting with the property management company. Tara had told him about it earlier, back when she'd thrown it in his face. Knowing Tara, she'd feel obligated to take the meeting. Canceling at this late date was out of the question. But he expected she'd send them packing now, politely. Although Tara had no idea he was planning to propose, it only made sense to leave things as they were while they pursued their relationship.

He'd looked NRMS up and perused their services. Tara had picked a good company. They were well respected and known for their successes. But they were pricey, too. Ryan couldn't see Harry wanting to hand over the kind of fees NRMS required. And now that Tara and Ryan were back together, there was no need for their services. Ryan would keep helping Harry out to ease his burden. At least, Ryan hoped Tara saw it that way.

But this was where things got tricky. Ten years ago their differing opinions about the lodge, career aspirations, and where to live had contributed to their breakup. Chad's death had just been the final blow. With them reconciling over that and getting past their grief and guilt, Ryan had high hopes they could overcome their other obstacles.

Hadn't ten years apart proven that they were meant to be together? No matter what?

Ryan had grown up since then, too. He realized how valuable career satisfaction was to life happiness, and he no longer intended to try to rob Tara of hers. If she still wanted to live and work in Seattle, they'd work some arrangement out. It was only a six-hour drive from Echo Bay to Seattle. It wouldn't be ideal, but he'd rather have her in his life, even part time, than lose her completely.

But surely she must realize that same thing about him? That she now held the power of his dreams in her hand. She could make them come true by marrying him. There was no longer any need for a property management company as the only way to keep Echo Bay Resort in the family.

Harry and Margie would be thrilled with the outcome. Tara would no longer have to fight them. They'd go willingly into retirement. Harry would be happy puttering around, doing as much as he wanted while Ryan shouldered the burden of day-to-day operations and all the financial worries. They could even keep their apartment in the lodge. Ryan would be happy to continue living in his cabin.

He grinned at the thought of Tara sharing it with him. And their children running around the resort, growing up like he and Tara had, loving the outdoors and the lake. There wasn't any place more fun for a kid to grow up than a year-round resort. Ryan was convinced of that.

He really didn't want to think of how Tara's Seattle job would mesh with these daydreams of children. They'd figure that all out when the time came.

He and Tara had dinner plans together—takeout. She'd offered to meet him in town, but it hadn't stopped snowing all day. And on top of what they already had, getting around was treacherous. Besides, he wanted a little privacy with her.

Ryan texted Tara that he was home. *Thank goodness.* He was late getting home and she was eager to see him and concerned about him on the roads. It hadn't stopped snowing all day. Tara bundled up for the walk to his cabin. Just outside the door to the lodge she ran into her grandfather.

Harry was bundled up as well, looking like an aging snowman—round, but not jolly—as he stared up into the sky and the falling snow.

"You'll catch your death out here, Grandpa." She mimicked Gram, smiling as she did.

"Huh?" He looked at her. "Oh, Tara."

"What are you doing out here in the dark? You can't be stargazing."

"No, no. Just checking out the roof." Harry pointed.

Tara followed his finger. "It looks like something out of a winter storybook."

Harry shook his head. "It looks like trouble, like too much weight for the roof. That's what it looks like."

Tara frowned. "It's cold and the snow is lightweight."

Harry kept shaking his head. "Even lightweight snow adds up. Like a lot of us, that roof is old and can't do as much as it used to." His breath came out in white wisps as he spoke. "It needs to be shoveled, and soon, or we'll have no end of trouble on our hands."

Tara studied Harry. "I hope you're not planning on getting up there." It was less a question and more a command.

"Me?" Harry was studying the roof again. "Not too many years ago I would've. But not now. No. I'm thinking of Ryan."

Tara looked up at the expanse of roof with all its peaks. She didn't like the idea of anyone going up on the roof, not in this weather. Not anytime, really. Especially not someone she loved. "Looks like an awful lot of roof for one person to clear. Did Ryan promise he'd do it?" She crossed her fingers, hoping not.

"A lot of work? Not for a young man. Especially if he's got a few friends to help." Harry smiled at her. "Yeah, Ryan said he'd do it. Get a few of his buds over here to help him."

Tara shielded her eyes from the falling snow and studied the roof again in the dim light. "You can't expect Ryan to do all our work here. There are services, professionals with professional snow-blowing equipment who'll do it for a reasonable fee. Let me call one."

"No, no, no. No use paying someone. Ryan will do it."

Sometimes Harry could be too tight with a dollar.

"Where you headed to this time of evening, missy?" Harry asked.

Oops. Here was her protective grandpa rearing his head.

"To Ryan's. For dinner." She tried not to sound belligerent and defensive. Challenging. Harry wasn't going to scare Ryan off. Not this time.

But her grandpa was getting old and losing his fight. "Huh. Well, you tell him to get his tail over here tomorrow evening and get this roof shoveled off before it collapses on our heads."

She shook her head. "Will do."

"You have a good time, then. And don't get back too late." Harry headed toward the lodge. "And make sure Ryan walks you home."

Right, Tara thought. *On all counts.*

It was a quick and beautiful walk through the woods to Ryan's. As she strolled up his driveway, she studied his roof. Judging from the scant amount of snow piled on it, it appeared he'd recently cleared it.

Smoke came out of his chimney, and the windows to his cabin were warmly lit and inviting. Ryan met her at the door.

"Watching for me?" She wrapped her arms around him.

"You took your time getting here." He kissed her lightly on the lips. "You're freezing. Get in here and warm up."

She pressed her cold cheek against his. "Grandpa waylaid me. Said something about telling you to get over to the lodge and shovel the roof. He's worried about it."

Ryan grabbed her hands and pulled her inside, shutting the door behind him. "I'll get over there tomorrow if I can."

"I'll call someone to come do it, Ry. I don't want you up on the roof in this weather." Tara slid her coat off and hung it on a rack next to the door before taking off her hat and boots. "Something smells good in here."

He slid her arms around her again and nuzzled her neck. "I think that's you."

"You're saying I smell like garlic bread?"

He laughed. "I picked up Italian—manicotti, garlic bread, and salad."

"Sounds good to me. I'm famished."

A timer went off. He released her, grabbed a pair of oven mitts, and pulled a pan of steaming manicotti from the oven.

"Anyone ever tell you that you look handsome in the kitchen?"

"Only in the kitchen?"

"What can I say? I'm hungry," she said. "Can I help you with something?"

He set the manicotti on the table. "Everything's ready. And waiting for you."

He'd put a red tablecloth on the table and white candles were lit. A fire crackled in the living room just across from the kitchen. She was touched by his romantic gesture and thinking how this little cabin had potential.

They ate dinner, making small talk and eyes at each other. After they finished and cleared the dishes, they retired to the sofa in front of the fireplace.

Ryan sat with his arm around her. "Only four days until Christmas Eve. Looks like we'll have a white one this year."

Something about his tone was a little too eager and made her laugh. "You sound like a kid. Eager."

"There's nothing wrong with being excited about Christmas."

"You must have asked Santa for something special," she said.

He grinned.

He's up to something. She realized with a start that in all probability he had a surprise for her. Up until that moment getting him a gift hadn't even crossed her mind. Things had happened so quickly and suddenly. And now, what was the gift giving protocol? She opened her mouth to tell him not to go overboard, but shut it again before speaking. What if she was wrong?

"Have you decided what you're wearing to the Christmas Eve party at the Basin?" he asked.

"I thought tacky Christmas sweaters were the re-quired dress." She was teasing him.

"Please. Spare me that."

"Reindeer ears?"

"I was thinking that white fuzzy sweater of yours, the one that makes you look like a sexy snow bunny, and your knee-high boots."

She laughed. "What kind of fantasy are you con-cocting?"

"None. I just want to show you off to the other guys at the party and make them jealous." He paused. "Good and jealous."

"In that case, I'll wear something that will make you proud." She leaned her head against his shoulder, won-dering how to bring up her meeting. All through din-ner they'd both danced around it.

She wanted to be honest and upfront with him and not let anything come between them again. "I met with the property management company today."

"Was that today?" He hugged her tightly against him.

He was just a little too casual.

"It was a good meeting." She was eager to make him the offer. It wasn't something physical, but she couldn't wait until Christmas to give him this gift.

"Was it?"

"Oh, Ryan! Don't play coy. You can ask about it." She pulled away and smiled at him. "Cheryl had some excellent ideas."

Ryan frowned. "Did she?"

"Yes, and one of them concerns you."

He perked up and gave her a hopeful look. "Really?"

"Yes, I'd like to make you an offer you can't refuse."

"Now that sounds intriguing."

She grinned. "How would you like to be the new manager of Echo Bay Resort?"

CHAPTER SIXTEEN

"Manager?" Ryan's throat constricted. He barely got the words out, feeling as if Tara had just kicked him in the gut. "You're still going to engage NRMS?"

Tara looked puzzled. "Yes, of course. And I'll make it a stipulation of our contract that they hire you as the manager."

"Nothing's changed?" He removed his arm from Tara's shoulder.

She frowned. "Why should it?"

"You've convinced Harry and Margie?"

"Not exactly. We all have our concerns. But I think we'll be able to work them out." She clutched his arm. "Especially with you on our team. I want you at the helm. You love the lodge. With their expertise and your love of the place, we'll have a winning team."

Ryan stared at her, wishing he'd heard her wrong and knowing he hadn't. She was starting to look worried.

"No." He fought to remain calm. "I won't be your manager."

"But it's what you've always dreamed of!" Her eyes were wide. "If it's money you're worried about, we'll do our best to be competitive with Copper Creek." She grinned, trying to make light. "And you'll have more control over the cookbook."

He shook his head.

"Oh, come on. Once we get the lodge back on its feet and more profitable, we'll be able to pay you more. Maybe even give you partial ownership."

He popped to his feet. "You don't get it, do you, Tara? I don't want to manage Echo Bay. I want to *own* it. I want to own it with *you*. Why do you need a property management company now?"

She stared at him and bit her lower lip, which meant she was nervous. "We have something special, Ryan. Or the start of it. I love you, but it's too soon to tell where it will go. In the meantime, I have to look out for Gram and Grandpa."

If he thought she'd kicked him in the gut earlier, she'd just stabbed him and twisted the knife. Too early? What was too early? He wasn't some whacko she'd met online or known a few days. They'd known each other their entire lives. And had wasted ten years of it. Or so he'd thought. But Tara wanted to treat him as some new relationship guy? Someone she couldn't trust?

He ran his hands through his hair until it stood up on end. The fire suddenly felt too hot and his heart too cold. He'd been a fool.

He took a deep breath. "I'm sorry you feel that way. I thought we had something. I stupidly assumed all our years together meant something to you."

He tried to keep the bitterness out of his voice, but he was failing miserably. "But, I guess not. The beginning?" He shook his head. He was just dumbfounded. Blindsided.

"Ryan. Please. Don't."

He shook his head again. Seemed he couldn't stop. "You don't get it, do you? This is about *us*. Having faith in us staying together." He paused, staring at her while wishing he had the strength to look away. "You still don't trust me. Not with your heart.

"Have it your way, then, Tara. If you don't want to be with me, so be it. But I'm still going to get the lodge."

She popped to her feet. He may have been mistaken, but he thought there were tears in her eyes. Or maybe he imagined it. "I'm sorry, Ryan. I do want to be with you, but if that's the way you feel, I'd better go."

She turned on her heel and walked to the door. Her coat caught as she pulled it off the rack, nearly toppling it. She yanked on her boots and jerked on her coat and hat, then reached for the doorknob.

For a moment, he thought she was going to leave without saying anything more. What was there to say?

But she did turn and tears were standing in her eyes. "You're being an ass. Just like before." She pulled the door open and strode out of the cabin, and possibly his life.

He was convinced she'd slam the door. To his surprise, she closed it softly, as if she was shutting the door on the chapter of their life that could have been, leaving him standing there watching her walk away. For the second time.

Blondie sensed something was up and whined and howled.

Ryan stared at the door. Ten years ago he hadn't gone after her. It looked like that had been the right decision after all.

Jim Dickson stopped by the lodge to shoot the breeze with Harry and discuss the Santa Ski. He looked like his jolly self, dressed in a red hat and sweatshirt that emphasized his round belly. His big white beard was immaculately trimmed to match the ideal of Santa. He sat at the counter with Harry, drinking coffee.

Margie served him a piece of her Dutch apple pie. "I'm thinking this is the pie flavor I'm going to donate. Everyone loves apple." She handed Jim a fork. "It's a universal standard."

Stormy came by with the coffee pot and grinned at Jim as she topped off his cup. "Shouldn't you be at the North Pole?"

"What?" He nodded toward the window and the heavily falling snow outside as he stirred a spoonful of sugar into his coffee. "I thought this was the North Pole. I practically had to use the sleigh and reindeer to get here. Don't know how I'm going to make it back to town."

Harry shook his head as Stormy disappeared to wait on another guest. "Stupid, stupid snow. I'm afraid it's going to cave in the roof."

Margie studied her husband, hoping he didn't let his worry affect his heart. Stress wasn't good for him. Which was why she had to make sure Ryan and Tara got together and took over the lodge. She resisted grinning to herself. In that regard, it was beginning to look like she'd be getting exactly what she wanted for Christmas this year.

"Oh, Harry," she said to him in that familiar tone she'd been using for at least forty of their last fifty years together. "Don't you go thinking about getting up on that roof. You just wait for Ryan."

"Wait for Ryan. Wait for Ryan! We may not have a roof over our heads if we wait for him much longer. If I were ten years younger I'd have shoveled the darn thing days ago."

Margie tried to hide her skepticism. But she was too late.

"Don't give me that look, woman. You know it's true." He was frowning at her.

Jim laughed, the deep merry rumble of a real Santa. "Speaking of Ryan..." He looked around the lodge. "Is Tara around?"

Margie shook her head. "No. She's over at Ryan's having dinner with him. I don't expect her back for quite a while."

"Well, good then." Jim leaned into her. "I probably shouldn't be telling you this, but Ryan paid me a visit today. He has a special gift he wants me to give Tara on Christmas Eve."

Margie gasped and clasped her hands in front of her. Jim's tone implied exactly what that gift was. "No!"

Jim put a finger to his lips. "Shhh. This is just between us. But if you have any doubts about how Tara might receive it, now's the time to tell me. If it's not on her Christmas list, better for all involved for Santa to cross it off." He winked.

Margie couldn't keep from grinning now. "Don't worry about Tara. She's had that on her list for years. She just hasn't always realized it."

But Harry was frowning. "Now, Margie, don't you go getting ideas. Or your hopes up. And don't you say so much as a peep to Tara. This is between those two young people. None of our business.

"And, Jim, I'm not so sure of Tara's intentions. This buddy-buddy business with Ryan again is all very sudden. Our Tara can be slow to change her mind about things and stubbornly independent—"

Margie flapped her hands at him as if she was shooing him off the subject. "Be quiet, old man."

Harry shook his head and frowned at her. "It's no secret what my wife wants for Christmas. But wanting doesn't make it so. In my opinion, Ryan's being reckless and moving too fast."

Just then the bell over the front door tinkled. Margie looked up to see who the new arrival was as a diversion from wanting to throttle her husband. "Tara?"

Uh-oh. Tara's face was pink, too pink to be just from the cold. Her nose was red and her eyes were watering. She dabbed at them with her gloved hand. *She's been crying.*

Tara looked surprised to see them all sitting at the counter. And in truth, they were all staring at her. Margie had to force herself not to ask Tara if her ears were burning.

"Gram, Grandpa, Jim." Tara nodded to them as she rushed past and raced up the stairs to her room.

Jim raised an eyebrow.

Harry scowled. "See what I mean? Never does any good to count chickens."

Margie ignored him and the implications of Tara's sudden arrival and abrupt departure for her room. Margie was tenacious and hopelessly optimistic. She refused to view this apparently unfortunate turn of events as the loss of her dreams for a grandson-in-law—in particular, Ryan. Just a temporary, hopefully very temporary, setback.

Margie leaned down and whispered to Jim. "Just ignore what you just saw. You keep that gift in Santa's pack until you hear different from me. Things are going to work out. This Christmas we're going to have something to celebrate." If she had to make it happen herself.

Margie had had enough sad Christmases to last a lifetime. And since, statistically speaking, she didn't have much lifetime left, she was going to make good and certain her few remaining Christmases were merry ones.

"No matter what Ryan asks or demands, be a good Santa and believe in Christmas miracles. Just keep that gift in your pack. Make yourself unavailable to Ryan for a few days if you have to." She nodded in the direction Tara had disappeared. "Give the two of them some time to cool down and work things out."

"Staying unavailable in this information age is asking the impossible," Jim said.

Margie shrugged. "You'll think of something, Santa. You wouldn't want to let down two of the best young people around, would you?"

Harry had been sitting with his coffee cup poised halfway to his mouth, looking lost in thought. He chimed in, almost off topic. "Guess Tara brought up asking Ryan to manage the lodge." He shook his head. "I told her there was no way that's what the boy wanted. Offering him that job was like putting a match to a powder keg."

Well, Harry had been right on that score.

"Give them time," Margie said. "They'll come around."

Harry sighed and shook his head. "What makes you so sure? They didn't last time."

"This isn't last time. They've had ten years to miss each other and come to terms with what happened to Chad." Margie felt particularly defensive of Tara. She didn't want, couldn't stand, to see her slip into that despair and depression again. Not when they'd finally gotten her back to the lodge. "And we still have the lodge to use as leverage."

In her warm, cozy room, Tara threw open the window and inhaled deeply, feeling as if she was suffocating. The mountain was obscured by cloud cover and the lake was nothing more than a dark gray mass in the dark.

She brushed a tear away. Why was she still crying over Ryan all these years later? How could he just expect her to rush into things?

Is it really too soon? Or are you just scared?

Ryan's words haunted her. *You still don't trust me. Not with your heart.*

Was this really about them? Was she afraid to trust him with either her heart or her future or even her past?

But things were so new, and their relationship so obviously tenuous—

A tiny light blazed in the distant gloom on the edge of the lake. *Ryan's cabin.* Tara blinked. She'd been staring at his place like the lovelorn heroine of a tragic romance wishing she could will her hero to her side. Only Ryan had the power to turn her into a moony, emotional mess.

She shut the window and pulled the curtains.

Time, she thought, as her heart ached. *I just need some time to think things through.*

In less than a week she'd be back in Seattle, where she was safe and her heart in no danger. Why didn't that sound as satisfying as it had when she'd first arrived?

There was another eight inches of snow on the ground when Ryan got up the next morning and pulled his bedroom curtains back to check the weather and get his morning fix of the lake. He'd had a restless night. He could use a little light to raise his spirits. Had it been only yesterday he'd been full of optimism and Christmas cheer?

The sun wasn't even close to up yet. And from the way it was still snowing, it didn't look like it was going to peek through when it did.

Great. Just great.

He was going to have to dig his way out of the driveway again and plow his way into town and hope he could make it without getting stuck in a drift. At that moment, he hated his usually beautiful commute.

Across the way the light of the lodge sparkled brightly, enticingly. His stomach growled. And his mouth watered thinking of Margie's gingerbread pancakes and a steaming cup of coffee—the comfortable breakfast routine he'd established before Tara had arrived in town to break his heart. No way he could stop by now. He wasn't in the mood to face her. Now he'd have to resort to eating a bowl of instant oatmeal alone here at the cabin.

If he owned the lodge—

He corrected himself. *When* he owned the lodge he'd eat all the pancakes or waffles or eggs he wanted and not have to commute again.

He let the curtains fall back into place and headed for the shower. Fifteen minutes later, he toweled his hair dry and headed to the kitchen. Blondie met him at his bedroom door, barking happily.

He reached down to scratch her ears. "Why did I ever name you after her, girl? Come on. Let's go get something to eat."

He flipped on the hall light and his Christmas tree came into full view. He froze, staring at it and all the memories it was filled with.

"Dashed hopes," he said aloud.

Blondie barked as if she agreed.

"Good girl. At least you understand." He knew there was a reason he kept the dog around. But he rued putting up the tree. What was he going to do about it now?

He shook his head. He was just going to have to leave the thing up until after Christmas. But the day after, it was coming down first thing.

As he microwaved his oatmeal, he remembered he'd promised to grab a few buddies and shovel the lodge roof. He fully intended to do it. But he couldn't face it tonight. In fact, he decided to cancel his next waxing workshop, too. He just needed a few days to put the armor back around his heart and then he'd be fine. Just a few days so he wouldn't be tempted to act like a jerk around Tara, or a love-struck boy.

Speaking of which...

He grabbed his phone and texted Jim Dickson, telling him to hold onto that present for Tara and not to put it in Santa's bag, and promising to pick it up before Christmas. Ryan supposed he should stop by to pick it up today, but he didn't want to see that ring just now.

Maybe the thing was bad luck. It certainly was a symbol of his stupidity and failed dreams.

Tara doesn't want you, buddy, he told himself. *Not the way you want her. And what's the use of a lopsided relationship?*

He thought about the look on her face when she'd offered him the position of managing the lodge. Maybe he was the problem. Maybe she was right and he *was* moving too fast. But he knew what he wanted. Had known since he was a teenager. And right now both things were slipping through his grasp.

When Tara came downstairs for breakfast, Gram was worrying over another cancellation with Kathleen. "With so much snow, people are afraid of they won't be able to get here.

"I avoided two more cancellations, assuring guests the roads are well plowed and the skiing not to be missed. Telling them they can't miss the excitement and adventure of our record snows. But if this keeps up much longer..." When she looked up and saw Tara, she trailed off and forced a too-bright smile. "And how's our girl this morning?"

Tara forced a smile back, wishing she'd had more composure when she'd returned last night and thinking again how much her grandparents needed to hand running the lodge off to someone else. "Hanging in."

"Well, good." Gram gave her a one-armed hug. "Sit down and I'll go make you some breakfast."

"Don't bother. I'm not hungry."

"You have to eat."

"I'll grab a bowl of cold cereal—"

Margie shook her head. "I'll make you a nice, hot bowl of our famous oatmeal with cranberries and walnuts. You can help yourself to coffee." She disappeared into the kitchen.

Harry was puttering around worrying about the roof again.

"Ryan canceled his waxing workshop tonight," Harry said to Tara, looking sympathetic and as if he was walking on thin ice. "Made some excuse." Her grandfather patted her awkwardly on the back.

Tara could barely stand all this sympathy, and the way her relationship—or lack of—was affecting everyone and everything, the odds for having her first truly happy Christmas in ten years were slipping away.

"I was hoping he'd come over today to shovel the roof," Harry said. "I don't think that's going to happen, though?" He looked to Tara for confirmation.

"No, I'm sorry, Grandpa. I wouldn't count on Ryan coming over for a while." She paused, trying to keep her emotions out of her voice. "He and I have had a falling out." She cursed herself for tearing up. "In fact, I don't think you'll see him until after I leave. But don't worry. I'm going to get someone over to clear the roof ASAP. I'll get on it right after breakfast."

Breakfast and forty-five minutes later, Tara sat in Harry's office trying to make good on her promise.

"Yes, I understand everyone's snowed under and demanding immediate service," she said into the phone to the twelfth company she'd called. "But my grandpa has a weak heart. He can't do it himself. And the stress of worrying about it is bad for his health.

"Is the roof flat? No. Well, yes, I understand that flat roofs have the greatest chance of collapsing and have to have top priority but—

"What's the pitch of our roof?" She peered out the window, trying to guess. How was she supposed to know? "It's just a normal roof." Pause. "No, not steeply pitched like an alpine roof. Just your average slope." That should have given the lodge some priority.

"The twenty-seventh? That's the earliest you can do?"

She'd called every company from here to the Canadian border and back again. This was the earliest anyone had even offered to come out.

"Fine. Yes, I'll take it. Put us on the schedule." She crossed her fingers, hoping that blasted snow would stop and the old roof would hold up.

Tara's cell phone buzzed as she was heading back to her room. "Laurel. What's up?"

"A pile of guilt," Laurel said. "I just realized how close it is to Christmas and we still haven't had our shopping trip to Old European." There was a tease in her voice and she was clearly digging for information.

If Laurel was plugged in to the town's gossip, which she clearly had to be, she already knew Tara had been to Old European with Ryan. And practically bought out the store.

Ah, two days ago—the good old days.

"My bad," Tara said, trying to sound cheery and up-beat. "I'm sure you heard about my trip there with Ryan. I pretty much own stock in that place now."

"Yeah, I heard. And I kept hoping you'd call and dish. And, you know, apologize profusely for standing me up, or whatever you call doing our thing with some-one else. And arrange some other get together before you disappear into the black hole of Seattle again after Christmas."

Yeah, Tara was screwing up on all fronts. In the background of Laurel's call, Tara heard Christmas mu-sic playing and the happy clatter of the café. Laurel must have been on her break.

"I'll be out of here the twenty-eighth," Tara said. There was no way, particularly now, that she was stick-ing around to be dateless on New Year's Eve. "What's your schedule like between then and now?"

"Hideously busy, except for Christmas Eve. At least the early part of it. Donny's on ski patrol and has to be at the Santa Ski. I'd go with him if I weren't eight months preggo. But as it is, I'll be stuck at my mom's cabin in Echo Bay watching old Christmas classics with her and waiting for him to get home."

"You're spending Christmas with your mom?" Tara asked.

"Oh, yeah. It's her year."

"Well then, why don't you pop over to the lodge and spend early Christmas Eve until Donny gets back with me here?"

"You're not going to the Santa Ski?" Laurel hesitat-ed. "But I thought... I mean, I heard a rumor..."

Oh, darn. Small towns.

"At one point, I was going. But since then Ryan and I have had a falling out. Which, given us, was probably inevitable. Same old issues," Tara said, trying to keep her voice from wavering and hoping Laurel wouldn't press for details. Really, "same old issues" said it all, and Laurel knew their history as well as anyone.

"I'm sorry, Tara. I'd hoped—"

"Yeah, we all did." A bitter laugh escaped before Tara could stop it. Apparently she wasn't the only naïve Pollyanna ninny in the area. "And so, no, I have no plans to go the Santa Ski and I'd love to see you and spend Christmas Eve here instead. Like old times.

"It'll be cheery and festive. Gram's going to make her Christmas pie. Carter has been collecting the best and most Christmassy fragranced kindling and logs for the blaze that night. We can't compete with the prizes and skiing, but I can promise good food and good company."

"You know what, you're on," Laurel said.

CHAPTER SEVENTEEN

It snowed another day and ten inches. On the second morning, two days before Christmas, Tara woke up and padded into the bathroom to take a shower. There was one small problem—the floor was wet. So was her towel. And water dripped from the ceiling and walls.

Shoot, shoot, shoot! If only the roof clearers had come.

She gazed up at the ceiling, half expecting to see she'd acquired a new skylight overnight. But aside from the water running where it shouldn't be, the roof was still intact. She was really going to be in deep trouble with Harry now. And she had to stop him before he did something crazy.

For half a manic second, she considered calling Ryan and begging him to come over and help. Texting him, at least.

As she grabbed her robe and raced out of the bathroom, the sound of prancing and pawing on her roof stopped her cold. Actually, more accurately it was the sound of a ladder being hefted onto the roof as it scraped along the eves.

Ryan. At least she hoped he'd come to the rescue.

She rushed to the window and threw open the sash. There was no moon, and no rising sun, either, to give the luster of midday to objects below. And all that appeared to her wondering eyes was more snow and a little old man in a red stocking hat who was not so lively and quick—her grandfather carrying a shovel as he climbed up the ladder and hoisted himself onto the roof. Not a miniature sleigh or eight tiny reindeer in sight. Definitely no Ryan. No whistling and calling his coursers by name. Just a bit of benign cursing beneath his breath.

Harry waved when he saw her. "Tara."

At least she hadn't startled him off the roof. "Grandpa, what are you doing up here? I hope you're not planning to shovel the roof by yourself."

He shook his head. "This danged snow. Dang, dang stuff. It's piled up higher than the steam vents that stick out of the roof. The warm air from the vents is melting the snow ledge that sticks up above the vents and it's dripping into the lodge. I'm going to clear out around the vents is all."

That explained the new fountain feature in her bathroom.

"I'll put some jeans on and help you."

He shook his head. "No need. I don't want you on the roof. You stay inside and make sure your gram doesn't worry too much. As soon as Carter arrives, send him up."

Gram would be terribly worried. Harry's balance had been off for years. Tara nodded. "You be careful."

"That goes without saying."

Tara closed her window and got dressed. By the time she got downstairs, a cluster of guests was discussing the situation.

A little boy, no more than three or four, kept grabbing his mom's hand and pointing to the ceiling. "Santa's on the roof and he's going to come down the chimney."

Oh, boy. Tara hoped not. If Harry came down the chimney, it wasn't going to be magical like Santa. It was going to be time to call 911.

"Your fool of a grandfather is up on that roof," Gram said the minute she spotted Tara. "I told him not to go up there, but would he listen?"

"Has anyone called Ryan?" Tara said. "I'm sure he'd come—"

Gram shook her head. "Harry has too much pride to ask him."

Tara knew the reason for that. Harry had always been fiercely protective of her. If some young man had hurt her, Grandpa was going to shelter her from him. Right now, Ryan was that man. As long as she was hurt

and on the outs with Ryan, no one would be calling
him. She was the same as giving Gram permission now
to defy Harry and just call Ryan for heaven's sake.

"If you won't, I'll call him." Tara reached for her cell
phone in her pocket.

Gram grabbed her arm. "Don't. We can't string
Ryan along and prey on his good graces any more.
We'll handle this ourselves."

Gram was usually sweet and amiable. But when her
tone was hard and serious like it was now, there was no
use arguing with her. She made a good point about
stringing Ryan along. Tara was guilty enough of that
as it was. She'd wanted to come back and make things
better for her grandparents. Instead, she'd messed
things up for them and Ryan.

"What can I do to help?" Tara asked.

"Round up as many buckets as you can find and go
door to door distributing them," Gram said. "I think
there are a couple, at least, in the shed. Then grab anything else you can find—empty bowls, wastebaskets,
and cans. We can try to minimize the damage. Get all
the clean towels you can find, too, and hand them out.
And some mops to wipe up."

Gram shook her head. "There might be an old one in
the shed, too. We don't use mops for much any more
with all these fancy new cleaning devices. I'll need help
with the extra laundry later. And call the laundry and
see if they can send more out."

Tara had just opened her mouth to agree when they
heard a heavy thud on the roof.

Tara froze. Gram stilled beside her. The buzz of guests having breakfast and getting ready to head for the slopes died into pin-drop silence.

The sound of rolling and skidding was followed by scream.

Gram gasped. "Harry, you old fool!"

Tara ran for the door and out into the cold and dark, skidding in her tennis shoes across the ice beneath the new blanket of snow, oblivious to the cold. Harry's ladder leaned against the building were he'd left it. Harry, white and pale and clutching his chest, lay in a five-foot high pile of snow next to it, made visible by the beam of the camping lantern he was still carrying.

"Grandpa! Grandpa!" Tara reached him first and scrambled up the snow pile to the light. She took the lantern from him and held it over him as she evaluated the situation.

Beads of sweat stood on Harry's forehead in the frigid twenty-degree weather. *Not good. So not good.*

"I got dizzy. So danged dizzy. And it felt like the roof pitched and I tumbled off into the snow," Harry said.

"The roof *is* pitched, Grandpa."

He gasped for breath. "The weight. My chest feels like Santa's fully loaded sleigh is sitting on it and the reindeer are doing a tap dance." He clutched his chest. "Danged reindeer. I can't breathe."

"I'll tell Santa to get his team under control." Tara patted his shoulder and tried to smile at him. "You're too old for jumping from roofs, Grandpa." She grabbed his hand and squeezed it. "Can you move? Is anything broken?"

"Hard to tell." Harry moved his arms and legs and wiggled his fingers. "Doesn't seem so. The snow"—he wheezed—"cushioned my fall."

As Tara pulled her cell phone from her pocket, headlights swung into the parking lot.

Ryan! Her heart leaped.

Her relief and joy were short-lived. Ranger Rick Dempsey was arriving for his morning cup of coffee in his park service pickup truck.

She squeezed Harry's hand again. "Hang on, Grandpa. You're going to be all right. I'm calling for help." Tara frantically dialed 911. While she waited for them to pick up, she called down to Gram. "Get some blankets and Grandpa's nitroglycerin."

The emergency dispatcher picked up. "9-1-1. What's your emergency?"

"This is Tara Clark from Echo Bay Resort. My grandfather Harry Jansen just fell off the roof. I think he's having a heart attack. He has a lot of pressure in his chest and is gasping as he breathes."

Rick Dempsey jumped out of his truck, waded through the crowd of guests that had gathered outside, and scrambled up the snow pile beside her with an emergency blanket and a first-aid kit in his hand. "How's the patient?"

Tara shook her head and put a finger to her lips. As she talked to 911 and relayed information, Rick wrapped Harry in the blanket and spoke reassuringly to him while performing a quick triage check.

Tara was relieved first-aid-trained Ranger Rick was there.

Rick leaned in and whispered to her. "Nothing appears broken. I think he's having a heart attack. We need to get him to the hospital. *Now.*"

Tara nodded and spoke to the operator. "Send an ambulance and the paramedics." She turned to Rick and relayed the news. "They say the roads are so bad it will take at least half an hour to reach us."

He motioned for the phone. "Tell them you're putting me on."

She handed it to him and spoke to Harry. "You picked a fine time to fall off the roof." She patted his gloved hand. "The roads are tricky, but we're going to get you help, I promise."

"Yeah, I have an extended cab service vehicle equipped with snow tires, chains, and a plow blade. Uh-huh. Okay. We're on our way." Rick hung up and handed Tara her phone. "They said to give Harry an aspirin and his nitroglycerin. Then they want us to take Harry in my truck to the hospital in town. They'll assess and stabilize him there and call for a life bird if he needs more serious care than they can give him."

Beside them, Harry gasped for breath, a heartbreaking, painful, scary sound that spurred Tara into action. She was not going to let her grandfather die two days before Christmas. Not on her watch.

"Margie can ride along." Rick looked Tara directly in the eye. "You'll have to drive so I can keep an eye on our patient here. Think you can do that, city girl?"

Right then Tara would do anything. "Can I do it? I've been driving these roads since I was a kid. Stay with him. We'll need help getting Grandpa to the truck."

Tara kissed Harry on the forehead. "Hang with us. I'll be right back."

She slid down the snow bank to where Margie was waiting, standing outside in her lightweight cardigan sweater with Harry's heart medicine and a bottle of water in her hand. The sight of her almost made Tara cry. Margie looked just like she had when Tara had arrived to spend the holidays. Tara loved her gram even more in that vulnerable moment. Gram had been strong for her when Chad died. Tara would be strong now. Gram needed her.

Tara explained the situation and hugged her. "911 said to give Grandpa some aspirin, too. Do you have any?"

Gram nodded.

"Good. It'll be okay. It will." Tara actually had no idea if that were true, but she was going to do her best to make it so. She would not let another Christmas tragedy haunt her family. It would kill Gram, too, and devastate Tara's mom.

Tara turned to the crowd of guests. "I need volunteers to carry my grandfather to Rick's truck. And someone to run into the lodge for aspirin."

The harrowing half-hour trip to the small hospital in town took both an eternity and a blink. Tara lowered the blade on Rick's truck and plowed their way out through ten miles of small, twisty, snow-laden, two-lane roads to the main highway. So much snow lined the roads that the plow blade had a hard time throwing the snow out of their way.

On either side of them, the trees in the forest stood like weary white soldiers and groaned with the weight of the snow. The always-narrow road had shrunk to barely a lane and a half. Each time Tara met a car she pulled to the side and prayed they wouldn't get stuck in the snow banks lining the road.

When they reached the highway, it wasn't in much better shape. The lanes were rutted with snow and ice and narrow with towering piles of snow piled in the center. Even with snow tires and chains, Tara had to take it slow while her heart hammered out a rhythm urging her to hurry, hurry, *hurry.*

Gram sat in the seat next to her. In the backseat, Rick spoke reassuringly to Harry and monitored his vitals. Tara whiteknuckled the steering wheel and tried to block out the sounds of what could be her grandpa dying as she appealed to God to save him.

Not this Christmas. Not another one.

If Harry died now, during the holiday season, Tara would not come back to Echo Bay again.

In town, the roads were crowded with skiers and boarders heading to the mountain and the going was even slower. Tara laid on the horn and worked her way through them.

"Turn on my yellow light." Rick gave her instructions as he texted the hospital to expect them within minutes.

The flashing yellow light helped, but only marginally. People didn't move out of the way for park service vehicles with the same speed and urgency they did for police and fire.

At last the hospital loomed ahead in the breaking gloom of a snowy dawn. As Tara pulled into the lot, her heart went wild, beating so fast she almost couldn't breathe. She'd never wanted to come back here. She had no faith in here.

The paramedics took Chad to this very hospital after his accident. He hadn't died here, not technically. His brain was dead, but life support kept him going for a while longer. The old wounds suddenly felt as fresh as they'd been after they'd happened. The memories were not any comfort to Tara as she pulled into the entrance for Emergency and came to a stop.

As a team of orderlies rushed out and unloaded Harry, Tara texted Ryan the news, including how Harry had fallen off the roof. She wasn't being malicious. Ryan deserved to know. He'd want to know. And right now, every part of her ached for him to come to the hospital and hold her and tell her things were going to be okay.

Gram held his hand as they strapped Harry onto the gurney. "You hang on, Harry. Do you hear me? It's only a couple of months until our fifty-fifth anniversary and you promised me you'd make it."

As Tara watched her grandma, a lump formed in her throat. Her grandparents had been together for nearly fifty-five years. Tara could have had a shot at making it to a fifty-fifth with Ryan if she'd married him as they'd planned when they were in college. Now the odds of making it to even a fiftieth with anyone seemed long.

Her grandma was still gently scolding Harry as she helped tuck the blankets around him. "I told you not to go up on that roof. You should listen to me, Harry. But make it through this, and I promise not to hold it over you." She bent down and kissed his forehead.

Tara thought she heard her grandma whisper that she loved him just before the orderlies wheeled him away. Tara put her arm around Gram as they walked into the waiting room, almost as much to steady herself as Gram. Rick was right behind them, quiet and sympathetic.

The hospital was bright and modern inside, obviously remodeled in the years since Chad died. But the layout was basically the same and the emphasis was obvious. County General was set up to care for broken bones, fractures, sprains and strains, and head injuries. Ski posters and posters about how to care for sprains and breaks covered one wall. This hospital was a mere way-station for anything serious, a place to stabilize and prepare patients for transport. So they could die in a big, fancy hospital elsewhere. That had been Tara's experience.

Even wrapped in a large down coat, Gram felt frail and small beneath Tara's embrace.

A Christmas tree sat in the center of the lobby in the same spot it had been when Tara had waited there for news of her brother. Different tree, different decorations, covered with tags to take to buy presents for different needy children. Still too eerily familiar. Color crayon drawings of Santa and his reindeer by local schoolchildren covered the bulletin boards and the wall opposite the ski posters. A plastic Santa sat in the corner, and Santa in a grass skirt, placed by someone who wasn't the fan of winter most of the town's guests were, did a hula on the counter of the admittance desk. A TV tuned to a national talk show hung above the plastic Santa. A weather forecaster was predicting more snow for North Idaho.

Tara blocked out his jovial comments about what a jolly white Christmas they were going to have as she led Gram to the desk.

Gram seemed stoic and in control until the nurse at the desk began asking questions. Then Gram fell apart and started to gently sob.

"I'll take care of it, Gram. Don't worry." She hugged her, thankful to Rick when he took charge and took Margie by the shoulders.

"Come with me. Let Tara handle this." He led Margie to a chair in the waiting area while Tara answered questions and the woman behind the desk entered her responses into the computer.

Can this really be called paperwork, anymore? Tara thought as she answered question after question and caught herself glancing at the door to the outside every time it opened, hoping it was Ryan.

Just as Tara finally finished with the admittance registration, the outside door did open up, followed by a cold blast of air, and a Sanders breezing in. Just one problem—the Sanders was Laura, Ryan's mom.

Laura caught Tara's eye too quickly for Tara to look away. Laura shook her head just slightly. Her eyes snapped with both compassion and anger. She was a mama bear defending her cub, Ryan. As angry with Tara as Harry was with Ryan.

Tara had once been close with Laura. She'd spent inordinate amounts of time at the Sanders' house when she was young. She'd hoped to see Laura again under better circumstances. She was grateful Laura had come despite the tension between them.

Laura hurried to Margie and put her arm around her while Tara railed inside at Ryan for being too much of a coward to show up. He sent his mother instead. Laura had worked as a maid at Echo Bay Resort for many years. She and Gram were close. She'd be good comfort for Gram, but that didn't make Ryan any less cowardly.

Rick stood and greeted Laura, whispered something to Margie, and walked over to Tara. "You look like hell. Have you eaten anything today?"

Tara stared at Margie and Laura. "No, but what does it matter? I should go to Gram."

Rick put a hand on her arm to stop her. "Let them talk. Let Laura take care of Margie. Come to the cafeteria with me. I haven't had my coffee yet and you need something to eat."

"You're very kind," she said to Rick. "But you don't need to stay."

"I absolutely need to stay." Rick took her arm and propelled her down the hall toward the cafeteria.

"They'll be okay. It will be a while before we get any news about Harry."

In the cafeteria, Rick maneuvered her into line. "What looks good? Breakfast is on me."

Tara just shook her head and shrugged. "I'm really not hungry—"

"Protein, then. And coffee." He grabbed a tray and filled it with fruit, a couple of pastries, two plates of eggs, and two cups of coffee. "Cream? Sugar?"

"Both."

He paid at the register and led her to a table by the windows that looked out on what would have been a view of the mountain if it hadn't been obscured by cloud cover. The sun was up fully now. Or rather, it was light out, but snowing heavily.

Rick set a plate of eggs and a pastry in front of her and handed her a cup of coffee. "Eat. You need your strength."

"You don't think—"

"No, I don't think. Harry is a tough old bird. He'll survive this out of sense of orneriness if nothing else. He's going to want bragging rights about falling off that roof at seventy-nine and surviving."

She smiled weakly. Rick certainly knew her grandfather. "You're right about that. It will give him bragging rights." She took a sip of coffee and a bite of eggs, and then she couldn't help herself—she held the steaming cup in front of her on the table with two hands and teared up. "I can't take this, Rick. This is a repeat of ten years ago and it's all my fault again."

"Good to know," Rick said. "Next year, or the next, when we're having a warm winter with little snow and the ski area's in trouble, we'll know who to call."

"Of course I didn't make it snow—"

"You mean you pushed Harry off the roof? Guess I'd better call the sheriff."

"Stop it." She couldn't help smiling through her tears. "Ryan and I did this. Again. Like we did to Chad. If we hadn't been fighting, Chad wouldn't have taken off down the slopes and crashed. If we hadn't been fighting now, Ryan would have come over and cleared the roof and Harry would never have been up there."

Rick pursed his lips, let out a deep breath, and blew on his coffee before speaking. "Tara, you don't control fate. Harry was ripe for a heart attack. If not on the roof, then while he shoveled the walk, or took a shower, or slept in his bed.

"Being on the roof, the fall he took, none of that is responsible for the condition he's in. And neither are you.

"You have to stop taking responsibility for the stuff that just happens in life. This is life. People get sick. They die in accidents. They get old and get heart disease. Ease up on yourself." He paused. "And Ryan."

She sighed and tried to smile at him. "When did you get so smart?"

He grinned back.

Laura was still sitting with Margie, chatting quietly with her when Tara returned to the waiting room with Rick.

"We should call your mom," Margie said as Tara sat down.

Tara was dreading calling her mom. She and her mom had had the same bad feeling about Christmas since Chad's accident. Her mom was even worse about it than she was.

Tara sat down beside Margie and patted her hand. "We'll call Mom once we know something definite. Until then, there's no reason to worry her."

"Yes." Margie nodded. "You're right. Of course you're right." She smiled weakly at Tara.

The doors to the surgery area opened and a middle-aged male doctor in scrubs strode out. "Mrs. Jansen?"

Margie stood. "Yes."

Tara stood with her and squeezed her hand as she gauged the doctor's demeanor. After Chad's accident she'd gotten pretty good at determining when medical professionals had bad news to deliver. This doctor didn't look worried.

"Harry's had a mild heart attack," he said. "Nothing too serious. He should be fine. We performed an angioplasty and cleared the blockage. No damage done to the heart as far as we can tell.

"And there's more good news—he didn't break anything in the fall. No internal injuries. Just some bumps and bruises. He'll be stiff and sore, but he should heal quickly."

Tara put her arm around Margie.

Her grandma slumped against her in relief. "Thank goodness."

The doctor smiled. "I'm going to keep Harry in the hospital for a few days to keep an eye on him. It's standard procedure. But he'll be home in time for Christmas Eve."

Gram asked the doctor a few more questions, but Tara was so relieved she barely heard them.

"You'll be able to see him when he comes out of recovery in about an hour. Until then, relax." The doctor took Margie's hand and squeezed it while she thanked him.

"I guess we can call Mom now." Tara smiled through her tears of relief.

Rick had been standing so quietly beside them that Tara had nearly forgotten he was there. When he spoke, he startled her.

"You'll want to stay to see Harry when he gets to his room. I have some business in town I may as well take care of while I'm here. But I'm at your disposal. Stay as long as you like and I'll take you home when you're ready."

"That's so kind—" Tara started to say.

Laura interrupted her and spoke to Margie. "I'm sure you'll want to be near Harry tonight. We're right here in town and we have an open guestroom. We'd love to have you stay with us. We insist. We can take you home tomorrow or whenever you're ready." Laura paused. "You too, Tara."

The last thing Tara wanted to do was spend the night with Ryan's parents. "Gram, you stay. But someone needs to get back and check on the lodge and I'm happy to do it."

Gram agreed, looking grateful that Tara was taking over. Someone needed to get back and deal with the roof and the leaks and all of it.

Tara turned to Rick. "I'll text you when I'm ready?"

"Sounds like a plan." Rick said his goodbyes and left.

Margie excused herself to use the ladies' room, leaving Tara abruptly alone with Laura Sanders. If Tara had been the suspicious type, she would have thought Gram did it on purpose. In fact, Tara *was* suspicious. Gram probably had.

They sat in silence until Gram disappeared down the hall.

"Thanks for coming," Tara said. "I appreciate it. And I know Gram does, too."

Laura shrugged. "Margie and Harry were good to me when the boys were young and I needed work. They never minded Ryan and the others tagging along and 'helping' me while I cleaned. More like the boys were bugging Harry and running wild. But Harry never did seem to mind." Laura laughed softly at the memory.

Tara agreed. "You know my grandpa, the great outdoorsman. He's a man's man and he's always liked boys and wished he'd had a son. Mom was too girly-girl for him. He loved having Chad and his friends around."

Laura nodded. "I'll always have a soft spot for Margie and Harry. Not just because of how they helped me, but because they helped make the boys' childhoods special. They have nothing but fond memories of the lodge."

Tara thought Laura gave her a rather pointed look. Spearing. As if the fond memories were despite Tara.

"I used to watch you and Chad and Ryan play together when you were little," Laura said, watching Tara closely. "Despite all the teasing your brother and Ryan did to you, you were always a good sport. You and Ryan got along better than any little girl and little boy I ever knew. I always thought what you had was special.

"I told Ryan, told all my boys, that when they found a woman who was their best friend, they should marry her. That's the kind of love that makes a marriage last."

Tara dropped Laura's gaze and stared in her lap, playing with her hands as she swallowed a lump. "Laura, I'm sorry about coming back and upsetting Ryan's life. I didn't mean—"

Laura cut her off. "You could do worse than my boy. He's a good man. He could be your best friend again, if you'd let him."

CHAPTER EIGHTEEN

Ryan never showed up at the hospital, the coward. Not while Tara, Gram, and Laura waited for Harry to come out of post-op. Not while Harry was being settled in his room. Not while Tara visited with Harry, thinking he looked smaller than life as he lay in his hospital bed connected to an IV and all sorts of monitors while an old Christmas classic movie played on the TV over-head. Not when relief surged through her that this was not going to be the tragic Christmas she'd feared. Not even when Rick picked Tara up to drive her home to the lodge.

Tara couldn't stay at the hospital until Christmas waiting for Ryan to show up. In fact, she came to the conclusion her presence was probably keeping him away. So reluctantly, she texted Rick and asked him to pick her up.

It was better this way. It really was. She couldn't face Ryan's cold shoulder and accusing eyes again. She was disappointed, terribly disappointed, in him, and in herself for being disappointed. Laura's little talk with Tara had given her hope again, and hope, in this case, was a dangerous and unreasonable creature.

What did she really think was going to happen between her and Ryan? A Christmas miracle?

Tara imagined Laura had texted Ryan the minute she left with Rick. And Ryan had probably swooped in to visit Harry as soon as the hospital was clear of her presence. At least, she hoped Ryan would visit Harry. He darn well should.

She and Rick rode in companionable silence for most of the half-hour trip on snowy roads through snowy woods to the lodge. But she was still fuming and silently berating Ryan.

Dusk was falling as they pulled into the long driveway into Echo Bay Resort. As they came around the corner and the lodge came into view, Tara gasped. No longer was the lodge roof piled high with snow. The roof, the actual roof, was clear. Piles of shoveled snow surrounded the lodge.

"Someone's cleared the roof." Tara's eyes clouded with tears.

"Looks like it," Rick said in his understated way.

"I wonder who—"

Rick shook his head. "Yeah, I wonder."

She wasn't looking at him. From the tone of his voice, she could only imagine him rolling his eyes.

He pulled directly in front of the front porch and came to a stop.

She smiled at him. "I take back every bad thing I ever said about you, Rick."

He grinned. "You said bad things about me?"

She laughed. "All the time. Back in the day, anyway. You and the boys were always merciless with me." She paused. "Thank you for today. I don't know what I would have done if you hadn't shown up when you did."

"You would have thought of something." He looked almost embarrassed.

"I owe you coffee, probably for life," she said.

"You can buy me a cup tomorrow. After that, we're even."

She jumped out of the truck and slammed the door tightly shut behind her. She didn't wait for him to pull away. She simply ran into the lodge. There was so much to do.

Clearing the roof would have fixed the leaks. But there was the cleanup and the laundry and the apologies...

Stormy met her at the door and pulled her into a hug. "You're back!"

"I am, indeed."

"How's Harry?"

"Up and ornery and asking for coffee." Tara looked around the lodge. The fire crackled happily. Groups of guests milled around contentedly. Someone was even playing Christmas songs on the piano. No one looked upset or worried or hassled.

"How are things here?" Tara asked, but she had the feeling she already knew.

"We're great. Everything's back to normal." Stormy pulled her inside as she pointed upward. "We're standing under the mistletoe. I don't want anyone getting ideas." She laughed. "Ryan was really a wonder. Once he stepped in and took charge, it was like magic. Everything fell into place. He charmed the guests, recruited a group of his friends, and cleared the roof while we cleaned the rooms."

Stormy smiled again. "You should have heard the ruckus they made up there—stomping and laughing and shoveling. Piles of snow flying off the roof past the windows. Someone was playing Christmas music. It sounded more like a party than a work crew. I was almost tempted to join them." Stormy winked. "I did bring them coffee once or twice, handed it right out the second floor windows.

"The guests made a joke of running out between shovelfuls of snow coming off the roof and the kids thought it was great fun.

"During all the festivities, Ryan got on the horn to the laundry service and somehow sweet-talked them into making an emergency delivery despite the snowy roads. As if that wasn't enough, he got a handyman from town to come out and repair the damage the leaks caused in the rooms.

"Now that we now that Harry's going to be all right, it was all simply an exciting morning adventure."

Tara's eyes misted up again. She'd misjudged Ryan so badly. "Ryan did all this?"

Stormy nodded. "He showed up shortly after you left. He just left about fifteen minutes ago. He raided the kitchen and fed his crew lunch on the house, but I don't think Harry will mind. If you want to catch him—"

Tara shook her head. "What a wonder. Did he cancel my roof-clearing service appointment for the twenty-seventh, too?"

"You'll have to ask him, but I wouldn't put it past him."

All day long Tara had been silently calling Ryan a coward and thinking all kinds of horrible things about him. And all the time he'd been taking care of them, doing what needed to be done here when she was sure he'd rather have been at the hospital.

"Hey?" Stormy looked concerned. "Are you okay?"

Tara nodded. "Ryan really loves this place."

Stormy nodded. "He certainly treated it like it was his own today, and I don't mean that in a bad way. You should have seen him with the guests. I think we're due for more repeat business because of the accident, rather than less."

Stormy paused and snapped her fingers. "I almost forgot. Ryan got a card for Harry and passed it around. Most of the guests have already signed it. You can take it to Harry when you visit him tomorrow. And Carter says to tell Harry he's saving the best kindling for the blaze he's going to make for Harry when he comes home.

"Come to think of it," Stormy said. "Ryan even ordered another couple of cords of wood and had them delivered. Carter complained to him that he was running low."

Was there anything Ryan hadn't done or thought of?

Stormy looked Tara over. "You look beat. Things are under control. Why don't you take a rest in your room?"

Tara nodded. "I think I will. Thank you."

Back in her room, Tara immediately noticed that the wet towels she'd used to mop up the leak were gone. The wall was dry. The bed neatly made. The curtains were open and there was a light on in Ryan's cabin across the way. The snow had finally stopped and it was just clear enough to make out the happy glow coming from Ryan's window.

Tara pulled out her cell phone. She owed Ryan a debt she'd never be able to repay. She stared at the phone and frowned. It was narcissistic to think he'd done any of this for her. If she were cynical, she would have said he'd done it to win points in his battle with her for the lodge. But she wasn't so jaded that she could overlook Ryan's true nature and love for this place and her grandparents. He'd done it for Harry and Margie. In a way, she didn't owe him any thanks at all.

In another, she owed him everything. Her grandfather's heart attack had made things clearer than they'd ever been. She had arrived just in time to take care of her grandparents with the purest of intentions and the worst-case scenario of an implementation strategy.

Would a manager appointed by Cheryl from North-west Resort Management Services have shown the love for the lodge and gone to such lengths to make sure the resort ran smoothly? Could that manager have rounded up volunteer locals to help out in an emergency the way Ryan had? Would the locals love the lodge as they had all these years Harry and Margie had run it if a big corporation took over? Would Harry's legacy die with him?

Maybe the best gift she could give her grandparents this season would be letting them decide what they wanted, really and truly wanted, for Echo Bay, even if that meant selling it to Ryan now rather than willing it to her.

She made up her mind to put the question to her grandfather when she visited him tomorrow.

She stared at her phone again, finally texting Ryan two simple words: *Thank you.*

Harry looked much better when Tara walked into his room the next day carrying a Christmas poinsettia. His color had returned and he sat up in bed finishing his breakfast. Gram sat next to him eating a Danish from the cafeteria.

"Look who's here, Margie!" Harry sounded happy to see Tara.

She walked over and gave him a kiss. "You look good. You scared us yesterday. I thought Gram told you to be careful up there. I did, too, and you laughed it off. So what is this disobeying orders business?"

Harry chuckled. "Henpecked, that's what I am. And paying the price for that disobedience. That snow may have been soft, but it wasn't soft enough. I'm bruised six ways from Sunday."

Tara set the plant on the nightstand next to his bed and hugged her grandmother. "You'll both be happy to know the lodge is back to normal and running like a well-oiled machine."

Harry's eyes lit up as he patted Margie's hand. "I knew our girl would take care of things!"

Tara removed her scarf and took a seat in the guest chair across the bed from Gram. "Not so fast. I'd love to take credit, but I think lying will get me on Santa's naughty list and I've been bad enough already this year."

Harry furrowed his forehead. "What do you mean? Did my excellent staff take care of things?"

"They helped and followed orders. But Ryan deserves the credit." She related everything he'd done.

Margie got tears in her eyes.

Harry looked moved, too. "Ryan's a good one."

"Yes, he is." And she meant it. Tara was nervous, but she'd just been handed her opportunity to bring up the lodge and its future. "And he loves Echo Bay Resort like no one else, except maybe you two." Tara winked at them and took a deep breath.

"I have to apologize to both of you. I came here for Christmas to do what I thought was best for you both and the lodge. But it turns out that although I acted in love and had the best of intentions, I pretty much was just forcing my opinions on you.

"As much as I love Echo Bay, I have no desire to run it." She swallowed hard. "That was always Chad and Ryan's dream. I thought hiring a company to manage it so you two could take it easy and semi-retire was the best alternative. But since I've arrived, I've realized that I'm not sure that's what you want." She bit her lip.

"So please answer me truthfully—my desires aside, what do you want to do with Echo Bay? Do you want to sell it to Ryan? He'd be really good for it, and owning it's the only way he'll take over as the manager."

She rushed on before they could cut her off and answer. "Because if you do, I have no objections. Truly. He'd be good for the place. There's no need to hang onto it and run yourself ragged just so you can leave it to me. If you want to sell to Ryan, I'll help you make the arrangements and call off my management company."

Harry and Margie looked at each other as if trying to get confirmation from each other that it was okay to say what they really thought.

"I'm serious," Tara said. "Chad's dream can live on through Ryan. He's not Chad, but he's been as much like a grandson to you as anyone." Tara choked up. "If we're all truthful, he's been a better grandchild to you than I've been.

"Look, I've seen how much you care for him and how much he loves Echo Bay. There's nothing wrong with wanting him to be the one to continue your tradition."

Harry cleared his throat. "You've been a good granddaughter to us, Tara. Don't ever think different."

Margie nodded as tears stood in her eyes. "We love you like nobody's business."

Tara had tears in her eyes now, too. Some cheering up she was doing. "I know. And I love you both so much, too. Which is why I want what you want and what's best for everyone, not just me."

Harry shot another glance at Margie. It wasn't like Harry not to speak up, but he seemed to be walking softly and afraid of something. "Ryan has the touch with the place. He just seems to know what to do and when to do it. It has to do with loving it. If you love something, you can't keep away from it. You get to know it." Harry smiled slightly and there was a tease in his eyes. "Kind of like I know that old girl over there." He nodded toward Margie.

"Oh, Harry." Gram used her embarrassed tone, but her expression said she was pleased.

"I've always thought Ryan would be a good choice for the lodge," Harry said. "He's offered me a fair price and he'll let Gram and me stay on until we die if that's what we want to do." Harry paused. "But I can tell from the look on her face, your grandma is worried that if we sell to Ryan, you'll never come see us here again. That would break her heart." His tone was gruff, which meant it would break his, too, the old softie. He was trying to act tough, but it was easy enough to see through him.

"So," Tara said, "let me see if I have this right. You want to sell to Ryan, and I agree with you that's the best solution for everyone. But if I refuse to visit once he's the owner, that's a deal breaker?"

"I think you about got it, kid," Harry said as Margie adjusted the pillow behind his back for him.

"Ryan's upset with me now," Tara said. "But once I bow out and give him my blessing to buy it, I think he'll forgive me." She hoped. "If I promise to come back and visit, we'll have a deal?"

Harry nodded. "We'll have a deal."

"Can I make it a condition of the sale that Ryan holds my room for me and gives it to me on the house whenever I want to come? Within reason, of course."

"Sounds reasonable to me." Harry's smile reached from ear to ear. He looked as pleased as the Grinch on Christmas Day as he carved the roast beast.

Margie beamed.

"Okay, then." Tara reached across and patted her grandfather's gnarled hands where they rested against the blankets. "You have a deal, on one more condition—let me tell Ryan. On Christmas. Bowing out of this battle will be my gift to him, if it's all right with the two of you."

"Sounds more than fair to me," Harry said.

"Good," Tara said. "And no more climbing on the roof for you. Let Ryan do it. From what Stormy said, he knows how to make a party of it."

Tara left the hospital with a light heart. Or, at least, a lighter heart. Her grandparents were ecstatic. The only thing that could have made them happier was Tara and Ryan getting back together and giving them the great-grandchild they longed for. And the truth was, if Tara had still really believed in Santa, she would have put that wish on top of her list, too. Realistically, she wasn't sure Ryan was ready to forgive her, or ever would be. After all, she'd already broken one engagement to him and all but turned him down a second time. How many chances did a girl get? Then again, that was only two. Wasn't three supposed to be the charm?

The least she could do was leave Echo Bay with a clear heart. And that meant coming clean with Ryan. She headed to a quaint little gift shop along Main Street and stopped in to buy a Christmas card with the right sentiments, not too optimistic they'd have an I'm-so-sorry-please-forgive-me-and-now-you-can-buy-the-lodge section.

How does one find a card that strikes perfect balance of true feeling, romance, and forgiveness? Did she go sappy sweet? Sexy come-on? Funny? This greeting card had the weight of her world on it. It had to immediately convey that she still loved Ryan, make him smile, and beg his forgiveness. A tall order, and one she was willing to pay a premium price for.

The clerk greeted her the minute she walked in the door. "Merry Christmas! Can I help you find something?"

"Just looking for a Christmas card."

"You've come to the right place." The middle-aged woman came out from behind the counter and showed Tara to the greeting-card section. Which she could have found on her own, but the woman seemed to want something to do. "We're a bit picked over."

"That's what I get for waiting until the last minute." Tara turned her attention to the cards. "Thanks for your help."

"You're Harry and Margie's granddaughter, aren't you?" The woman just would not leave.

"Yes."

"I heard Harry fell off the roof yesterday." The woman sounded and looked concerned. "How is he doing?"

"Great. He's recovering quickly. He'll be home for Christmas Eve."

"That is a relief." The woman smiled. "We all love Harry. He's a fixture around here. What would we do without him?"

Fortunately, another customer came in and diverted the clerk's attention. "Let me know if you need any help." She wandered off to help the new arrival.

She browsed the Christmas-card section, hoping no one she knew came in and caught her in the act of buying a mushy card for Ryan. This was a top-secret mission, after all. She picked up the first card and read it: *Let's Get Caught Under the Mistletoe.*

Not bad. Good sentiment. A bit of innuendo. And a little humorous given how she'd almost kissed Ryan beneath the mistletoe the night she arrived and it had surprised them both.

She moved on to the next one. *I loved you yesterday. I love you still. I always have. I always will. Merry Christmas.*

Yes, perfect sentiment. This would definitely get her message across, but—hadn't she seen this, minus the "Merry Christmas," on a decal on a friend's wall? Was impersonal wall sentiment the way to go in this delicate, critical situation?

She picked up a card with cartoon drawings. *You're the holly to my berries. You're the marshmallows to my hot chocolate. You're the merry to my Christmas. We belong together. I love you.*

Corny. But it made her smile. One Valentine's Day when they were college, she and Ryan had had a competition to see who could give the other the corniest card. He'd appreciate the effort.

She bought it and escaped to the coffee shop next door. She ordered a peppermint mocha and drank it at a small table by the window as she poured out her heart to Ryan.

I could go on—you're the kiss beneath my mistletoe. You're the bindings to my snowboard. Wait, that's not any better, is it? Worse?

I've been a fool and I've hurt you and I'm sorry. I thought I wasn't ready for commitment. I thought I had to give us time to reconnect. But these last few days I've realized I've let too much time pass already. We could have had ten wonderful years together. Let's not waste ten more days.

I love you. I want you in my life. And, whether you still want me in yours or not, I want you to have the lodge.

I talked to Gram and Grandpa. They're in agreement. They want to sell the lodge to you. You're the best person in the world to hand their legacy over to. Make them an offer they can't refuse.

Merry Christmas!
I love you.
Tara

She stared out the window at the white winter wonderland and the record snowfall. People her grandparents' age were saying they'd never seen as much snow as this, certainly never at Christmastime. This was probably going to be the whitest Christmas she'd see in her lifetime. She hoped it wasn't the bleakest. It certainly would be one to remember.

She closed the card, put her pen back in her purse, slid the card into the envelope, and sealed it with a kiss just for fun. It was what she did as a silly, moony preteen in love with Ryan. Then she wrote *SWAK* on the back and drew a little heart as laughed to herself, remembering her ten-year-old self giving the twelve-year-old Ryan a card with *SWAK* on the back. This was just her silly way of reminding him of their shared history and all the silly, happy, and sometimes painful times they'd been through.

She grabbed her purse and picked up the card and her coffee. Before she headed back to Echo Bay, she had to stop by Jim Dickson's and ask the town Santa to stuff this in his Santa bag for Ryan. Jim was a good sport. She doubted she'd have too much trouble getting him to deliver her card to Ryan at the big Basin Santa Ski and Christmas extravaganza.

It was too bad she wouldn't be at the party to see Ryan open it.

CHAPTER NINETEEN

It was Christmas Eve and Ryan was going to be spending it alone in the midst of thousands of happy Santa Skiers. It wasn't like this was the first Christmas Eve he'd ever been dateless. It was more that until a few days ago, he'd had such high, foolish hopes for this one. Maybe he *was* being an ass. He'd thought a lot about things since his blowup with Tara. Maybe he'd been wrong not to give her more time.

Her rejection, or rather her lack of trust in him, still stung. Even if they didn't work out as a couple, or in spite of the fact that it appeared they weren't going to work out as a couple, he'd take good care of the lodge and of Harry and Margie. Did Tara honestly think that an impersonal property management company would look after Harry and Margie if they got sick? Or needed to be driven somewhere? Or their health deteriorated to the point someone needed to contact the family?

Maybe not. But even if he was right, what good was being right when he'd lost Tara and Echo Bay both in one dumb move?

Harry was being discharged this afternoon. Ryan wanted to see him and wish him a merry Christmas before Harry went home. Ryan thought it would be more respectful to let Margie and Harry have their first Christmas in years alone with Tara without the tension and drama of his presence.

On his way to the hospital, Ryan had stopped by Jim Dickson's to get Tara's old engagement ring back. But Jim was mysteriously out again, like he'd been every time Ryan had stopped by these last few days. The holidays were a busy time, and it probably didn't matter in the long run. Ryan could pick up the ring any time. He was pretty sure Jim had gotten his messages not to put the ring in his Santa bag.

Ryan swallowed a lump and pulled into a parking spot in the hospital's visitor parking lot. It was a clear, sunny, bitterly cold day, the first day it hadn't snowed, and wasn't predicted to, for what seemed like weeks. The skiing and boarding should be excellent. Under different circumstances, Ryan would have been looking forward to the evening. Maybe the boarding would clear his head, if he wasn't too busy playing cop to guests who were celebrating a little too hard.

Ryan jumped out of the car, grabbed the gifts he had for Harry and Margie, and went to Harry's room.

Harry was alone, sitting up and looking ready to blow the place.

Ryan knocked on the doorjamb. "Glad I caught you. I was afraid you'd have escaped this place already."

Harry chuckled. "Don't I wish. It's not the best place to spend Christmas Eve. But don't tell the nurses that. They've done their best to make the place cheery and add a little holiday spirit. I hear Santa's even going to make a visit tonight to the little kids."

"Yeah, that Santa," Ryan said as he came in and stood next to Harry's bed. "He's going to be a busy one tonight."

Harry nodded. "Off work early?"

Ryan nodded. "In a manner of speaking. We closed the plant at noon. I stopped by Mom and Dad's for lunch. I'm heading up to the Basin for my Santa shift in a few."

"You're carrying presents, but you don't look like you're dressed for the big event." Harry sat up straighter.

"My gear and suit are in the car." Ryan paused. "I got you and Margie each a little something." He set them on the stand next to Harry.

"A case of salad dressing apiece?" Harry's eyes sparkled. "You know, you could just bring them by the lodge after the big doings tonight."

Ryan shook his head. "I'm not going back to the cabin. I'm spending tonight and Christmas day with Mom and Dad. In fact, I might not make it home until the twenty-seventh or twenty-eighth. Mom will want someone to drive her to Spokane for the big after-

Christmas sales. Dad hates that duty, so I think I'm it. Part of my gift to him."

Harry studied Ryan and nodded sagely. "Well then, you'll have to come when you come home. It's too bad you won't be around until after Tara leaves. She'll be sorry she didn't get a chance to say goodbye."

Ryan snorted. "Yeah, sure."

Harry was still studying him. "I'm serious, Ryan. She'll be sorry. I'm not supposed to mention it, but she has something she wants to tell you."

Like "go to hell"? Ryan thought. "If I don't see her, tell her she can tell me next time. Or send me a text."

"Don't be too hard on her," Harry said. "This trip has been tough on her. Me falling off the roof didn't help things any. You'll want to hear what she has to say. If she gets the chance, listen to her, will you? Really listen. That will mean more to me than any gift."

Ryan frowned. *What is Harry getting at?* Ryan hated himself for the way his heart raced with hope. "Sure." He nodded toward the door. He wanted to be well gone before Tara and Margie came by to pick Harry up and take him home.

"I'd better be going," Ryan said. "Merry Christmas, Harry."

Tara picked Laurel up on her way to take Harry home from the hospital. "You look ready to pop," Tara said to her as she loaded Laurel's suitcase in the trunk. "Donny really has to go on ski patrol duty this evening?"

Laurel laughed and grabbed her baby bump. "He's looking forward to it and I wouldn't deprive him of the pleasure." She winced and made a pained face.

"Hey, are you okay?"

"Just another Braxton Hicks. I've been having them all day." She took a deep breath and smiled. "Don't worry. I'm fine. They're nothing."

"They don't look like nothing. Good thing we're on our way to the hospital. Maybe I should drop you off there for the evening."

"Nothing doing. We're picking up Harry and hanging at the lodge like old times. I'm not about to miss Margie's Christmas pie." She opened the door and got in the car.

Harry and Margie were waiting for them at the hospital. Tara grabbed Harry's bags and loaded them into the car while he groused about having to be brought out in a wheelchair.

Margie patted him on the shoulder. "Perk up. You're living to see another Christmas. What do you have to complain about?"

Harry grinned. "You're right, old woman. I'm going to enjoy this Christmas if it kills me."

"Watch what you say." Tara opened the car door for him. "It nearly did kill you."

"That was just winter." Harry winked and got in the car.

Half an hour later, just as dusk was falling, they pulled into the lodge parking lot. The Christmas lights were just coming on and the moon and stars were coming out.

"It looks like a Christmas card," Margie said as she got out.

"You always say that." Harry got out.

Tara let Laurel out, too, and parked the car. She entered the lodge to find her grandparents standing beneath the mistletoe, kissing while a small cluster of staff applauded.

Except for the staff, and Laurel's mom Carol, who was Harry and Margie's guest for dinner, the lobby was quiet. This was that wonderful lull time when most of the guests were up on the mountain and wouldn't return until late. Everyone could breathe and relax, joke and laugh, and enjoy the holiday spirit.

The fire blazed brightly. The Christmas tree Ryan had helped Tara cut and buy decorations for was lit up. The ornaments glittered in the firelight and the tree filled the lodge with the scent of fresh forest. Tara couldn't banish the image of kissing him beneath that tree. She wanted to feel that passion again, his arms around her, and his kiss on her lips. Presents from the staff to each other for the Christmas gift exchange were piled beneath the tree. Holiday tunes played over the speakers.

"Can't a guy kiss the missus without an audience?" Harry joked.

Tara rolled her eyes and whispered to Laurel, "Grandpa is in his element." But she was thinking of Ryan again.

If Ryan had a change of heart and accepted her apology, forty years from now, the old couple kissing beneath the mistletoe could be them.

Just a year ago, she couldn't have imagined wanting that future, let alone being nervous that she'd very likely blown it. Could Ryan's love for her have lasted all these years, only to be lost so easily? She hoped not. She wanted a future with Ryan at Echo Bay, wanted it more than she'd ever wanted anything.

She glanced at the clock. Just before four. The Christmas party at the Basin would begin at seven. She smiled at the thought of how happy Ryan would be to get the lodge. Would he be as happy at the sentiment her card expressed?

Harry gave Margie a squeeze around her shoulders and faced the staff members, those who were really like family, who were still on duty. Harry gave as many staff members as he could possibly afford to do without Christmas Eve afternoon off. The few who remained were those who either volunteered or were particularly close to Harry and Margie, like Kathleen and Stormy.

Harry inhaled deeply. "It smells great in here. Is that Kathleen's famous oyster stew I smell?"

It was also tradition to have an early Christmas Eve dinner and close the kitchen so the kitchen and wait staff could go home to be with their families. Anyone who wanted to dine with Harry and Margie, be they staff, family, or guest, was heartily welcomed.

On Christmas Day, Harry ordered dinner served later, a real feast of prime rib and spiral-cut ham, salads, potatoes, rolls, pies, Christmas cookies, and plenty of holiday cheer. The guests would arrive late off the mountain and it was a festive time that Tara had almost forgotten about.

But Christmas Eve, particularly this one with the big party at the Basin, was a quiet, much more intimate affair. Oyster stew, plenty of oyster crackers, salad, lake fish Harry had caught and frozen, venison from local hunters, and a great big Christmas pie made from an old family recipe.

"That is indeed oyster stew," Kathleen said. As she came forward and hugged Harry, tears stood in her eyes. "Welcome back, boss."

Half an hour later, Harry was settled in and seated at the head of the head table. The dining room had been transformed—the tables covered with snowy white tablecloths, lit with candles, and decorated with fir boughs and red Christmas balls. A buffet lined with food in warming trays lined one wall. The curtains were open to the snowy woods outside. Tara had a perfect view out the French double doors to the Basin beyond.

She couldn't keep her mind off the Basin and the party and Ryan up there. She was suddenly having second thoughts about her decision to avoid the party at the Basin. If Chad had been alive, that was where he'd be. What about her desire to honor his memory by going up on the mountain? With Ryan by her side, she'd thought she could do it. Why had she chickened out? What if something went wrong and Ryan decided not to go to the party after all? What if he didn't stay for the Santa giveaway? What if Jim wasn't able to give him her card? What if Ryan missed getting her Christmas gift to him? The what-ifs weighed her down.

Her mind was elsewhere as Harry said a Christmas blessing and they dug into steaming bowls of oyster stew. It stayed elsewhere through a delicious meal she barely tasted. Her gaze kept drifting toward the clock. Just a few more hours.

They retired to the lobby, where Harry took his favorite chair in front of the fire Carter had carefully built and stoked for him.

"I do love a good blaze." Harry sighed happily, but he looked tired.

Gram took a chair next to him while Laurel and Carol took the sofa and Tara sat opposite Gram.

"It's a shame you girls are missing the big party at the Basin. Everyone will be there. We're old stick-in-the-muds here." Margie glanced at Harry.

He yawned.

Poor Grandpa. He really did look worse for the mild celebrating.

"It's not even six and Grandpa's ready for bed." Margie looked at him fondly. "I'm sorry, Tara. This isn't the evening we'd planned. I was looking forward to our traditional gift exchange and game night. But I don't think Grandpa is going to make it." She paused. "But there's no reason you two young women shouldn't have fun. Why don't you go to the party at the Basin?"

Gram sounded way too encouraging and hopeful, as if she was eager for Tara to go. Highly suspicious.

Tara shot a look at Laurel. "I don't think so, Gram. Laurel's in no condition to go—"

"Oh, nonsense." Carol startled everyone. "She should go and have fun. Sit in the lodge and visit. Be with her husband at the party." She patted her daughter's hand. "Have fun before the responsibilities of parenthood settle in. Donny would love the surprise."

"But I thought..." Laurel frowned. "I don't want to leave you alone until late."

Carol waved her hand. "I'll keep Margie and Kathleen company. I'll be fine. I've told you that all along."

Harry suddenly chimed in. "The skiing and boarding will be perfect. If I hadn't fallen off a roof a few days ago, I'd be tempted to go myself." He smiled at Tara. "You should go and have a run or two before they close. It would do you good. Make you feel young again. The young Tara never missed a chance to snowboard."

She couldn't argue with that. But the mature Tara had other reasons besides great powder for wanting to be up at the Basin.

"Laurel? What do you think?" Tara said.

Before Tara could answer, Kathleen came hustling out of the kitchen, carrying a beautifully boxed Dutch apple pie. "We have a problem." She held the pie up. "Somehow this got missed when the guy from the Santa Ski committee stopped by earlier. It's part of the gift package."

Margie smiled at Tara. "Sweetie, you have to go now and play delivery girl for me."

Tara smelled a setup. She turned to Laurel.

Laurel nodded. "We can't let Margie down. Let's go."

Tara laughed. "We'll be the only two on the mountain not decked out in Christmas lights."

"Not so fast." Margie got out of her chair and pulled a package from beneath the tree. She held it out to Tara. "Open it."

Tara arched a brow and pulled the lid off the box. A beautiful, green, home-sewn Santa's elf hat complete with fake ears, a sprig of felt mistletoe tucked behind one, fur trim laced with a string of red battery-operated Christmas lights, and a white puffball on top lay beneath layers of white tissue. Tara recognized Gram's handiwork at once. She was a sewing whiz, and extremely crafty in more than one sense of the word. Beneath the hat sat an assortment of Christmas necklaces with lights that lit up, glow necklaces, and a pair of reindeer ears.

"Gram, what did you do—buy out the craft store? There's enough for the full twelve days of Christmas in here, more than enough to share," she said to Laurel as she gave Gram an openly suspicious look.

Gram smiled and shrugged. "I made the hat and got the other things for you before you cancelled your plans to go to the party..." She trailed off without adding, "with Ryan."

"It would be a shame for them to go to waste."

That was fast work. Tara only had those original plans for a few days.

Gram looked way too pleased with herself. She wore the same look she'd had the night Tara arrived and Gram was expecting the salad dressing man and singing his praises. The salad dressing man who turned out to be Ryan.

Tara hadn't been happy with Gram at all that night. Now, however, she gladly accepted Gram's help, cautiously optimistic as she wondered what Gram knew that she didn't. Or was Gram merely being hopeful?

Tara held the box out to Laurel. "What would you rather be—the elf or the reindeer?"

"I think the elf is definitely you."

Yeah, the elf on the shelf, Tara thought. *Watching love and life go by.*

Laurel picked the reindeer headband out of the box. "I've always been more of a reindeer girl. Does this come with a red nose?"

CHAPTER TWENTY

The Santa Ski was a huge success, at least if the size of the crowds was any indication. Fate had conspired to make the evening perfect for the event—clear skies, stars sparkling, full moon, perfect powder, dramatic temperatures, no breeze. Skiers and boarders dressed in holiday gear, wearing glo necklaces and flashing battery-operated LED lights, tacky Christmas sweaters over ski coats, reindeer ears over their helmets, all manner of whacky Christmas outfits packed the slopes. Some men even wore "beardskis"—ski masks with long fake beards attached, Santa white being the most prevalent.

Ryan had opted to go beardless. He looked tacky enough with a red Santa coat on over his ski coat, and a ski patrol vest over that. Unfortunately, this was the regulation ski patrol outfit today and tomorrow. He felt more like the Grinch than Santa. If there had been a way to stop Christmas from coming, or even a way to simply avoid it, Ryan would have latched onto it.

Ryan had hoped the joy in the air and the perfect powder would distract him from his loneliness and thoughts of what might have been. He'd planned to break the Christmas curse and end the evening an engaged man. Now he was just another lonely guy on the slopes all too aware of the coupledom around him. Couples, couples everywhere. Young couples. Old couples. Couples with kids. Couples without. Every stag had a doe. Everyone but him.

And so, with flashing lights on his helmet, he played cop and sidelined revelers who'd imbibed one too many holiday spirits. He helped a few celebrators to the first-aid station, nothing serious so far, and tried to mend his own broken heart as the Ghost of Christmas Future haunted him—a future without Tara. Unless a miracle occurred. Or maybe unless he got up the balls to try again. Or maybe he'd spent too much time trying already and should give up.

He looked up at the stars sparkling in the skies. He needed a sign, a Christmas sign.

The parking lots were packed and cars lined the road for what seemed like halfway down the mountain.

"I've never seen it so busy," Laurel said. "And that's saying something. Looks like the Santa Ski will be here to stay. And look at the village." She pointed out the window. "It looks like a Bavarian Christmas village.

They've done a great job." She smiled at Tara. "Thanks for bringing me up here."

"Don't thank me," Tara said wryly. "It's all for Gram's pie." She laughed, but she was nervous. "Was it just me, or did you notice that Gram and your mom were eager to get us up here?"

"Yeah," Laurel said. "I had that distinct impression, too. What do you think they're up to?"

"I wish I knew," Tara said. Or maybe she didn't. "Last time Gram acted suspicious, she was playing matchmaker between Ryan and me. Somehow I don't think Gram has changed MOs. I wonder who the new victim is?"

Laurel laughed. "Could be the same old victim." She wiggled her eyebrows.

"Shut up." But Tara was way too hopeful it was.

"Whoever it is, she thinks they go for garish girls. Look at the way she tricked us out." Laurel held up her LED Christmas-light necklace.

"Yeah, I'm not sure we're exactly Christmas candy," Tara said as a group of skiers walked in front of the car. "But look at them. We do fit in." She laughed. "In fact, maybe Gram's right. We're pretty smoking in our tacky finery."

"You are. I'm roly-poly, a right jolly pregnant reindeer."

"Oh, I don't know. Now when people say you're glowing, you literally are. Especially if you put on that flashing Rudolph nose Digger gave me."

"Gee, thanks. Glowing is always the way I've wanted to be described." Laurel gasped. "Baby kick."

"Cute. Baby's excited to be here, too. See? We made the right choice to come." Tara hoped. "Your baby daddy will think you're hot, I'm sure."

Laurel's phone buzzed. "I am hot. Constantly. All that extra blood in my system. But at least it's winter." Laurel looked at her text. "Donny's waiting for me in the lodge. He talked his way into getting off his shift early."

"Isn't that sweet. Mom and Gram were right—he really does want you up here with him." Tara scanned the road ahead and wasn't optimistic about finding parking. "I'm going to try the lots," Tara said to Laurel. "But first I'll drop you and the pie off at the lodge."

"No way! I can walk. Exercise is good for pregnant women."

"But slipping on the snow and ice and falling face first into a pie isn't. I'm dropping you off. I'll feel a lot more confident that both you and the pie will make it to the party in one piece that way. And I don't need to get on the outs with Donny for not taking care of you. Besides, I don't want to have to carry the pie all that way, either."

Tara inched the car through the streets, finally arriving at a drop-off spot in front of the main ski lodge. "I'm going to make a few runs first." Tara swallowed a lump. "In memory of Chad."

Laurel squeezed her arm in support. "You going to be okay?"

"I'll be great. I'll join you at the party later," she said as she helped Laurel out and handed her the pie. "Save me a seat."

"You got it."

As Laurel stepped out of the car, Donny came out of the ski lodge, wearing a great big grin. He'd obviously been watching for them. He pulled Laurel into a bear hug and a passionate kiss. Laurel hadn't even needed a sprig of mistletoe behind her fake ear.

When the kiss ended, Donny waved at Tara through the open car door. "Hey, Tara, merry Christmas. Thanks for bringing my girl."

"You're welcome. Now help her with the pie and get in to that party and have some fun," Tara said and laughed.

"Aye, aye." He grabbed the pie, slammed the car door, and put his arm around Laurel as he walked her into the ski lodge. Tara smiled after them, thinking how nice it would be to be part of a couple.

Without the benefit of Ryan's ski patrol pass, Tara was lucky to find a spot in the far end of the farthest lot from the ski lodge. She grabbed her gear, put on her elf hat, and headed for the lifts and the very run where Chad had died. She was going to board down that run and enjoy it for his sake and her own.

Speaking of Ryan's ski patrol parking pass, Tara couldn't help herself. She had to make sure he hadn't already left. She swung by the special lot and looked for his car, letting out a sigh of relief when she spotted it. Now she had a dilemma. How did she make sure he didn't leave while she was up on the run? If only she had a wheel lock on her. Short of that, she could lean against his car and wait for him. It was an awfully cold night for that. Or she could trust. Waiting at the car for him almost won. She was that desperate to make sure he got her card.

But looking like a stalker in the lot and developing hypothermia weren't as enticing as the slopes. Instead, she resorted to childish superstitions and wished on a Christmas star as she headed for the lifts.

As she waited her turn for the chair lift, Tara looked up the slopes at the colorful, flashing, crazy, happy skiers and boarders. It was an awesome, joyous sight to behold. Even if this was all the better the night got, she owed Gram a big one for making Tara come to this party.

The ride up the lift was the most beautiful one Tara could remember. The forest below was pure white winter wonderland. The moon lit the surrounding mountains and hills and the lake below glowed silver and spectacular. As Tara stared at the moon, she imagined the silhouette of Santa's sleigh sliding across it. And the stars twinkled so brightly it was easy to picture the Wise Men following one of them.

At the top, she got off the chair lift and boarded to the top of the crowded run.

Ryan was ready to call it quits and head to his parents' house to lick his wounds in private. One final run down the mountain, down the run where Chad had died in honor of his friend, as he did every Christmas Eve, and he was out of here. No Christmas party and Santa Claus for him this year.

He was almost to the top of the run when his heart stopped. There was Tara, standing at the top of the run on her bright polka-dot snowboard looking like every vision of a Christmas sugar plum he'd ever had—sweet, tasty, and gorgeous in her green elf hat beanie, goggles on her head as she admired the view.

It was stupid. He was foolhardy, but he couldn't help himself. He rushed to her side before she could snowboard away, out of his grasp. "Tara?"

His heart hammered in his ears. His pulse raced. And then she turned to face him.

As recognition dawned, her eyes lit up and she smiled at him as if she was genuinely overjoyed to see him. "Ryan?"

"What are you doing here?" They asked each other in unison and laughed.

Ryan stared at her, willing himself not to blow what might be his final chance to talk to her in person before she left.

"I'm facing my fears," she said, nodding toward the slope. "And making happy memories. For Chad."

He nodded. "I do this run every year on Christmas Eve for him, too."

Her eyes misted.

He'd said the wrong thing.

He took a step closer to her, standing so close it was tempting to hold her in his arms. "I'm sorry."

She looked up into his eyes. "Don't be sorry. That's sweet. That's nice of you. He'd love that you do." Her voice broke.

"Yeah." Ryan cleared his throat and shoved his hands in his pockets to keep them under control and stop himself from making a pass at her that she wouldn't appreciate. He ached to touch her, and that fake mistletoe behind her felt ear was practically begging him to kiss her. He had to extricate himself from this mess. "I'm heading down. And heading out."

"What?" She looked alarmed. "You aren't staying for the party? When did you become an old man? Have you forgotten how to have fun?" She paused and lightly touched his arm, imploring him. "You can't leave until you've seen Santa. Who knows? Maybe you'll win a present."

Was it his imagination or was she hinting at something? It was too easy to get his hopes up. "I'm not lucky. I never win."

"Maybe you'll get lucky this time." She set her jaw, giving him her determined look.

He laughed. "Careful what you say."

She surprised him by simply smiling back at him. "I'm perfectly serious, Ryan. You can't leave. What do you have to rush home for?"

What was she telling him? What reason did he have to stay?

"Harry said you have something to tell me? Something you wanted to say in person?"

"I do," she said. "But not here." She flashed him a crooked smile. "See you at the bottom of the hill. I'll tell you in the lodge over a drink. I'll buy."

His heart raced so quickly, he was quickly becoming breathless. Tara had always had the power to take his breath away. He hoped she wasn't stringing him along again. Before he could answer, she pushed off.

He pushed off after her.

Snowboarding was like flying. Tara let herself go and simply enjoyed the feel of the board beneath her feet, of cutting down the mountain in the fresh, cold air. Of breathing and feeling alive and really and truly hopeful again.

Ryan caught up to her. He'd always been the faster snowboarder. Once he came even with her, he stayed beside her as they cut their way down the mountain. Tara embraced the joy that bubbled inside her. She felt young again and free from all the pain of the past.

She hoped she wouldn't have to hang onto these few minutes in her memory forever. She prayed they wouldn't be the last, that she and Ryan would have years and years more of them together.

At the bottom of the hill, she braked in front of Ryan, nearly cutting him off on purpose just to rattle him. As she laughed, he wobbled and grabbed her, pulling her into his arms to steady himself.

As if a miracle had occurred, he was wrapped around her, breathing hard. Their eyes met. Their lips inched closer. "Ryan, I'm—"

"Ryan!" Someone slapped him on the back.

Ryan pulled away.

"Grab your girl and get inside. Santa's already handing out presents."

"Yeah, yeah, we'll be there in a minute." Ryan ignored his buddy and turned back to her.

She pulled away from him. Ryan looked confused.

"He's right," she said, trying not to let her eagerness show. "We can't miss Santa. What if you win?" She stepped off her board, grabbed Ryan's hand, and pulled him toward the lodge with one hand, her snowboard in the other.

"Whoa! Let me get my gear off. My car's just over there. We can stash our boards in it."

"Hurry." She pulled him along. "Who knows? I might win something, too."

She was impatient as they put their gear in Ryan's car. As soon as he closed the car door, she pulled him into the warmth of the lodge, dragging him to the front of the room right beneath the stage.

"Do we need to be so close?" he asked.

"I think we do." She pulled off her elf hat and shook out her hair as she caught Jim Dickson's eye and signaled him to pull Ryan's card from his pack.

The Christmas giveaway was a raffle. Santa's helper pulled a raffle ticket from a bin and called out the winner. The winner generally screamed with joy, jumped up and down, and ran for the stage, where Santa pulled the prize from the bag and handed it to them.

Ryan had been watching the action as Tara pulled him toward the stage. In that brief time, two winners had been announced. Tara had dragged him to the party in the nick of time. Santa's bag was already looking deflated.

As Ryan stood next to Tara, wishing he could talk to her over a drink and waiting for the minute the raffle ended, Jim as Santa interrupted the general giveaway process.

"Wait!" Santa held up a hand to stop his helper. "Hold on, head elf. What's this? I have a present here that has a name on it."

For a minute, Ryan's heart stopped dead in his chest. *No, please, Jim. No. Not Tara's ring.*

"How did this get in here?" Jim Dickson, who did a convincingly jolly Santa as he pulled a red envelope from his bag.

Ryan relaxed. He was off the hook.

Santa adjusted his glasses. "Who's the lucky person?" He peered at the envelope and squinted for effect. "Well, well, well, one of our fine ski patrol members. Ryan Sanders, come on up. This has your name on it."

Ryan froze and frowned, puzzled.

Tara gave him a push. "Go on. Get up there." She leaned in and whispered. "I told you you'd win something."

"If it has my name on it, this is a rigged win."

Tara seemed way too eager for him to go on stage and trying to act too casual about it.

"Ryan, I see you there right in the front row," Santa said. "We don't have all night." Santa handed the envelope to his helper, who handed it down to Ryan.

His name was written neatly on the envelope in Tara's small, feminine printing. Ryan would recognize it anywhere. His heart pounded and his hand trembled as he took it from the elf.

Ryan looked at Tara.

"I told you I had something to say. Open it." Her eyes were shining.

Santa and the raffle had moved on. Ryan felt frozen in time as he turned the envelope over and saw *SWAK* written in Tara's hand. He arched a brow. "SWAK? Really?"

"Really," she said, softly. "You used to like it."

Heart hammering, he slid his finger under the flap and pulled out the card and read it.

You're the holly to my berries. You're the marsh-mallows to my hot chocolate. You're the merry to my Christmas. We belong together. I love you.

The more he read, the bigger his smile grew—and his heart, too. She wanted Harry to sell the lodge to him. She was conceding, giving him his dream. It was the best gift anyone had ever, or could ever, give him. And she loved him?

"Really?" he said.

She looked him in the eye and nodded. "Really. All of it. Every word."

As he broke into a grin, ready to take her in his arms and kiss her, Jim Dickson caught his eye. Jim held a jewelry box discreetly in his hand. He arched a brow, asking the question—*Do you want to give this to Tara now?*

Ryan grinned and nodded.

Santa's voice boomed out. "Looks like we have another present with a name on it. Looks like jewelry. Tara Clark, you're a lucky girl."

Santa walked to the edge of the stage, but he didn't hand Tara the box. He handed it to Ryan. "I think you'd better do the honors."

Tara's heart hammered a rhythm that twelve drummers drumming would be hard pressed to match. The noisy crowd surrounding them went silent-night quiet as Ryan opened the box and held it out to her, balanced on his fingertips.

She gasped. Her original engagement ring sparkled in its cushion of velvet. Her eyes clouded with tears, but she was smiling and couldn't help it. "Really, Ryan?"

"Yeah, really." He was smiling at her with the same hopeful look he'd had the first time he'd asked her to marry him. "It's just a placeholder. I'll get you a nicer one. Will you—"

"Yes, I will. This time I *really* will."

He slid it on her finger, right where it belonged and should have been these past ten years.

She held her hand out to admire it while she clutched her elf hat in the other. "I like this one."

She threw herself into his arms and held the elf hat with its fake mistletoe over his head to make it perfectly clear what she wanted.

As Ryan pulled her into a passionate kiss, she wrapped her arms around him and the crowd erupted in applause.

Piles of snow, mistletoe. The man I've always loved. Best Christmas ever.

She belonged in Ryan's arms now and forever. And she belonged in Echo Bay.

ABOUT THE AUTHOR

Gina Robinson lives in the Pacific Northwest with her husband and children. She loves humor, romance, suspense, and spies. Not necessarily in that order. She writes humorous romantic suspense, contemporary romance, historical romance, and women's fiction.

If she could meet just one fictional spy, she'd be hard pressed to choose between James Bond and Max Smart. In her opinion, the perfect spy would be a combination of the two. Most days she writes while wearing slippers, flip-flops, or tennis shoes, depending on the season. But she loves a great, sexy heel and has a closet full for special occasions.

Connect with Gina online at www.ginarobinson.com